Todd Grimson lives in L.A.
Until he can't stand it anymore.

BRAND NEW CHERRY FLAVOR

STAINLESS

TODD GRIMSON

QUARTET BOOKS

The author would like to extend special thanks to
Ruth Witham and Jane Galen.

First published in Great Britain by Quartet Books Limited in 1997
A member of the Namara Group
27 Goodge Street
London W1P 2LD

This edition published by Quartet Books in 1998

This is a work of fiction. The characters, incidents and dialogues
are products of the author's imagination and are not to be
construed as real. Any resemblance to actual events or persons,
living or dead, is entirely coincidental.

A catalogue record for this title is available from the British Library

ISBN 0 7043 8083 8

Phototypset by The F.S.H. Group
Printed and bound in Great Britain by Caledonian International

For Sally Wofford-Girand

PART ONE

ONE

Sunlight is spliced into the afternoon. Soft dead unmoving air. Keith doesn't know what time it is, what day. Shadows tremble, and he forgets for a moment—until reaching for a glass, he sees the bandage wrapped around. He forgets again, choosing to ignore the matter of his twisted hands.

There are flowers in this garden, red hibiscus, lavender and jasmine, and over there, several cacti amongst hard stones. A song goes through his mind. Something partially familiar, nothing that he ever played. He can't get to the end of it. It slips away. Fades out and then picks up, with only a momentary glitch, back at the start.

What do deaf people hear? Not just silence, surely: no, they must hear all kinds of noise. Buzzes, murmurs, soft roars. Whispers, hissing, a humming, and maybe the ocean, the tides of the blood. A steady dreamy orchestra, warming up slowly, forever, in the distant wilderness of the nerves.

The wind starts up, touching him for an instant, a phantom hand, and Keith considers going inside. He wonders if Justine will go out tonight. Really, he doesn't want to do anything, but if there's some reason to go somewhere that's okay too. He'll live. That's the stupid part.

TWO

Justine is a vampire, and Keith is the human she keeps around to take care of things during the day. It's more complicated, but that's the general outline. A little over a year ago, she bit him on the neck. At that time, he was a junkie. He had, before the "accident" to his hands, been in a band that had a successful album. They were called SMX. Keith's girlfriend committed suicide, his hands were grievously injured, he dropped out of sight and became addicted to painkillers, ultimately to heroin.

When Justine put him into a trance, prior to biting him, he sensed what was happening and he was terrified, sure. But he was also somehow exhilarated—at least he would die knowing that there were wonders and surprises in this life on earth, even if he only had a few moments to marvel, it was all right, he accepted the surprise. But vampires possess a highly evolved faculty of taste, and Justine would never take more than a small sample of blood from a drug addict, or an alcoholic, or someone with a blood disease. So she spared him, but something in the telepathic bond moved her, interested her, and she kept him, injecting a small amount of "venom" to maintain the hypnotic tie. But she did not enslave him, as she might have, as she has done at other times.

Maybe because he loved a dead girl, or because he has known suffering, or perhaps simply because he was handsome, and she was lonely. She likes him. They spend many nights talking, sitting together on the couch. She has difficulty describing her past to him, for her memory is bad, she forgets a great deal. There are just these huge blanks, sometimes all she'll be able to remember from what would have been a whole lifetime is a single scene, or a picture of a room.

She does not require human blood on anything like the scale of killing someone every night. Often, in fact, she puts a spell on someone, bites them on the wrist or behind the knee, on the foot . . . takes only a little, disguises the wound with an incision or two, induces amnesia in the victim . . . and the person is left with a "blackout" and a minor wound, no lasting damage at all. The spell wears off.

Now and then, however, she must kill. It is an imperative of her being, an imperative of the strange species she has been for so long. If such a creature exists in Nature, then does it not have a right to live? If she kills, then, she does not feel bad about this.

She is both a manifestation of Death and, not dying herself, apart from Death, unaging, and thus she still holds in herself a freshness, perhaps even an immaturity. She looks young, younger than Keith's twenty-eight. Slender, pale, with dark hair and large hooded dark eyes. The fangs truly extend only when she is about to strike, but those teeth are always a bit prominent, lupine and sharp.

Tonight is humid and warm, and as they lie together on the couch Justine's flesh is very cool against Keith's. He says, "You're so cold."

"Do you mind? Does it bother you?"

"No, I like it. It feels good."

The house is not air-conditioned. There are ceiling fans, but they make a faint whirring noise. When everything else is so quiet, why have something whir? Keith does not mind the heated air, the breathing of this room.

He has been telling Justine about his fateful affair with Renata Spengler. "Leggy supermodel, Renata Spengler." Justine is especially curious, and he feels like telling her things he has never told anyone else.

"When I came back to the States, I kept thinking of this image, it had stuck in my mind, I was sure that somewhere along the way I had seen it. A photograph of Renata, naked, her pubic hair shaven, with a hand coming out of her vagina, or a hand there instead . . . and I imagined that it had been inside of her, it had grabbed hold of me and pulled me in, all the way in, like I had gone into another room . . . I don't know, I probably haven't looked hard enough, but I haven't been able to locate this photograph, so I don't know, I might have just made it up."

"Go back," Justine asks. "Why did you go with her to Venezuela?"

"She said she had to attend the funeral of a childhood friend. She went to school in Caracas when she was eight or nine. And she'd gone back a couple of times. She had a boyfriend whose father owned Maracaibo Oil. Gilberto."

"And he's the one who had your fingers broken."

"I think so. As far as I can tell."

"I'm sorry," Justine says, lightly caressing his forehead, her hand then brushing back his short hair.

"I *want* to tell you about Renata. It's okay. The funeral was for her. I mean the childhood friend was herself. I was only with her, off and on, for nine months. I didn't really *know* her, and if I was in love with her, it was that kind of hot, ignorant love that doesn't exactly give you time to think and figure things out. I knew she was fucked-up, that she had very poor, uh, self-esteem, that she was a liar and a masochist and all that. But it's not like you give somebody a test to see if they're worthy of your love. It's just chemical, or electric, magic, and then you're in too deep to know how to breathe."

Keith hesitates, finding himself suddenly unwilling—much to his surprise—to revisit Renata's self-hating adventures. They seem too sordid, too sensational. So he says nothing, for the moment. There's no hurry. The cold fingers caress him absently. He doesn't want to tell her about the time in Cannes when Renata went to bed with a famous French actress, and had herself peed on and tied up. Then spent the next night with a black rapper who was in some gangster movie.

Renata then flew to Amsterdam, to meet Keith there, on tour with SMX. In the hotel room, after they'd fucked, she told Keith what she'd been up to, using her body. She was trying to get him to hit her, he knew it, and Keith remembers the bottomless hopeless feeling as she watched him, her eyes waiting, in mad insolent pain, for his response. Jon Jon, she told him, wasn't as good a fuck, but he did have a much bigger dick. Keith slapped her, hard, hoping she would cry and that would end it, but she wanted a bigger scene. She told him she hated him, he didn't really love her, and on this occasion she fought him with all her strength, making his mouth bleed with a flailing elbow as he—

feeling like a rapist—just sought to hold her thrashing body down. It can be harder to simply hold someone down, trying not to hurt them, than to use your strength freely and rough them up.

Abjectly, later, after all the tears were spent, she whimpered, begging for forgiveness, saying that if he didn't love her she would have nothing left, no reason to live. She was ugly, she would say. I hate myself. I have demons. I want to die.

Keith says, "I wasn't equipped to deal with her problems. I didn't know how to save her. I didn't really want to, in a way. I resented it, that she made her problems more dramatic than mine. After all, I'd suffered through my own unhappy childhood, which I've told you about. I had survived. But . . . in my relations with women, I was used to being the troubled *artiste*. That was what . . . oh, I don't know, I was going to say that was what attracted Renata to me, but actually I think . . . I don't think at this point I'm vain about it, or have any reason to be . . . but I think we connected on a much deeper level than that. Almost immediately. Like we had been children together. There was so much we never had to say. We just *knew*."

He sees the dead girl again as he speaks, vividly, sees her eyes, Renata turning to look at him across a crowded room, that flash of *one mind*, just for a moment, evanescent but real. What did Renata look like? What does anyone look like who's on the cover of *Mademoiselle*, *Elle*, and *Vogue*? Cheekbones, full lips, perfect teeth, gray eyes like changing, moving, bluish clouds. A thousand expressions on her face. She was tall, brown-haired, with beautiful legs, augmented breasts above her ribcage, her belly . . . a hand coming out of the taut cleft. Whose hand? Is it feminine? Is it hers?

Yes, Keith tentatively assesses. The picture is in black and white and looks like an antique, like it was taken in some impossible 1913. The model's faint, tantalizing smile. Wet, slicked-back hair. Her body is definitely modern, not pre-World War I.

His own hands. In the semi-darkness, he dares touch Justine, when she can't look and see his hand. His left hand is worse, partially numb and clumsy. Neither has much strength, both give him a lot of pain after much use. He has difficulty buttoning his shirt.

How much does Justine know? It's hard to tell. Sometimes she seems so sensitive and subtle, beyond anyone he's ever known. Yet to some extent he's guessing, because she's mostly inarticulate, and sometimes, like an animal, she can even seem downright dumb. Uncomprehending. Shading from absentmindedness to a sort of frightening state in which she looks at you without seeing, if you speak you are sure she does not hear. Yet she may move about in this condition. When she is like this Keith feels that she will kill him. He has made up his mind not to fight it, not to resist.

"Why did Gilberto blame you for Renata's suicide? He must have been aware of how she was."

"Yes," Keith answers. "She was a torment to him . . . I'm sure of it. She visited him, once, when she was with me in England. He was a student at the London School of Economics."

"He was jealous of you," Justine says. "She drove him mad."

Keith listens. Justine yawns, and in the light her fangs shine white with a sparkle of green. It's the yellow in the light. The entire room seems umber shadows and melted gold.

It is a large room, high-ceilinged. The coffee table is sand-blasted glass. A large painting is off to the right, geometric, two hexagon radials seen not quite front on, with lots of black scuffs and lines on sort of a turquoise to green-blue, with brick-red and dirty cream.

Justine wears a black mini-dress, and as it rides up on her thighs the skin looks so vulnerable, so naked and white.

"What?" she says, suddenly looking at him, smiling, after they have been silent for a long time.

He shakes his head, shrugs. She reaches over to her glass of water, brings it back to her lips, and carefully takes a little sip.

"I have a memory," she announces. "I just saw it. I was in a field, with my sister, Fleur. Our dresses are soiled. The sun is shining . . . yes, if I look up, there it is, I can't believe it, the sun is a bright, white . . . star. The sky is blue. Ah, damn. I want to say more, but I'd just be making it up."

The hexagon radials seem about to fall out of the metal frame.

THREE

The full creepiness of the situation is not lost on him. He is in the position of serving as Justine's imp, her familiar, her "Igor," assisting her as she preys upon the world. It's like she is a dominatrix, and he a slave. If anyone knew of his allegiance, they would despise him. Were the villagers to come up to the castle, torches ablaze, like in an old black-and-white movie, they would kill him without a second thought.

The question of what he ought to do absorbs all of his spiritual energies, in a way the heroin addiction never did. That was wholesome by comparison. Understandable, given his broken hands, the loss of his career. It was weakness, he was weak, but this is sick.

He sees now the radical uneasiness caused by the undead; how, being neither truly one thing nor the other, they make everyone very nervous. He fully comprehends the anxiety experienced as long as the vampire thrives nearby. It seems like it must be destroyed, if there is to be any peace.

But Keith does not expect to have any peace inside him, he has never been at peace unless he was kidding himself, or the peace, in the form of heroin, was artificially imposed. Then his inner kingdom was serene, green meadows with sheep and trees and blue sky and fluffy little clouds. This was a landscape he has only seen, in real life, from afar.

Some sort of boiled down vision of happiness, simple enough, not too different from that of anyone else. The heroin relieved physical pain, and mental distress, it simplified things. Everything seemed all right, he saw things in an optimistic, positive light. Of course, coming down from that, waking up the next day, on the edge of withdrawal, he was nervous about everything, he saw all the multifarious painful details that slipped by unnoticed in the high.

His life was simple then. It was maybe stupid, worthless, and contemptible, but he had his assigned task. He needed to get some more heroin, before he started falling apart. Everything would be ugliness as withdrawal took hold. Everything hurt, everything made him want to throw up.

Doing some smack in that circumstance was like coming back from the dead. That's an exaggeration, but the euphoria was so sweet, so heavenly—Keith wonders if it's like that for Justine. If, more than keeping her alive forever, the fresh blood makes her high.

One night he asks her, and she doesn't answer for a long time. Then she says, "Do you mean, does it make me drunk?"

Artless, she seems genuinely puzzled that he would guess this, or have the nerve to bring it up. Keith never knows when or if she is playing the *faux-naif*. Never, perhaps.

"Yes," she says. "Not every time."

"Sometimes it just gets you straight."

"Yes."

He kisses her hand. He means it ironically, or would to anyone else, but he also just wants to kiss her hand.

He likes her. In some ways—probably his false interpretation—she seems shy. He takes certain liberties with this.

Undead. Both of them are in between, living but dead. Undead.

Keith listens to music, to tapes sped up so that a fifty-minute side of a cassette takes about half that time.

He puts headphones on, and lies there, waiting for the sun to go down. There's a particular silence when the burning orange-pink sun goes down behind the distant line marking the end of the world, there's a silence in which the birds pause for an instant, the dogs don't bark, that moment when the vampire's eyes come open, safe from the light.

Keith listens to music, out in the air, at the ordinary, usual speed. He waits. He has no thoughts. He is in a state of unpeace.

FOUR

Ever since she began coming here to clean, Consuela has been curious about these locked doors. She has been coming once a week, on Monday afternoon, for three months. Just another expensive house in Beverly Glen. But these locked doors.

Consuela has tried to look into the rooms from outside, but there are plum-colored drapes concealing the interiors, drapes which are always drawn. The only person she's ever seen here is a young, good-looking Anglo, twenty-five or so . . . but he's not the owner, she understands. He's house-sitting. From what she has seen, he sleeps well into the afternoon. Something is wrong with his hands.

He's amiable, he is nice. She will tell Elvis not to hurt him. It's going to be bad enough, they'll scrutinize her very closely after a burglary at one of her houses, she's been through it before. She doesn't want to hear about any violence. Otherwise, well, there's a lot of crime in L.A., and this place doesn't have the best security, places a lot more protected than this get hit every day. There's no "pattern." It's not as if the houses Consuela cleans sooner or later all get robbed.

This house . . . its time has come, that's all. Elvis has problems, he needs money bad, so finally she said, "Look, I might know a place with a lot of good stuff."

They'd never be able to prove anything. Most crimes like this are solved by somebody talking, somebody copping a plea. (That is, if they're ever solved, which most are not.) Nobody here would ever talk. The Rodriguez brothers are Elvis's cousins, they've been tight since they were kids. It's their truck, and it's Victor Rodriguez's father-in-law who's the fence.

Consuela doesn't even know the rich people who own this house, she's never seen them, and this guy who hangs around, yeah his hands are fucked up, something happened to him, but even so he's not poor—look at the beautiful house he gets to stay in while he gets well.

She doesn't feel great about it, but the finder's fee will sure help and sometimes you just have to do something bad. Once it's occurred to you, and you know it's possible, and when you add everything up it doesn't seem that risky after all. Once she mentioned it to Elvis . . . it's become a little like being in a movie, working undercover, pretending like everything's the same. It makes all the rest of her week a little more exciting, waiting to come back here. Elvis lent her a little camera, and she discreetly, like a spy, used up a roll of film.

It remains frustrating, however, not to be able to sneak a look into the locked rooms. What treasures might be hidden behind those doors?

Consuela studies all the furnishings and art objects with a different eye, appraising in the dining room the eight high-backed Louis XIII chairs, the pewter table service, the tall sculptures which cast such intricate shadows on the walls. She turns a critical eye on the many paintings, which might end up in South America, Miami, or Guadalajara.

She particularly likes, in the study, the Bessarabian carpet, dark blue and gold and wine red, and in the bedroom, the twelve-fold screen painted with some scene out of the Crusades. Wonderful booty, *meant* to be stolen, to travel mysteriously all over the world.

Outside, she gets in her car and lights a cigarette. She's not allowed to smoke, or use strong-smelling cleaning solvents, inside.

She feels nervous as Keith comes out of the shadows, watching her, electronically closing the gate as she drives out. The place is so very silent and still. She feels a stab of fear.

FIVE

Some miles from Richmond, Virginia, in April of 1837, James Robert Ward continued walking at a brisk pace steadily home. It was quite dark, and he reckoned he had at least another two hours or ten miles to go. He was a strong and healthy twenty-one years of age, accustomed to walking tours and long strolls.

By now, after walking alone for many hours, his earlier concerns had faded away—foremost among these a mis-understanding he had suffered with his prickly brother-in-law, upon whose wealth both he and his widowed mother were somewhat dependent—and his thoughts had settled into contemplation of his last meeting with Ermina, whom he loved. The ringlets of her hair, the charm of her unaffected smile . . . he pondered her every aspect in the light of Universal Redeeming Love. Oh, if she truly returned his love, every obstacle could be surmounted!

Surely, for instance, in his absence, his sister would now work to soften her husband, to make him see how light a favor was required to put James on his own footing from now on. This material question once settled, James would feel free to ask Ermina for her hand. He had already pledged her his love, through poetry, and although she had not come out and said she returned his emotion, she must— he had seen the answer in her shining eyes!

James was an optimist. All would be well.

It was pitch black now. He was walking, on this road, through a low-lying glade where the trees formed a canopy obscuring the stars. The air seemed preternaturally hushed, and James found himself thinking, just for a moment, of ghosts. And then, more frighteningly, somehow, because more concretely, of runaway slaves.

Yesterday he had seen some newly arrived slaves, manacled and unhappy, on their way to be shipped over the mountains, to the Ohio River. Like cornmeal, tobacco, barrels of herring, or hams. His brother-in-law dealt in such wares.

James came out from the peculiarly dark corridor, into a more open space, under the sky. He was somehow relieved. And yet, strange, there was absolutely no sound but for his own hushed footsteps. It had been windy earlier on, so that he had been glad to have his Marseilles greatcoat, but all the entranced boughs remained perfectly still.

He walked on, gazing about attentively, but there was nothing, no reason to fear. He relaxed, and began to enjoy the quiet. It was a poetic, a magical night.

But then . . . he did not believe it at first, but then he clearly perceived, standing there, seemingly staring at him, a young woman. Clearly, she saw him. Indeed, it was as if she had been waiting for him! She advanced, at the edge of the meadow, and he moved to greet her, wondering if she needed his aid.

She was dressed in mourning, pale and melancholy, of a waif-like thinness perhaps somewhat consumptive, with hot, liquescent eyes and long black hair. She gave James a nervous smile, and said, "Please, sir, you must help me. Can you? I do pray that you may help."

"Yes," James said, feeling an attraction intermingled with dread. "What is it? Yes, I will assist you in any way that I can."

"Come then," she said, taking him by the hand, and he dropped his walking stick and followed her. Her hand was *so cold*, so cold! He smelled violets, or orris root, and all at once the wind swelled up, rustling the leaves.

"What is it?" he asked, as she led him into the woods, but he hardly knew if he spoke aloud or within his head. She turned to him every so often, with a sorrowful smile, and he felt keenly that there was something *wrong*, and yet he was so dreamy, he could not resist. Something like the promise of forbidden, horrid voluptuousness seemed to lie waiting, just ahead, as they penetrated the woods.

They stopped in a clearing; it was so black all he could see was the pallor of her face and hands. He was suddenly so afraid, so unbelievably afraid, as she stared, much less shy, into his eyes. Gently, she touched his face with both of her cold hands.

James found himself falling, slowly, ever so slowly, swooning, and a cat or some such creature bit him sharply on the neck, he wanted to push it away but he found that he could not.

Oh please, if he could only move one hand! Or, failing that, if he could only manage to utter one sound, even if he should just cry like a child or squeak like a mouse!

. . . so heavy and hot, his body was so heavy it should sink into the earth, heavier than lead and now burning, molten, molten like some new amalgam, some unholy alchemy transforming his entire being as the sky swarmed at him, he was unparticled, blind, as he surged up into the sky.

SIX

She's not sure, not positive, but she believes that the blood tastes different now than it did in the faraway past. It seems like it is fouler now, also more complicated, more of a metallic mineral tang to it, like licking the hood of a warm automobile. Somebody told her once about the minerals in the blood. She remembers magnesium and zinc. It flows through the veins and, deeper and richer, the arteries, through the pumping heart, the organs, the brain.

It's possible that any perceived difference is imaginary, or inconsequential. The same dark salty ancient flow is certainly present, unmistakable, probably the same as it was in the time of the Romans, the pharaohs, or back further than that.

They used to say, "Evil is in the blood." Or, "They are of noble blood." They used to put leeches on people to try to get rid of the "bad" blood.

Justine was a peasant. She had peasant blood. After she became a vampire, she used both kinds, noble and peasant, but whenever it dwelt inside her, it was the same. Evil. She used it up, in some fashion, and always needed more.

When she thirsts, and the first gout comes into her through her fangs, it hits her body like magic. A magical, sustaining fluid. She is infinitely familiar with blood in its different temperatures, with how it stains, or dries, or how fast it will bleed out of a wound. It is nothing to her to wake up with caked blood in her hair, dried brownish flaking blood to rub off of her face.

It doesn't feel to her like she's been alive so long, it doesn't feel like she's old. All the past is so indistinct, or nonexistent—it's more like she's a creature, reborn anew, with certain instincts but no real history, only occasional fragments which she dreams of during the inanimate long days.

At night, when she arises, she washes her face and wonders if there's anything important she's forgotten, and it takes a while for present circumstances to come back.

A long time ago, she might have compared her existence to that of a rat, or a worm, a maggot, and she feared sometimes that she was hideous, that she imagined she stayed young but was deceived.

She became much more dispassionate, bit by bit. She did things, and they made a big impression on her at the time, but in many ways no single night was more important than the next, and she forgot.

SEVEN

There's a lot of time to think and he thinks about how Ornette Coleman said that if the sound of a clarinet is two inches, the sound of an electric guitar is at least twelve. Somebody once told Keith, on the telephone in New York, about "sex chocolate." "It's new," the person said, and started to laugh. "I'm serious. It wears off too soon, though."

Everything wears off, he thinks. He wonders, not for the first time, if death is like sleep. If it is, what does that mean? Everyone dies. When this cat of his died, put to sleep after a bad illness, no hope left, the cat looked like he accepted it. He was relaxed, like he knew this was an inevitable part of life. If there are billions of people all over the world, each with his or her individual consciousness, what can be said about their little lives, their struggles, and their deaths? Beethoven died. Gandhi died. It's not like you get some prize. Like the cat, there are other cats to take your place. That's it.

A vampire is just an animal. It lives by what you might call abnormal means, but its physiology has its logic, it's a metamorphosis of what used to be human, of what started out as a human being like anyone else.

He talks to Justine sometimes about things he knows she doesn't understand. She listens, and he says at a midnight show of some band, "Repetition is change," and how Africans like buzztones, then the band bums him out and he says, later on, outside, "You play your guitar a while, then step up to the mike and sing your little song—about pain, and loss, or love—how can this be significant to anyone anymore?"

They get in the car and he feels antagonistic, he's sick of her, the suspense she keeps him in, and he says, "You know, I don't give a shit about you. I'm not even curious. So you exist. So what?

It's just a job. You do your job. It seems pretty boring to me. How can you stand it?"

She just looks at him. He drives them into the desert, under the moon.

Blur, blur. Smear.

The black desert is never-ending. That's all the world is now. Endless desert, endless unchanging night. If there are habitations, they are nothing more than gas stations and all-night diners, places where if you stop you might be killed. Your head might end up in the fridge. Justine accepts this situation, naturally, as she would accept burial in a shallow grave out by the railroad tracks. He stops the car and gets the shovel out of the trunk. He leaves the car running so he can see what he's doing, digs in the glare of the headlights. He buries her, tamps down the sandy dirt.

Then when he begins driving again she is soon there next to him in the front seat, uncommunicative and cold, pale as moonlight in a dark blue scary room. He stops and buries her again, drives a stake through her heart, but she turns up once more, his silent passenger, nothing to say.

He is weary. "What do you want from me?" he asks, and she seems not to hear, to be listening at all. He comes to a police roadblock. They look inside, check his driver's license, then wave him on. The sign says Flagstaff, Arizona, Tombstone, Death Valley, Dodge, Nowheresville. They are below sea level, they are on a highway underground.

Keith stops the car and runs out into a graveyard, in a ghost town. Justine claws her way up out of the dirt, blood on her mouth, a worm crawling down her face. She sits in the car, a blanket around her, dirt in her hair. Keith smokes a cigarette, standing at the side of the road, looking around, then gets back in to drive the car.

In a cheap hotel room, she lies on the bed, her dress carelessly up over her thighs, while he uses his tie to make a vein stand out in his arm. He melts the heroin, while Justine pays no attention, and he shoots up, sighing, releasing the tie. Pantomime.

'He' puts out a cigarette on her calf. She fails to respond. He says, "Honey, you're either dead or a real good faker." He waves his hand in front of her eyes.

Driving again. He yawns, big time. Suddenly, no apparent change, but he sees that she has fangs. Oh boy. He buries her again by the side of the road, but by the time he finishes, dropping the shovel and planting a wooden cross, she is already back in the passenger seat as before.

At a diner, he mashes a cheeseburger against her lips, to no avail. In the bathroom, he sits her on the toilet and waits, then stands her up and wipes her pubic hair, throws the tissue in the water and flushes it down. He washes her face, saying, "There, that's a good girl." He puts fresh lipstick on her mouth, and holds up her compact mirror.

In the car, she suddenly awakens, mouth open, turning to him with her hungry fangs. He steps on the gas, floors it, 80, 90, 100, but she doesn't care. She hisses, going for his throat.

Then nothing has happened. He's driving, she is his passenger on the desert highway in the night.

She says, "How far do we have to go?"

EIGHT

The second-youngest of five children, Keith could not remember a time when he was not at odds with his parents, a scapegoat, blamed for all manner of sins and petty crimes. His father was an alcoholic, and this condition worsened considerably when Keith was about eleven or twelve. His mother found Keith rebellious and unmanageable, and regularly told on him, so that his father would focus on Keith, drunkenly hitting him or whatever, ugly scenes, to make him sorry for upsetting his mom. The boy remained unredeemably stubborn; he would never give in.

When he was thirteen, during a particularly hot St. Louis summer, he spent all three months sleeping out in a hammock in the backyard. His parents disliked this situation, but if he agreed to stay inside, by midnight or 1:00 A.M. he'd be back out in his hammock, listening to his Walkman or to the ambient sounds of the night. Friends came over, bringing beer or pot, and on a few occasions he managed daring romantic rendezvous. Many, many nights he wandered the streets. At 5:30 A.M. he'd be off on his bicycle to deliver the *St. Louis Herald-Dispatch*.

He shoplifted batteries for his Walkman, anything else he thought he really needed, and never once was caught. His mother wouldn't allow him to play the family piano, so he got a guitar instead. He practiced it quietly, with damped strings, out in the backyard.

His oldest brother and sister, safely off to college before their father really degenerated, blamed Keith for causing trouble. He in turn disliked them. They were ignorant, they had never experienced what he had. He wouldn't explain it to them, either. It was too shameful, having your arm twisted up behind you in a hammerlock until you thought it would break, one fraction of an inch from snapping like the slim bone of a bird.

He hated his parents. He was not afraid to say that he'd be glad when they were dead. They were in perpetual opposition, perpetual conflict. Both his mom and his dad told him he would never amount to anything. He was lazy and never listened, he had a high opinion of himself based on nothing in the real world.

NINE

When Keith was eighteen, he got into some trouble with the law. He was actually charged with attempted murder, though that was never likely to stick.

What happened was that there was this nightclub owner,

Walter Baumgartner, who was a notorious scumbag, but in St. Louis there wasn't much of a scene, so if you wanted to play you pretty much had to deal with him at some point. Baumgartner would do things like agree to pay you half of the gate, and then at the end of the night he'd say, "Here's your three hundred bucks," and you'd have to start all over again, he'd argue forever, acting amazed, saying, "But that's what we *agreed*."

This when you'd had your own person in on the count and your band should be getting eight hundred or so.

In a million other ways besides being a total liar and asshole he was a scumbag, supposedly he owned an escort service and his bouncers sold all sorts of imported drugs. Rumors galore.

Well, one Saturday night after Keith's band Cum played late and it was really raining outside, a monsoon, Walter said, "Why don't you guys leave your equipment overnight? You can pick it up tomorrow afternoon."

Michael was worried about security but Baumgartner said there was an alarm system with a motion detector, plus he had insurance, and so, yawning, Cum went home to go to sleep. Keith, for his part, had no suspicion whatsoever that anything could go wrong.

The next day, when they came to get the equipment, both of the guitar amps were missing. Baumgartner's minion, Reg, acted shocked, and called Walter at home. He said, no problem, my insurance, etc.

It was only in the next few days that Keith found out that Baumgartner had pulled this before, bands had lost their equipment and the insurance was some shady company that never paid anyone off.

The particular outrage here for Keith was that he was *extremely* close to his amp, it was a modified Kustom Reverb Special that he thought of as one-of-a-kind. He loved his machine. He was close to his guitar, of course, but there were certain crucial sounds he could only get out of this one irreplaceable amp.

It was even more maddening, in his grief, to have the feeling that Baumgartner might think Keith was afraid of him. Physically afraid. There was this legend that, a few years ago, up in Chicago, Walter Baumgartner had murdered someone who could have testified against him in a counterfeit-ticket case that never came to trial. The guy had just disappeared, his body had never been found. And Walter was a big guy, with a mustache, who came on aggressively, surrounded by his bouncers and assorted criminal-seeming types.

So Keith bought a gun, a .32 revolver, from a drug dealer he knew. He went into the club and right into the office, late one night, put the loaded gun to Baumgartner's head, and said, "I want you to give me back my amp."

"Have you gone fucking crazy?"

Walter seemed to take it pretty well, having a gun held up to his head. He must not have believed it was loaded, or that Keith would shoot. Like he was in a movie, Keith shot out the window. To demonstrate his sincerity.

"You don't understand, Walter. That amp's not worth much, it's an antique, but I need it."

Just when it looked like Baumgartner was ready to come through, the police arrived. Keith surrendered.

His mother and father were vindicated in their low judgment of him by the arrest. Baumgartner wanted to drop charges, probably because he didn't want his business scrutinized, but in addition to attempted murder there were things like unlawful possession of a firearm, unlawful discharge of a firearm, menacing, a lot of shit like that.

Keith got to find out about jail. His father wouldn't bail him out, or at least was taking his time about it—Michael's dad, an attorney himself, put up the necessary funds.

Ultimately, Keith never had to do any time, though it looked bad there for a while. His amp was gone forever, never to return. Keith expressed remorse, in front of a judge whom Michael's father knew, and got off with a suspended sentence.

In another year, Keith and Michael Stein went to New York. Keith had saved up money, working as a messenger for Mr. Stein's law firm. Stein liked him, and he did a good job.

Walter Baumgartner closed his nightclub, and started having some problems with the IRS.

Keith can still remember, very clearly, how Baumgartner didn't crack, he was ready to die so as not to give in. If the police hadn't entered the equation, Keith might have shot him, out of irresistible curiosity to see what would happen next.

TEN

In New York, that's when Keith got obsessive about music on a higher level than before—he made breakthrough after breakthrough, hearing new things in his head all the time.

He had a girlfriend then who was very important to his development; he treated her badly and knew it at the time. She probably forgave him, for she was that kind of person, but he feels a twinge whenever he thinks of her now. Her name was Barbara, and she wasn't especially pretty or hip; in fact, she made jokes sometimes about how unstylish she was. Keith was never in love with her, but he loved her, in a way, and she listened to all his new music, whatever he composed she was delighted to hear it and respond. She was his best audience, for a long time. She encouraged him, flattered and cajoled him when he really needed some emotional support.

The problem was, in the social circles he was drawn into, he didn't especially like to be seen with Barbara, she seemed corny to him then, and he was secretly vain enough to think it was better for his "image" to turn up with some audaciously ornamental slut.

Barbara was hurt. Keith tried to make it all right, but he could see her side of it, that his behavior could be regarded as shallow and disloyal. Sure it was. But he found that, as the new band, SMX, became a happening commodity, he could get any number of dumb bunnies to listen to his latest new song. It all came to the same thing.

Was he so insufferable? Mostly what he thought about was the actual music. There was an ideal utopian space into which he went more or less at will. The actual sonic field blended with imagined, suggestive possibilities, hypothetical moments of transcendence and rhythmic flow. The music he heard gave hints of a perfect understanding of this world, a harmonious soundtrack where your body and mind connect in one blissful electrochemical wave. You are removed from time, from gravity's tie to the heavy spinning earth.

Keith was an idealist. The name SMX meant nothing in particular. It was close to SEX, or S&M, or SPX, a guitar effects unit both Keith and Michael used. SMX could be pronounced "Smacks," in which case it had druggy overtones, or was a breakfast cereal; spelled out it sounded like a car.

On stage, Keith often wore sunglasses, a white shirt, and short hair. The sunglasses helped him with his stage fright: he really hated the bright hot lights. It felt like coming out of a spaceship on superheated Venus—always unreal, as if you were in a film full of unsupervised special effects.

Guitars that sounded like backwards woodwind orchestras, or like grand pianos cut in half by melodious chainsaws. The Devil's smeary wah wah pedal feedback.

Keith met Renata Spengler at a photo shoot. She knew the photographer, and had some reason to come and speak with him. Then, she hung around. Keith felt an absurd confidence trying to pick her up.

SMX was asked to pose in leather jackets for French Vogue. Tania, the bass player, removed her top. The intoxication of glitter and praise and the constant undertow of ridiculous sleaze affected them all. Early friends went by the wayside, right and left. No one who wasn't there could understand.

ELEVEN

It's an old-fashioned alarm system, easy to disconnect. And Consuela said there isn't a dog. The front gate is far enough from the house that it seems all right to bring the truck in, away from the street. They can back it up to the house and take their time, once the house-sitting motherfucker is secure.

Elvis Morales. Victor and Teddy Rodriguez. They creep around a bit, outside, looking in the windows and seeing very little, checking to see if the Mercedes-Benz (which they also intend to steal) is in the garage. Yes, it is.

They can hear music playing within the house, and since there are several lights on, they are not sure where the guy might be at. It's 2:30 A.M. They reluctantly don ski masks, so he won't see their faces. It is possible that they will be pretty rough, but they have no intention of killing him. That would be an entirely different category of crime. Forget it. You'd never come out, if you went away for it. Or if you did, you'd come out an old man.

Nevertheless, everyone is carrying. Elvis has a 9mm which has jammed on him a couple times when he's test-fired it. He's worked on it and had Victor take a look and these days it seems to work okay. If he needed to really kill someone, or defend himself, he'd carry something else. The Rodriguez brothers each have Smith & Wesson .38s. Teddy's the young one, with the hot temper. Victor will try to keep him away from the Anglo, just in case the man behaves stupidly, or begins talking in a way that might piss Teddy off. Victor just wants everything to go down like they've planned. All of them are nervous, exhilarated and excited, but also kind of scared. Even with the easiest-seeming job, you never can be sure. God can decide to fuck you up, put you down. Man, put you in the ground.

So they're careful. They're trying to be careful. Elvis feels some responsibility toward the others, because it's a place his girlfriend has set up.

The thieves enter the house. They have found a door that is unlocked. This is a classy place, with classy stuff. Maybe they feel a little awed by the splendor, but they will have no qualms about disassembling and carrying away everything they can fit into the truck. It's like they're professional furniture movers. Once they get going, they will feel matter-of-fact and dry.

Ski masks on, they finally locate the house-sitter. He's listening to a CD, or maybe a tape. Great system. Elvis says, "If you cooperate, I promise you won't get hurt. Stay cool."

The Anglo has stood up, backing away a little, looking scared, though not as completely paralyzed as he ought to be by the gun. Only Elvis has his out, pointing at the dude. Teddy has the rope, to tie him up. Victor is down the hall, checking other rooms to make sure no one else is here.

Teddy pulls out a roll of white tape, to tape the guy's eyes and mouth shut.

'You understand?" Elvis asks, and the Anglo says, "Yeah, I understand. It would be better for you if you'd just leave, but I don't think you'll trust me on that, will you? I wish you would."

"No, man," Elvis says, smiling in the stuffy mask, wondering where Victor is, as Teddy goes forward with the rope, shoving the guy without any reason. Elvis doesn't feel like he can say anything critical to Teddy in front of the guy.

Where's Victor? Elvis turns around to look and there's this girl, he's shocked, it's just not what he expects at all, out of the corner of his eye he has the impression that something's happening with Teddy, this chick has blood on her lips and she's staring at him, coming closer, reflexively he pulls the trigger and the 9mm pumps a couple of bullets into her, the impact jolts her but then she just smiles and comes on. He's flat on his back and feels frozen, he can't move. It all happens in slow motion but so fucking fast.

He feels like he should be dead, like he's dying, but it's like one time when he was stabbed and woke up in the hospital, he doesn't care about anything at all.

There's some kind of a disturbance, over to one side of him, but he can't make the effort to turn his head and see. Something with Teddy. And then Teddy is done.

The ski mask is pulled off Elvis's head. There, that's better. They look down at him.

"Can you talk?"

He cannot. He can still blink his eyes. No, he can't.

The girl says, "This is the best one. I'm going to take some from him. There's another one out in the kitchen."

It feels so good to have her warm breath come down to his neck. Elvis gasps. There is music. He hears some classical piano music all over the world. He stares and forgets.

TWELVE

Before the three got into the house, Justine had come into the room and said, "We have visitors." She looked spooked. Keith asked her what she wanted him to do. He was willing, his manner said, to do whatever she required. This violation of their home . . . he could tell that it was something she truly hated and feared. She panted, just for a second, as if panicked, while Glenn Gould's piano transcription of Wagner resounded, schmaltzy and slowly melodramatic, building forever—and then she was gone.

When they came in, Keith felt like Justine would do something, he didn't know what. These guys just picked the wrong house to try and rob.

As Justine appeared and the guy tried to shoot her, Keith grabbed the other one and got him down onto the floor. The fellow was trying to get a gun out of his jacket, and this preoccupation enabled Keith to knee him in the groin and hold him down until Justine came over and bit his neck. It was harder than usual because the guy wasn't prepared, no trance to relax him, just fangs tearing into his throat.

Keith is not disgusted by the blood. He feels a kind of wonderment at himself that he can stand it, that he can participate in evil, but this vampire business still seems so surreal, and he has such a strange bond with Justine—you do what you have to.

When Keith used to do heroin, every time he jugged into a vein he thought maybe he'd die. It crossed his mind every single motherfucking time. He is so weak. He's beyond weakness. Helpless. It's all right. Killing these guys, seeing them killed, is in some tiny way like some sympathetic shiver of revenge—revenge on the Venezuelan gangsters who broke his fingers one by one in the Venezuelan jail.

His hands hurt really bad as he drags these two outside. It takes him a while. The pain makes him hate them more. He feels ugly, and ashamed. He doesn't want to go back in, to the light, but he does.

Justine is still sucking on the good-looking one, taking her time. When she looks up at Keith it's as if she is drunk, and he feels pleasure for her, that she has sustenance, nourishment . . . it puts roses in her cheeks.

She gets up, wiping her mouth on her sleeve. "Come here," she says, and he does, he shuts his eyes as he embraces her; he must have been frightened for he can feel himself tremble in her arms.

"Are you okay?" she asks.

"Yes. Did those bullets—did they hit you?"

"They went through," Justine says. "They passed on through."

Together, they drag this dead, drained thief outside. They don't want to get blood on the carpet. Justine comes back from the kitchen with a carving knife, and they cut all three of the throats upon the lawn, under the moon. Keith cuts the one of the guy who wrestled with him, whom he hurt his hands on. He has done this before, one time, to somebody who was already dead. This time, as he slices he feels murder. It's murder. He feels possessed by a sick electrical fizz. A weird jangly buzz. He could keep going, he can tell. He could saw off this dude's head. It is not lost on him that these guys all have had their own separate consciousnesses, their "I"'s. Keith trembles, but goes on. The mystery of death is before him, in the flesh.

It's work—though Justine is surprisingly strong. A quickness, really. They put the bodies in the back of the moving van. Keith will drive it away someplace and maybe set it on fire. There's a can of gasoline here in the back.

"Are you sure you can do all this? How will you get back?"

"I'll take the motorcycle," he rashly says. There's a motorcycle in the garage. He has never wondered whom it might have belonged to once upon a time.

4:30 A.M. When dawn comes, Justine has to be well removed from the rays of the sun. Keith may be a little photosensitive, but he doesn't anticipate any problem.

He hugs Justine, and she kisses him on the cheek. She's unbelievably warm. Like a madman, he shifts gears ultracarefully and soon leaves this neighborhood behind. It feels like he might never find his way back, like he's on his way to Mars. He feels reckless and scared to the bone.

THIRTEEN

It is of some comfort to Justine to clean up, down on her hands and knees, the blood spilled inside the house. She has not had a scene like this for a long time. But she can remember, quite vividly if chaotically, being hunted like an animal, that awful feeling of not knowing anywhere safe to hide.

She hopes Keith will be all right. Justine needs him. So many years spent in desolate, horrible quietness, inhuman, incurable . . . she has truly gazed upon and experienced the aching loneliness of a universe without God, and she has benumbed herself, existed like a creature made out of wood, or stone, or shit.

No, it's better to imagine God watching you, aware of everything within your soul, even if by your very existence you must sin, even if you might be understood in ordinary terms as a demon from hell.

They say the earth is young, as planets go; therefore, too, the life-forms are young, children really, childish, striving ever so slowly toward becoming pure spirit, the realm of what one might think of as Light.

Justine and others like her may have to exist in the Darkness, she reasons, through no fault, or choice—the why must be so very much larger and more complicated than anyone can conceive. In the face of such mystery, she is humble. Why are babies born blind, or deaf, all of those things? All of the mundane horrors. Justine seeks to understand, patiently, as one who has been given a difficult gift. She has been allowed to die and yet still live. Of what use is this, given the terms of her existence, one might ask. She doesn't know.

As she falls asleep she remembers—a memory consciously sought, and found—she remembers the devout young priest, so long ago, whom she visited one night, meaning to confess.

What was it that he said? Oh, she had been hungry, she put her spell on him, but lightly . . . and then they had talked, at midnight in the village church. He said that the wickedness of her existence was not for him to judge, that it was not of this world . . . it was older than that, older than sin itself perhaps— it came from before the fall of the angels.

Justine has often thought about this since. Or endeavored to thrust the thought away, as dangerous and absurd.

The priest said, when she asked him about hell, that hell is a place where no one is able to love. Not to love. And he said, You think that sounds ordinary . . . but even to understand what love is is a manner of love. A gift of God. Love comes from God. It was surprising, given the times, that he did not conjure up torments and exotic fire. Maybe her "venom" (which she always thought of as being like sugar-syrup) made him somewhat drunk, so that he was moved to a more personal utterance, or maybe the extraordinary circumstance affected him in this way.

The candles were burning, the cross towered above them as they approached the narthex. Outside it was dreary winter, it was endless night. Justine did not kill the priest. She left him unconscious, having fallen and gashed his poor neck. He would recover. He would be fine.

Keith reminds her, she realizes now, of that young priest in Provence. The priest was so innocent, so unworldly, devoid of any vanity. Is Keith like that, really? She tries to concentrate, to bring it back. The priest was plain-featured, even homely, frail and thin. No, the resemblance, if there is one, isn't physical. It's like some sort of indefinable *rhyme*.

FOURTEEN

Dissociated, yet feeling quite sane, Keith finds himself talking to Renata, "Look what you've driven me to," somehow believing that, from the grave, scattered, her problems solved, she'll understand. Perhaps even forgive.

This is the worst thing he has ever done. It was so easy. He slaps his own face at one point, as if to make himself realize the full gravity of his crime—but the slap and the talking are for his own benefit, and he sees this even as he cannot stop playing dumb. The truth is that he knows very well what's going on, and what is his role.

Formerly, before Justine, there were many things he had done that he was ashamed of. Most dramatically, he mistreated Renata, he misunderstood her, he was right there looking at her as she fell into the abyss. He looked right into her face, and he didn't save her.

Before that, there were many other things, but in comparison they all seem trivial and small. Renata saw right through him. She *knew*, she knew him, she chose him because she knew he'd help her fall.

One night, after he'd been with Justine for only a couple of weeks, maybe a month, when they were still getting used to the new situation . . . one night he drove her down to Venice, they went into this nightclub together and then separated. Keith was nervous, so he soon left to go wait in the car. He was afraid (probably groundlessly) that someone from the music scene might recognize him, that he might run into someone he knew.

Soon Justine came out, along with a young man. "He's my driver," Keith heard her say, and the young man laughed low, murmuring something. Then there was silence. Keith did not even glance in the rearview mirror.

He heard some sort of a sound. It went on for a while, and then Justine said his name. "Keith." He turned the key to start up the automobile. "No," she said. "No, stop. Look at me. *Look at me*."

And he turned and saw the blood, the fangs, the puncture wounds black in the shadowy light. It was some kind of a test. Keith put out his hand, and she kissed him on the back of the wrist, looking up at his face in a moment, grazing the fangs tantalizingly on his sensitive skin.

"Will you help me?"

Keith nodded, then said aloud: "Yes. It's okay."

They drove the kid to a park, carried him out onto the grass. Keith knelt there, took the knife from her, and cut into the throat to make some kind of a plausible wound.

Justine never asked him to do anything like that again. If she killed, he didn't know it.

Tonight, though, Keith knew that that thief was still alive.

When he cut his throat. Extenuating circumstances, sure, but a murder. Something permanent and unfixable. Consciousness and personality violently stopped. He tries to forget. There are these things he needs to do, so he tries to lose himself in the details, one by one.

Having driven the truck to a remote spot, he sets it on fire. This will draw attention at the same time as it obliterates clues. He has already taken all identification from the men, and retrieved from Justine's victim's pocket a map of the house and grounds, with the address. He rides away on the motorcycle, as the morning turns steel-gray to silver and rose-blue. Let them burn. The fire may be unnecessary, he realizes, but it seems necessary to *him*. As a ritual, a gesture of sacrifice. He feels like a lawless motherfucker back in the time when Justine was only a child. Exults in the destruction. Let them burn.

FIFTEEN

Michelle is wearing a dull silver way-too-large t-shirt with the sleeves ripped off; it hangs down over her right shoulder. The strap of a black bra is visible, in amongst sundry other black strings, a leather thong, and thin silver chains. A double-link piece of chain serves as a necklace, or loose choker. Elaborate custom or homemade earrings, continuing the chain motif. On the t-shirt, in red letters, it says SAINT AGATHA.

But most notable, to anyone even glancing at her, is the fact that Michelle's head is mostly shaved. She has a mohawk, though it is not, at this moment, moussed or otherwise greased to stick up. The henna'd brunette hair looks basically combable and soft. Michelle has had this hairstyle for a month, long enough so that her scalp no longer looks that sickly gray. Not that she would care. She liked the gray. The truth is, as far as outsiders are concerned, she doesn't care if they think she looks bad or good. Fuck all of them. If it freaks them out, that's their problem. She wants to make them unhappy like that, if only for a few moments, in the middle of their boring day. Her friends gave her this haircut, one night when she was on acid, but it wasn't like she was out of her mind.

She has somewhat of a roundish head, a roundish face, though she isn't fat. Her mother once said, in typically casual, hurtful fashion, that she has "chipmunk cheeks." Her friend Jason has said, thoughtfully, that she looks a bit like Linda Blair, when Linda Blair was young. But better, he said, sensing her frown.

Well, since the haircut, within her circle she's been more in demand. Jason is going to use her for the cover of the next issue of *The Darkest Night*, this magazine he publishes and edits, which Michelle does record reviews and interviews for. Their favorite band, goth-rock death-rock Saint Agatha . . . Michelle has got something going with the bass player, though she doesn't think it adds up to much. Michelle is nineteen.

Right now she is stopped at a gas station putting five dollars' worth of gas in the van. It's 10:30 A.M., usually very early for Michelle, in this case very late. She's been up all night. She's on her way home from a party at Saint Agatha's house. Nothing happened with the bass player, Fred. She doesn't know what's going on there. She doesn't like him that much, anyway. At about 6:30, she fell asleep on the rug. Curled up next to Jeff.

She yawns. It's a cloudy, gray, dirty, warm day. Across from the gas station is an aging bar and grill, maybe from the sixties, with these painted-on shadows of tall palm trees on the stucco wall, spiky silhouettes—while the actual, real trees seem to be dying, one of them is bent over, it looks sick.

Out of nowhere, then, at the Coke machine, when she pulls over and jumps out to get a can of Coke, this guy comes up to her and says, "Listen, can you give me a ride home? I'll pay you. How about, mm—really, fifty bucks?"

Some other time it might be like one of her fantasies come to life, because he's handsome, pale, kind of sad . . . a chance meeting with a stranger. She shades her eyes against the sun, looking around, past the traffic and the telephone poles, the wires, and he says, "My bike broke down. I don't want to fuck with calling a cab."

Michelle doesn't ask why not, but she does look him up and down, like checking him for dangerousness or the possibility of weapons. He seems to read her mind, and smiles. He's not too eager, so she says, "How far?"

"Beverly Glen."

"Give me the fifty bucks first."

"Okay," he says, and counts it out. His hands are in bandages, fresh bandages with some bloodstains.

"What happened to you?"

"Oh," he says, and she thinks he might not answer, but then as they start to pull into traffic he says, "They got slammed in some car doors."

"Ouch," she says. "That's harsh."

They go past some Vietnamese signs, stoplight to stoplight, and she thinks of mustard, blood, and gasoline. Pops in a cassette.

"What's your name?" she asks, as they go down this xerox'd gaudy, forlorn section of strip.

"Keith."

He looks vaguely familiar. She says, "My name is Michelle."

"I really appreciate this," he says, as if she is just doing him a favor, no money being involved. She can really use it, actually. She's poor. Actually, this will allow her to go a little longer without asking her mom for money. They're not getting along. Her mom, Brenda, is a CPA. She's so full of shit, with her sorry-ass boyfriends, her desperate dating.

Keith is thinking, *Just get me home. Please, just let me get home.* It had seemed like he deserved it when the motorcycle conked out, after hissing and dying all the way from San Bernardino. He abandoned it in an alley, near a used-car lot with colored little flags flapping in the wind. He was feeling very shaky when, at the gas station, he suddenly walked up to Michelle. She reminded him of the kind of girls he used to meet when he was in the band, before they were a success.

Perhaps unfairly, he has instantly assessed her. He thinks he knows her type. Poor self-esteem, mostly dumb but sometimes more intelligent then she needs to be, morbid, self-conscious, a sucker for "bad boy" *poseurs*. She talks, overcoming her initial awkwardness, and he encourages her, although he's not really curious about any of this stuff.

Groupies, parasites, hangers-on. Every group accumulates them. People who will go get you a Coke, a takeout meal, or some MDA. Girls who will give you a blow job, etc. No, he doesn't want to remember. But he can't help himself.

To interrupt, he asks Michelle to tell him more about this business of *The Darkest Night*. This leads to a discourse on Jason, the prime organizer of everything. Jason started out by doing videos in high school, and charging admission to his parties. You wouldn't know the location for sure until the final day. They were always jammed, totally jammed, like turning kids away. He's a true bisexual, too. Now besides the magazine, he has a cable show, and he's getting into booking bands. It all fits together, it's all part of the same thing. He has like a vision, a highly developed aesthetic.

Keith nods, as they travel past hundreds of car lots, used and new. Numbers, promises, gray cement. He understands that this is Saint Agatha, the band she and Jason and the rest are hot on, high on—that's their album playing on the cassette.

"What do you think?"

"I like it," Keith says, faking interest, just like when somebody back when would make him listen to a tape.

"Really?"

"Yeah."

She grins. A large healthy child. Teenage nihilism's always in style.

SIXTEEN

Michelle is yawning. She confides to Keith that she's been up all night, that she's very sleepy. He doesn't seem impressed.

"I need to come in," she says. "I have to go to the bathroom. And if you don't mind, I sort of want to see where you live."

She refrains from saying anything about the evident wealth. The van is parked and turned off. She comes inside, annoyed by the feeling she gets that he doesn't want her here now. It makes her want to bug him, to test him right away.

Does she make him nervous? He's so polite, it's hard to tell whether he likes her or not, or in what way. She strolls out of the bathroom, gazing around at the spaciousness, and the art. Keith is looking down at a spot on the floor. When he sees that she's observing him, he smiles and says, "Go ahead, look around."

"Do you live here by yourself?"

"No," he says. "But the other person . . . she's gone a lot. She travels all over the world."

"Oh? What does she do?"

"She's an art consultant," Keith says, as Michelle bends over, scanning the titles of his CDs, not exactly expecting to see much that she likes.

"Would you like something to drink? I know I have iced tea."

It dawns on her. It's like she's known for a while, she's known there was *something*: seeing the band's name makes her fully realize, she looks at him, eye contact, and says, "I thought I recognized you. You used to be the guitar player in SMX."

"No," he says. "It's somebody that looks like me."

She laughs and shakes her head. "No, it's you. Keith . . van der something. I've seen your picture, I've seen you in your videos." She glances at his hands. "I remember that there were these rumors . . . and you dropped out of sight."

"I'm okay now," he says. "But I don't want anyone to know where I am. Can you keep this a secret? Really. I'm out of all that."

"What about your hands? What happened to them? You've got bloodstains . . . are you all right?"

"This? Oh, it's not . . . don't worry, it's not anything. When they were broken, they weren't set properly, so they're still kind of fucked up. I do rehab, and occupational therapy. But sometimes . . . they're easily hurt."

He comes close, puts his hands on her bare shoulders. Michelle knows it's important to him, and so she doesn't want to give in.

"Michelle, please, will you promise me? Don't tell anyone about me. It's not much of a story, even to the alternative press. SMX is over. I had my day. I just wanna be left alone. I don't want people talking about me, or even thinking about me. Don't tell Jason. . . . "

He holds onto her wrists and lightly drags her to the couch, so they're sitting together.

"It could really fuck things up for me," he says, and something in his tone makes her think this might be true, or that he believes it might be true, and she stops feeling like being a bitch to him, and says, in a different voice, "I won't say anything. I can keep my mouth shut if I want to. There're plenty of secrets that I never . . . I never say a word."

"Okay," Keith says, very quietly, and she thinks, *God, what's wrong with him? What is he so afraid of? It's not like anybody really cares.* At the same time, his vulnerability and everything makes him terrifically attractive, even more so than before . . . and she just barely senses or imagines that there's probably some mystery here she doesn't understand. She's drawn to him, and curious, very curious.

After they're silent for a few minutes, they look into each other's eyes, and Michelle smiles in a way that she guesses he understands. She says, "Can I come visit you?" and he says,

"Yeah, sure. Come in the afternoon. That's the best time. The nights aren't so good."

SEVENTEEN

1950. It's a rainy, humid night. So sticky and damp you're not sure when it is raining and when it has stopped.

Frank McKenna, homicide detective, has seen some bad juju, but this time he knows he's in deeper than he can ever get out of, he's at the bottom of a hole going clear down dark to the endless void at the center of the earth. To hell, in other words.

He strangles Justine, sort of experimentally, hard enough to kill just about anyone, make them stick their tongue out, eyeballs pop, for sure leave big handprints on her white throat, he strangles her but doesn't really believe that she will die.

She goes limp, her eyes stare at nothing, it's like she's mocking him because she suddenly with a *jerk* is out of his hands, standing a few feet away. He wishes she would at least ask him why, but she doesn't bother, isn't curious, doesn't want to know. Isn't even mad. She owns him; they both know it well.

Okay. He lights a cigarette, trying to steady his trembling hands. They stand there, in the run-down house in the Hollywood hills.

Frank makes himself tough it out, smooth out his voice, interrogation technique, says, "You ought to put Gloria in the ground. She's drawing flies. You'll have coyotes soon enough, they smell that meat."

Gloria is the big-breasted bleached-blond whore who used to be Frank's snitch. He shacked up with her sometimes. Now she lies there dead in a coffin, turning colors, just out the sliding glass doors. Guess Justine got tired of having her around, running her errands in the daylight, driving her places at night.

"I'm watching her change," Justine says, no huskiness evident from the strong thumbs on her throat. "I want to see what happens, day by day."

"Is she going to . . . ?"

"No. I didn't bite her."

"How'd she die then? Natural causes?"

Justine shrugs, like how would I know, though Frank had noticed Gloria's neck cut open ear to ear, as if with a jagged saw.

He goes over to the bar, pours himself a drink. Straight bourbon. Knocks it back. The room is hot, perspiring.

He's been bringing people to Justine, white trash and drifters, prostitutes and spic pimps, mostly she just takes a pint or so but a few times in his presence she's gone all the way.

It's bad. It gives him an unbelievably bad hink, Justine wanting to watch Gloria decompose. He turns on the radio to country swing. Bob Wills and his Texas Playboys.

"Listen," Frank says, "you can't just keep Gloria out there like that."

"Why not?"

"Because . . . it's not wise." Frank wants to leave, to get out; at the same time he wants to stay, he wants her to hold him in her arms, he wants that sweet dangerous amnesiac high. On one level, he knows what she does to him. But he wants it anyway, those fangs, that feeling like magical forgiveness of all his sins.

"Let me get rid of her," Frank says. "She's far gone enough, you must be gettin' the drift."

'What will you do with her?" Justine asks, after a while.

"I don't know. Steal a car and put her in the trunk. I'm not sure."

"You know how to fix these things." Justine states this as a fact, and he's proud. Sure, he knows how to fix these things. He's shaken down pansy movie stars, beat the fuck out of their blackmailing boyfriends, set up city councilmen to be photographed in bed with nigger whores, leaned on them to plead health reasons to resign their seats or else the pictures come out, he's framed commies for reefer or chicken out in the park. He's framed spics and covered up evidence on guilty but connected wops. He's done it all.

"I'll get you a Filipino maid," he says, and Justine doesn't say thank you, doesn't seem grateful, instead goes out to cop a few last looks at Gloria, in the plain unvarnished coffin up on a picnic tabletop to keep away some of the mice.

Frank decides not to wait. He goes out the front door to his car, backs up into the add-on garage. Before he can handle touching poor Gloria, he needs another drink.

Then, when he's calm enough to gaze upon the vampire of his dreams studying the face of the purplish, greenish, livid corpse— Justine turns her eyes to him, and she comes in, and without saying a word she lifts his wrist to her mouth and gently, painlessly injects some of her serum. She looks at him almost with some sort of compassion—it isn't compassion—the injected vampire saliva or whatever it is cuts through all of the bennies and coffee and alcohol and pure fear, he collects himself and does the awful job of somehow lifting the week-old corpse out of the coffin, carrying it wrapped in a blanket to the trunk of his car. It stinks, but he is immune for the moment to the horrid smell.

It's a sucker play, and he knows it. Still, he has to do it. He drives into town at 3:00 A.M. and has some sort of half-developed plan now of planting the body in the bungalow of this religious sex freak named Reichardt, maybe do a real grandstand play and plug him for resisting arrest, set up some kind of sick scene there before calling it in. What's fishy about this plan is that some guys on the Squad know about Frank and Gloria, that he used to take it out in trade. A lot of the guys in Vice used to fuck her, Frank wasn't the only one. Back in 1945 or so, '46, she was hot stuff. The last couple of years she's been fading fast.

Frank rolls to his apartment, meaning to run in and get a throw-down piece, only as he parks his car and gets out of the DeSoto some unfriendly Narco bulls come out of the shadows and brace him, one of them says, "Where's that scag from the Epley scene?"

"Yeah, cut us in, Frank. You been acting strange."

Epley is this hepcat trumpet player who caught an axe in the forehead, unsolved, Frank's case, rumor has it some jigaboos from South Central followed him home.

"I don't have any heroin," Frank says. "Epley was clean. What's the fucking skinny, you show up here at my pad?"

Lieutenant Davies says, "Let's see what's in your trunk."

Something in Frank's face maybe gives him away—when he makes a play for his gun, Randolph the ex-Marine grabs his arm and breaks it, snaps the elbow the wrong way and Frank falls to his knees, hat falling off his head into the street.

Davies says, "Check the trunk. It better be here."

The pain is bearable, because of Justine's bite. The funny thing is, Frank *did* cop the heroin. It's hidden at his sister's, he intended to lay it off through this pachuco he's used before, Tommy Diaz. Maybe Diaz talked. These guys are pissed. They want their cut.

Their payoff for breaking his arm is they find Gloria. Other guys, he could tell them something, they could work it out. Davies here hates his guts. It's just bad luck. Davies wants to see him fry in the electric chair, since they busted his arm there's no going back.

'Why'd you do it, man? The cooze just get into your head?"

"Shut up, Oscar. Who gives a shit why he went off. He's been walking on razors for years. Now he got cut. He's gonna bleed all the way to the chair."

Frank McKenna keeps his mouth shut. At the station, they try to sweat him, ignoring his broken arm. His story is that he found her dead, went mad with grief and the combination of not having slept for three days: he'll take a lie detector test on whether he snuffed her or not, nothing else. Inadvertently, yes, he tampered with a crime scene. The chief comes in to see him, says he can be on inactive duty till he gets his twenty in another few months.

Then he will resign. This whore-killing is buried, kiboshed.

"Lieutenant Davies shouldn't have let his men come on so strong."

Days later, arm in a cast, Frank has a pal drive him up into the Hollywood hills. Check the house. Nothing doing. Justine is gone. He never sees her again.

He gets a job as head of security at one of the studios. He puts on weight, takes up with an ex-starlet-turned-agent named Roxanne. His right arm is never the same. You might say he's haunted. Every single night, he remembers. Even on vacation in Havana, playing blackjack, watching a sex show, he never forgets. All the alcohol in the world.

He's lost his edge. Roxanne leaves him. He's fired from his job. "New blood," they say they want. He's a drunk. They start showing *Dracula* on late night TV and he tells people he used to know a vampire. Nobody's interested. It's 1956.

EIGHTEEN

"Do you ever . . . does it ever feel like, through the blood, that you really *experience* the life, or the mind, of this stranger you're preying upon?"

"I try to seal myself off," Justine answers.

"Then there *is* something. Some communication . . . outside the normal channels."

"I don't know what I'd call it," Justine says.

They are in darkness, in Keith's bedroom. He is hesitant to touch her, because of the bullet holes. He doesn't want to be indelicate.

"I just wondered," he says, "if you ever felt . . . like all these people—were *contained* in you, somehow. And then, beyond that, I wondered . . . if there is some kind of collective memory, something like that, some element that continues, that endures.

Or if the blood is just like food, with nothing to say."

"It says something," she replies, slowly. "But I am not a worthy vessel. I am not sensitive enough to understand."

"Oh, I think you're sensitive."

Justine looks at him anew; he can feel the movement of her eyes. She seems to be concentrating. A long silence ensues.

"I have never loved," she says, after a long time. "Not like you loved your Renata. You still love her, even now."

"You're wrong. I hate her. She was crazy, and we collided, it was a collision, I hate her for what happened to me. I should never have told you about her."

"Are you lying to me?"

"No. I hate her. I've hated her for a long time. If what happened was random, bad luck, I hate her like you'd hate a wasp that stings you in the eye. If it wasn't random, if you want to say she was my fate . . . then she is my enemy, and that's worse. I want to totally forget about her, to be indifferent. . . . The heroin used to help me with that."

"You think about her," Justine says, with some confusion, "you see her. She's alive to you."

"No."

Justine waits. He can see her face in the moonlight now.

"You're beautiful," he says, the first time he's ever thought this, or maybe the first time she has looked like this to him. "You have the face of an angel."

The words trouble her, judging by her expression. He doesn't care.

"Why do you want to die?" she asks.

"What do you mean?"

"Well, you know that if you want to, I will make you like me. Many people," she moves to push her hair out of her face, "want this very much. I've known them. As soon as they find out what I am, they want to be one too. They don't want to die, not in the ordinary way."

"I'm afraid of dying," he says. "I'm not brave. But one's life . . . only has shape when it has an end. People die constantly, all over the world. It can't be so hard. What would I accomplish if I hung around, hiding out and drinking blood? What would be the point?"

"Yes," Justine says, and she's smiling in such a way that he's not sure whether she's offended or not. She feels something. He cannot tell what.

She may kill him now, to call his bluff. He stares at what he cannot see in the darkness and is ready, he dares her, he is sincere.

NINETEEN

"My stepfather gave me the first orgasm I ever had," Renata said, as she and Keith lay, half-entangled in the sheets. This was four years earlier, in her apartment, Upper East Side in New York.

"Didn't you know how to masturbate?" Keith asked, rather coolly, unwilling to make a show out of being provoked by such provocative material.

"No," she said, rolling over, onto her back. "Not until he showed me how." She sighed, and he watched her face closely, she had such a repertoire of expressions, modeling does this . . . it's like silent-film acting. "It sounds bad, I know," she said, staring up at the skylight, "but it wasn't as sordid . . . it didn't seem sordid at the time. It was like . . ." she moved again, "he was a man of the world, and he was teaching me these secrets, he was initiating me. Like," she said, "Babylonian fathers used to initiate their daughters, in Babylon. That's what he told me." Renata laughed, briefly, and Keith continued squeezing her hand, perhaps he squeezed it harder for a moment—he regarded her warily, not really knowing how to respond. Already he withheld judgment, as she had once or twice been proven, circumstantially, to have told him some melodramatic untruths. So the sympathy he extended for what struck him as this revelation of terrible pain . . . the sympathy was tentative and restrained, not wanting one thing or the other, waiting to really understand.

"My stepfather was very charismatic and strong willed, and charming. He said that I was a natural-born *nymphet*, I was irresistible, if I learned to use this I would have a wonderful career. He liked to be naked, he liked all of us to be naked. My mother . . . couldn't keep up with his Dionysian side, she wouldn't *let go*."

There was bitterness toward the mother here. Keith asked, "Did she know?"

"I think so," Renata said. "They had big arguments . . . behind closed doors. My mother was jealous of me."

A tear made its way out of Keith's right eye. He knew the mother had died of breast cancer. He wanted to ask about Renata's younger sister, but he did not, remembering that Renata had said they did not get along. The sister was three years younger, a student at Sarah Lawrence.

"I'm sorry about telling you all this," Renata said, tracing Keith's tear with her finger, wetting her index finger in it, as another followed, slowly. "It's a mess."

"I don't know what to say," Keith said.

"Don't worry," she said, lightly kissing him on the cheek. "I love you. It's all in the past."

Renata's "beauty" meant nothing to him then. It was unlucky. She was way inside there, far far away from her flesh, her perfect skin. He wasn't a doctor, he couldn't fix her, and he didn't want her to feel like her past, her problems, hung there between them like a living ball of hell. He didn't want her to feel that he was expecting something, so that if she did not behave in therapeutic fashion, do "x" or "y," that therefore she was letting him down. He didn't want her to have any possibility of thinking she'd failed, or that he was disappointed in her.

"Anything you do," he said, "is all right with me. I mean forever. If you sometime want to stab me through the heart, I mean it will hurt, I'll die . . . but I forgive you in advance. I just wish we could be happy together somewhere, just ordinary, maybe live together in Switzerland or something and forget everything else. Take the cows out into the field and bring them back at night. Like that."

Renata smiled, really smiled, and they lay close together, gazing into each other's faces. That was the extent of the landscape they knew, for a while they didn't know anything else.

Oh, and they walked outside into a big park, it was different, the world had changed and when they came out it was all new: It turned out that Renata's room was on the second story of a Japanese-style little building, there were shops on the ground floor, they were in the midst of a park that stretched out for miles and miles in every direction. There were no cars, no paved streets, just untrampled green lawns, people walking everywhere, everything clean, everyone friendly and smiling, strolling about hand in hand. Renata and Keith walked over a hill with their friends and down to more small buildings and large tents. A procession of large puppets, led by harlequin-clad jugglers, the music of tambourines and drums and big bells. It was not New York. Maybe someplace in California. Such a gigantic green park! The sun shining down on the colors and faces and wonderful skin. It was paradise. Renata cut her finger, and it bled. It's nothing, she said. Keith's same finger bled in the same exact place. The pain was okay. They smiled at each other. The pain was just fine.

No, that part was just a dream.

45

TWENTY

Renata, at twenty-two, could look world-weary, jaded, as though she understood sorrow beyond her years; at the same time she was young and heartbreakingly innocent. She could go from complicated interest mingled with contempt to a nine-year-old who'd been early corrupted, yet now had been saved and was lost in the moment, lost in a moment of pure joy, the child's perception, awake and alive to the unselfconsciousness of pure *fun*.

Often, in many of the photos, one wanted to protect her, to cheer her up, to show her that the world was not so bad.

She had an innate grace. She held and moved her body gracefully, fluidly—the photographers all loved the way she walked, the way she stood or sat at rest. She could turn on a knowledge of sexiness, a smoldering gaze and a new tilt to her pelvis, subtle but real, she could turn it on and off.

Once she came to have power as a model, she sometimes threw tantrums, or burst into tears, say, when she was bored and they couldn't get the reflectors the way they wanted them, but it wasn't personal, the storm passed in a moment, it was easy to get her to laugh. Renata wasn't a bitch in the sense of fucking with those lower on the totem pole, she wasn't stuck up at all with underlings and technicians, she might not necessarily go out of her way to learn their names but she would talk to them with genuine friendliness, and recognized repeat faces from one shoot to the next. She was a pro. Everyone got tired and out of sorts now and then.

Renata wore a black Calvin Klein jacket in washed silk crepe, along with matching trousers and three different complex silver bracelets on the left wrist, two on the right. Hands in her pants pockets. No top on under the jacket. No necklace or earrings, other than, in the visible right lobe, one plain pearl stud.

Renata wore a lace evening gown, form-fitting, at first glance lingerie. Her expression was unreadable, hint of a secret smile.

A gray jacket with a man's silk tie, hair blown by a wind from her left. Renata's lips, her as-if-Russian, nineteenth-century gaze.

In a composition that was blown up bigger than life-size to appear in an exhibition by the *au courant* art-porn photographer Cesar Sutherland (who is gay, and black) Renata reclined with her hair tied back, holding a clarinet across her hips, a jeweled choker around her neck, otherwise naked but for ritual black nylon stockings and garter belt, spiked heels, a tiny black g-string tightly hugging her vulva—a weird, strangely excited but also perhaps embarrassed, excited-by-shame smile there in her lips and glittering eyes.

In another one she just stood naked, sullen really, hair messy and sweaty, lips puffy, her left hand's fingers touching her semi-shaven sex. Byzantine-style antique bracelets and an elaborate earring in the exposed left ear. In black and white. Really, sort of a typical, "arty," quasi-pornographic pose. Renata never had too much modesty about her breasts. She was fond of them. They'd been augmented when she was seventeen, and they were perfect, not too big, perfectly shaped. The nipples were not very sensitive, however, since the surgery. They came erect at temperature changes and at being rubbed but she really didn't feel much, in an erotic sense, anymore. These breasts also were not as soft as others Keith had known. They were problematic.

Renata called up Keith one night and told him, low-key and subdued, so low-key as to seem pharmaceutically tranquilized, that she was all right, not to think about it, she was going to have an abortion in the morning and she thought he ought to know. "I'm just informing you of a *fait accompli*." He hadn't known she was pregnant. He said, "Wait. Let's talk about this." He didn't know what he wanted, there wasn't enough time. He was in New York with the band. Renata was calling him from Copenhagen. He wanted her to wait.

They had gone together, in France, to the nude beach. All he could remember was the blue water, and this hushed feeling, like sound didn't carry very far. The violent contrast of the sand, all of this white sand, and the soft (or not-so-soft) oiled, raw skin. The sun cooking them slowly into a stupor, one's normal social consciousness melting into this elemental, light- and heat-drunk daze. The sensuous here and now. Complicated and complicating, even as they spoke to each other in low voices, imagining they were talking, that they could speak and the other would hear.

After the abortion, when he put it in too far she said it hurt. Keith didn't believe it, or thought she was exaggerating, or that she should see another gynecologist, but she didn't want to. He thought this phase would pass. He held her, hugged her, whispered to her, and kissed away her tears. And so, there wasn't that much fucking going on. But they were in love. They were a couple. If they had to be in two separate places on earth, because of career, they ran up big long-distance bills. They talked every day. "Where were you?" the other would ask if one missed.

So Renata knew Keith's latest thoughts on feedback and its effects on the brain and nervous system, and the latest music-world gossip, and what was going on between the members of the band. Renata talked about what she did during her day, the art and fashion people she met and what she thought of them, what trends were in the air—and Keith was always very interested in all this, and interested to hear about how for instance navy was being used instead of black.

Black wasn't going anywhere, but navy looked newer. Keith loved details like that, which he would then let drop to Tania and Shawn. Or Renata might tell him about how Julia Raspberry was in withdrawal, nine months pregnant, and gave birth while sitting on a toilet bowl, Sheila, her lover, using a broken hundred-dollar bottle of Barbaresco to cut the cord.

Renata was one-fourth Jewish. One time, she had gone to Israel, but she said she didn't feel Jewish in that way. She had never been in a synagogue. But Hitler would have seen her as a Jew. The SS would have put her on one of those trains. She had gone to Smith, flunked out, then gone to Syracuse University for about a year. She affected to despise her younger sister, Sasha, for reasons that were unclear.

Renata arranged herself on the bed in the hotel room, in Venezuela, nude, a composition for Keith to come back and view. A picture he'd never forget. She had taken several Roxicet, a narcotic pain pill roughly equal to Percodan, and slashed both of her wrists, and then perhaps, not getting anywhere, the veins in her right elbow to much greater effect. She was left-handed. There was blood all over the sheets and on the floor, crimson and wet, attracting a half-dozen flies. The glass doors to the balcony were open, letting in a warm breeze that smelled of *empanadas* sold on the street.

Gilberto, whom Renata had known briefly two years before, who still sent her flowers, birthday presents, the occasional letter—Gilberto approached Keith three days after the death, when Keith sat alone in a restaurant, trying to make himself eat.

That night, Keith was arrested for heroin possession. They planted it in his room. In those days, the only drug he used was alcohol, and not too much of that.

He wondered, later, if Renata had contacted Gilberto. He wondered how much of all this she had planned, beyond her actual death. She admired greatly such suicides as Sylvia Plath, Yukio Mishima, Ian Curtis, Anne Sexton. She thought people who lived on "as less than themselves" were cowards. Gilberto blamed Keith for drug taking and emotional scars which led to Renata taking her life. In the restaurant, he said, "You killed her. You drove her to it." Keith couldn't defend himself, not to a stranger, but he thought this was unfair.

Guilty or not, he was punished. They broke his fingers, one by one, all ten. Then at least one of them raped him, though it hardly mattered to him by then. A month later, Tony, the band's manager, was able to get the charges dropped, paying a large fee. Keith was a heroin addict, having taken it for the pain and to blot out all thought. A nice homosexual named Pascual had taken care of him, washing him and shooting him up. Sucking his penis now and then as a reward.

Renata had killed herself and killed him too, like a pharaoh's household, annihilated as a sacrifice to the holy dead. She had left him around to know about it, to remember her, to see her naked, a hand coming out of her sex.

TWENTY-ONE

Keith comes to meet Consuela at the gate. He is wearing a cinnamon-colored shirt, light tan or natural loose-fitting trousers, and he says, confirming her nervousness, "I'm sorry, but we've made other arrangements. The owner was here late last week and over the weekend, and she wants to use the same service that her brother recommends. I'm sorry . . . I thought it would be better to tell you in person than just call the agency, and also—here." He hands her an envelope. "Severance pay, since this is so sudden. You don't have to report it, mm, for your taxes."

He almost smiles, but not quite. Consuela is stunned; she nods, she says thank you, he nods and turns to go, wishes her luck.

Back in her car, Consuela finds that the envelope contains three hundred dollars cash. She realizes that they know something but it's all so puzzling. The theory in the neighborhood is that Elvis and the Rodriguez brothers were hijacked, that they stole something and had it taken from them, maybe some Vietnamese gang or something, because the killings were not in the style of the barrio, nor of the shoot-em-up Uzi overkill blacks.

But they planned to come here, to the Durand house. Elvis actually never said when, however, so they might have been out on another job, something he never mentioned. It seems too much of a coincidence that they would just happen to fire her now, today, unless they suspect something. And if nothing happened here, what would there be to suspect?

Consuela finds that for some reason, as she drives off, the money makes her cry, somehow it brings back the shock of finding out, the other day, that Elvis was dead. His body burned. The police won't exactly be breaking their necks trying to find out who did it, either. Who knows? It might have been the LAPD themselves. There might have been some chance encounter, some words exchanged. That Teddy was such a hothead.

Consuela shakes her head. She still can't believe it. This morning, cleaning the Japanese man's apartment, she kept thinking when am I gonna wake up? She better go to the agency, she realizes. Explain what Keith said. She's been terminated, but it's not her fault. He said she didn't have to say anything about this money, didn't he? It's just for her and her kids.

Big sigh. Maybe tonight she'll call up her friend Peppa, hire a babysitter, they can go down to Richie's cantina and get drunk. She feels the need to talk to someone about Elvis, to confess.

TWENTY-TWO

"Feel my wounds," says Justine, sitting in the raised bathtub, art deco carved gold feet on a floor of black-and-white checkerboard tile. Her hair is wet, so that her pierced ears show. Keith, who has been sitting on the closed toilet seat, comes over to her, hesitates, looking from her frail body up to her eyes and back down to her small white breasts and then her ribs. "Don't be afraid," she says, somehow amused. "Touch them. Put your finger in."

There's a little circle of red, swollen flesh around each of the bullet holes. Keith touches the fast-closing central dime-shaped entry, and gently presses his right index finger into the yielding puzzle-pull, tactilely experiencing the heat generated by the healing, the gunk as hot as interplanetary soup.

"Is it sore?" he asks, looking up to her face.

"No," she says. "It's more like it's itchy, and, I don't know, hungry. I need more blood."

He nods. He thinks he understands. The tepid bathwater is a brick red swirly color, from the blackish discharge she emits when she sleeps, and which was caked in the front and back wound sites. The exit wounds are larger, yet seem to be healing just as swiftly.

When someone is bitten by a vampire and sucked unto death,

that person will turn into a vampire after two or three nights, generally, unless exposed to sunlight all day, or beheaded, burned, subjected to an autopsy, or left in water, either fresh or salt. The stake through the heart has a paralyzing effect, and can be fatal if left in for a long enough time.

The "sugar-syrup" that Justine has injected a few times into Keith has almost entirely worn off: the telepathic link is quite faint.

As she puts on makeup, she complains to Keith, "I don't really feel like doing this. I can't talk to people."

"You don't have to say much," he replies.

When dressed, Justine takes her time, bandaging Keith's hands in a special way she's learned to give them support. He groans at one point, but when she looks up he nods, he says it's fine.

Out in the car, the Mercedes, as they come into the sea of lights Justine becomes a little excited, it amazes her, just for a moment, how much things have changed. This endless electric urban cosmic swarm of fallen stars is incomprehensible in terms of rural, fifteenth–century France.

They drive to Santa Monica, go into Stephen's, to reconnoitre over a glass of wine. Yes, Justine will drink red wine, although only a few sips at a time. It is early, not even midnight. There are many places one can go, to find a stray. In her simple but somewhat slinky "little black dress" she would immediately be prey to adventures were she to enter a lesbian bar, and then it's very simple. Somebody desires her, in any case an impossible desire, a desire for something that in real life does not exist. Desire that leaves them in most cases with a wound, and perhaps sometimes an indistinct memory that comes now and then in their sleep, in their dreams. On occasion the impossible desire will leave them *all used up*.

Keith says, "Someone I know," lightly touching her hand, and Justine looks up to see someone—a young woman— approaching their little table, smiling unaffectedly, and as it develops she is a doctor, she once was one of Keith's doctors, she mentions that she hasn't seen him now for over a year. When he begins to introduce her as "Dr. Rothschild," she dismisses the formality, her name is Tamara, and as such she introduces herself to Justine.

Modern medicine in general, much less women doctors— it's all very foreign to Justine, outside of her experience, so she studies Tamara as the latter, unafraid, having been invited to sit down, soon takes the liberty of asking Keith about his hands. From her eyes, although she will not bring it up, one can see that the last she knew, Keith was back on heroin. She seems to like him, though, and not to judge him.

Tamara is not beautiful, but she is certainly attractive, the more so perhaps for the clean gaze of intelligence without arrogance or evident vanity in her pale blue eyes. Why this should tend to provoke her, Justine does not know, all she understands is that she feels provoked.

"Well, you look good," Tamara says. "You look like you're doing well." Presumably here indirectly she's referring to the drugs. Only now, socially, when her putative reason for sitting here, her "excuse"—Keith being a former patient whom she is interested in—only now, when this has begun to seem played out, is she a bit awkward, or shy.

She explains that she came here with a colleague, after attending the symposium on nerve damage that's part of a week-long conference being held at a nearby hotel.

"So when I saw you, after you'd just dropped out of sight . . . I had to see how you've been getting along."

She smiles then at Justine, nonverbally apologizing for having registered her in only a rather cursory way. Justine holds her gaze, and puts something into it, and Keith notices this, possibly with alarm.

"I have to visit the ladies room," Tamara says, and Justine nods. "So do I."

On the way there, Tamara says, "All of the nurses and therapists, everyone liked Keith and wished him well."

"Yes," Justine says, a bit unconnectedly. "He is very nice."

In the large, hypermodern bathroom, two young blondes, in dresses with cleavage, are discussing some young male actor they know, who has used steroids to overnight pump up his pecs. They have considerable makeup on, and one of them, with a huge wave of tinted hair, adds a tad more blush. "Do you have a Xanax?" the other asks, going through the contents of her purse. Yes. It is swallowed, with water, and they depart.

Justine stands outside the cubicle, listening to the sound of Tamara's micturition. She seems young to actually be a doctor, and not a medical student. Brown hair, modest blouse and skirt. Hardly any makeup. Earthtone lipstick. She has a fleeting awkwardness, occasionally, in how she holds her body, her head on her neck.

When she flushes, and comes out, she is slightly nonplussed to find Justine right there, close. Really, she is too innocent. Justine asks her, Where do you live? Tamara's eyes dilate. If she had contact lenses, or wore glasses, it would be more difficult to achieve the rapport. Is your friend gone? Good. Drive home, and wait for us in the lobby. Here, write down the address.

Usually, when someone is bitten, the venom injected, after they have a long sleep they can act naturally, and yet function as hypnotically agreed. In *this* state, however, Tamara may act spacey, and the trance is something fragile, it can be broken. All Tamara has to do here is get her car back from the valet, tip him, drive home, and wait. She can accomplish these things on automatic pilot.

Keith is unhappy when he realizes the plan. He leaves money and they follow Tamara to her apartment, making all the green lights. She is in the lobby, awaiting their arrival, her purse in her lap.

"Justine," Keith says, before they enter. "This is a bad idea.

She's a good person. She's been kind to me."

"She won't know anything happened. She'll just think she had a little too much to drink. I won't hurt her."

Tamara opens the front door and lets them in. She appears deep in thought, or as if concentrating on a hard important problem, oblivious to her surroundings.

They take the elevator up to the fifth floor. It is a new building. The halls have thick plush carpeting. Tamara opens her two locks and they go in. Justine notices that Keith says nothing now in the presence of the young doctor, afraid of disturbing the spell. Not wanting her to remember any of this later on.

He does say to Justine, "You promised. You won't take very much."

Justine's fangs are fully out now. In the bedroom, lit by the bedside lamp, she has Tamara undress. Keith leaves, or at least begins to, lingering in the living room, torn. Justine assists the somnolent one, pulling down the pantyhose. In lacy rose-beige bra and underpants, Tamara lies on her side on the bed. Justine pushes her gently onto her stomach, and bites into the good blue vein behind the right knee. It is excellent, hot blood. Speeding, secret blood.

Justine gasps, and momentarily swoons. She is with her sister, Fleur, it is sunny out and they are in a rowboat. The rowboat moves without oars. In a big river, silent, no sound anywhere, no sound of water lapping or wind blowing, they come to an island and debark. Off in the distance, there are people sunbathing on the sand. Some of them may have wings.

The main feature of this island in the big river is a hill. Justine and Fleur set off on the road that winds around the hill. Out of sunlight into cool, refreshing shade. Fleur carries a box. They are going to bury this small box. Around the spiral, they come upon an old car, maybe a Packard, a Stutz-Bearcat, a convertible, and there is a man sitting behind the wheel of this car. Justine seizes this man. She and Fleur overpower him, and leave him lying by the side of this dirt road. They take his car, and the car takes them away. The ascension along the curve of the spiral inexplicably turns into a descent. They drive down into the interior of the island, down, down, into a big cavern underneath the river.

There is a sound. What is it? A tortured rooster? A dog? A man, screaming at the top of his lungs? Winged creatures—are they angels?—approach Justine and Fleur. Around them, in the deep black dirt, tiny frogs are hopping, little ducklings hatch forth from eggs. There are children, mournful children with grotesque fully adult growths of dark pubic hair, adult penises and testes, vulvas developing like sticky plant mouths, sped-up flowers blossoming, now a black penis, wet, on a white angelic child with wings who suddenly smiles a disturbing smile. The strange box is dropped to the ground. What is inside?

Tamara groans. Justine, leaning back against the wall, viewing the room in a kind of strobe effect, shudders, oh she feels it, as Keith sadly, mercilessly, slashes with a knife to connect the bite marks into one cut. He dabs at the blood. The sugar-syrup venom has a clotting effect. The purple wound-mouth swells. Tamara pulls away, turns more fully onto her side, knees coming up into fetal position, warm body, intimate, revealed. Eyes shut, she says, "Ow. Ow." Justine drools blood. Keith rises, turns, comes to her. He wipes her mouth on his sleeve. She breathes.

TWENTY-THREE

Keith wakes up at 2:30 or so in the afternoon. He'd like to sleep longer, but he cannot. It seems a drag, to wash, to perform these ordinary ablutions, it's always somewhat difficult and slow because of his hands. When he was a junkie, he often stayed dirty for days. He didn't care. Or rather: it was an experiment, seeing how it felt. His hands were worse back then. Something like washing his hair, or shaving, was slow. You have the bottle of shampoo in your right hand, and your hair is wet, under the shower; you squirt out an appropriate amount onto the palm of your left hand, and rub this into your scalp. You have to use your left hand as simply a way station, and slap it on top of your head. Then use the right to do the rest. Just little things. Minor inconveniences. Things slipping out of his hands. He could not, for instance, carry a plate and glass out of the kitchen, to have his dinner in front of the TV. His left hand was out of the question, it was too weak for a plate with food, and if it held a glass—he'd start out okay, then just be unable to hold it, his hand would disobey his will and let it go. Buttons, shoelaces, carrying a sack back from the store. It was different. He'd reach out for something and fumble it, or drop it—he was weak.

He had junkie friends. One couple in particular. David and Lorene. Sometimes Lorene danced nude, in a club, but she never seemed to hang on to a job. They were very nice to Keith, in their way. They made money off him, but he didn't mind. They helped him deal with the tougher, more paranoid pushers, who didn't want to sell to anyone they didn't know. Usually Hispanics, but sometimes white or black. One black one named Ricky was very scary, Ricky'd been awake for three nights and he had a gun, he was in the backseat of the car and he pulled out this gun. He asked Keith . . . did he like The Cure?

Later, Lorene said that Ricky had supposedly raped another dancer she knew, he was going to deliver some heroin up to her room after she got off work and he just did it . . . and then didn't charge her for the stuff. He'd only been out of prison for a month. The police were already sort of looking for him, 'cause he hadn't been in to see his parole officer since the first time. The p.o. would be able to tell he was fucked-up.

Keith is in a terrible mood. He feels bad about what happened to Dr. Rothschild. He's worried about her. What time is it? 3:15. Keith wonders if it would be possible to reach her through the hospital switchboard. He doesn't know if, given the conference, she'll be wearing her pager or not. It would be weird to talk to her on the phone. He decides against the attempt. The operator would ask him who he is. She's probably fine.

Dressed, Keith wanders outside. The gardener is here, with his young son. Keith nods at them, goes for a somewhat inhibited stroll, and re-enters the house.

He misses his pals from the band. Just having them around. He knows he didn't necessarily appreciate them so much at the time. They were always present, and sometimes they got on his nerves. But they liked him, they upheld him with their affection, and that environment of camaraderie is something he misses. It seems like it was seventy-five years ago, or a hundred. He dreams, now and then, that he's making up new songs, demonstrating them to his band, and his fingers work, better than they ever did in the real world. Trying to impress Michael with the brand-new song. He's known Michael since he was eight.

Okay. It's 3:49. He gets the phone book out. It makes him nervous, imagining the purposeful, orderly world on the other end of the line.

"Would you page Dr. Rothschild for me?"

"Just a moment please."

And Keith is left on hold. He thinks about hanging up. He doesn't really know Tamara. At one point, while being passed amongst others, orthopedists and hand specialists, he was her patient for a while. She's a neurologist. It was funny. When she came into the examination room, they got along immediately, or at least, perhaps, Keith was more than usually responsive to what she put of herself into her professional friendliness, her manner. She seemed to be in no hurry, to have all day. Like she was reluctant, even, to go back to her grind. Somehow, he was more honest and open with her, admitting his pain, and the mental torment occasioned by the whole situation. He felt he could talk to her, in her white jacket, why not? She wasn't a type of person he'd known before. Afterwards, it felt strange.

The next time Keith came, she said that she had bought the SMX CD, and liked it. He was embarrassed. For one thing, he didn't like to think about that stuff anymore. Second, by "violating" the separation between their two specialties, Tamara revealed her innocence, her unworldliness, and Keith didn't want to make her feel this. He didn't believe, for instance, that she had the background or whatever to really enjoy SMX, to abandon herself to their noise. But he didn't want to make her feel unhip. Maybe she did like it. If so, that was good. He was glad.

When she called him at home about a prescription, she would say, "This is Tamara," identifying herself, not "Dr. Rothschild." Keith was initially flattered by this, until he decided it didn't mean anything, it was just part of her "new physician" style.

Of course she had seen people in all kinds of extremity, dealt with them, street people, gang members, liars and assholes and people at the end of their rope, all of which had no doubt contributed to the steadiness of her gaze, an unflinching quality she had. No, strictly speaking, she cannot be said to be naive.

"Go ahead," the operator says and clicks off. "This is Dr. Rothschild," Tamara announces, neutral but friendly, professional, not knowing who it might be.

"This is Keith. I hope I'm not interrupting you."

TWENTY-FOUR

Tamara is having a rotten day. She woke up late, really late, and she's been behind ever since. When the phone call comes from Keith, she's glad to hear from him, it's like this is what she's been unconsciously waiting for all day.

"Are you okay?" he asks, and she's embarrassed. She doesn't know what happened last night, she's been leaving it unexamined for the moment, but the very fact that he would ask such a question means quite a lot.

"I'm all right," she answers. "I don't remember very well . . . exactly what happened after I met you and your girlfriend."

"You might have had a little too much to drink, that's all."

"Oh God." This is so against her normal practice that she can only shake her head at herself.

"Do you have a hangover?"

"Do I ever," she says. "I've been feeling very weird ever since I woke up."

"How is work?" he asks, and the ease of their familiarity makes her realize they're behaving as if they're friends, and she thinks this is good, it pleases her, even as it seems accidental and strange.

"It's been terrible. I'm not functioning."

She hesitates. There's something in the back of her mind, but she can't remember what it is. She worries for half a second that Keith might think she's coming on to him if she suggests further contact, but she has her secure relationship with Patrick, and Keith has—Justine. Tamara can only dimly recall Justine's face. She is suddenly intensely curious about them, and asks Keith if he'll meet her for coffee—tomorrow, since she's so messed up today.

Sure, he says.

Tamara goes back to her stack of charts. A year ago, when Keith was a patient, she bought his band's CD. It became a point of contention between her and her boyfriend, because she liked it and wanted to play it all the time, and Patrick said it drove him crazy, it was like being on the runway when planes were landing and crashing at LAX. It was too hypermodern for him.

Tamara thought he wasn't listening to it right. To her, it suggested all these realms of experience and imagining, dreams of unknown splendor, that sort of thing. It sounded different to her every time out.

It's funny. She's not sure why, but she's pretty sure Keith isn't on heroin anymore. But there's something essentially mysterious about his life now with this young woman from France. Tamara sees Justine's eyes staring into hers, she has a flash of memory, and for one shaming moment she wonders if what she has forgotten is a ménage-à-trois. No, that's a ridiculous idea. Keith wouldn't have taken part in something like that. He wouldn't do that to her.

Still, there does seem to be some kind of real flavor of danger in the air. I'm too dull, she thinks. She has come to live so straight a life, any little variation seems scary to her. The routine of the medical profession has made her timid, against her nature, which has always been to take chances, to follow her curiosity. One can be so prudent one might as well just hide away from life and die.

TWENTY-FIVE

Andy calls and says that two large Hawaiian pizzas have come back as undeliverable, are you interested? Jason says I'll be right there. Out back behind the pizza place, the usual traffic noise making it hard to hear, Andy says, "You'll get me into Saint Agatha Saturday? Backstage?"

"Sure," Jason says. He can't believe he and Andy once fooled around together for an afternoon, home from school. Andy's so weak. The pizzas are placed in the van.

When Jason held his Ian Curtis party, celebrating the famous suicide of the Joy Division singer, who sang incredibly depressed lyrics and then hanged himself on the eve of the band's U.S. tour, this was way back in 1980, before anyone's time, since legendary—Andy was one of the boofs who got carried away, cutting his wrist superficially and then smearing the blood on car windshields. . . . All that got out of hand, what with the hangman's noose around all these guys' necks, when the cops came in, everyone's dicks hard out to *here*. Actually, it was great. Jason's status only grew. Now he was *extreme*.

Across the street is this late fifties version of space-age architecture, closed up. It's faded rose-pink. Next door on the white wall is painted an image of the Virgin of Guadalupe, bigger than life-size.

"Gotta buzz," Jason says, and Andy, ridiculous in his pizza uniform, looking like he expected a kiss or something, stands there forlorn as Jason drives off.

Jason is thin, blond, and frail. Sometimes he wears eye makeup and black lipstick, his hair coming in kind of a *swathe* over the left side of his face, pulled back behind his ear on the right. He has a severe (or "brooding") stare. He proudly feels that he has started some fashions here amongst the youth of L.A. Purple or wine-colored velvet jackets, or green, with frilly ruffled white shirts. He thinks maybe he helped bring that back. He's ambitious to do much more.

This afternoon, he had watched a black-and-white movie on TV. It was called *The Courage of Robert Greasewell*. As it turned out, that was the name of a ship. This was back in the Cold War. The ship's captain, Robert Mitchum, had a bunch of problems. They were docked at Helsinki, or maybe Stockholm, and Robert Mitchum's best friend was found dead, washed up in the waves. Then there was a dwarf on the big Navy ship, there kept being reports of this dwarf. "Well *find* him," Robert Mitchum said. "I don't care if we have to tear the ship apart." Ashore, Robert Mitchum's girlfriend, Elke Sommer, was called "Miss Stenko," which struck Jason as an interestingly ugly name. There were Japanese sailors dancing in this nightclub, and Robert Mitchum was getting drunk, he'd been relieved of his command. He thought it was an ominous sign, he said to Miss Stenko, that "the dancing has gone downhill."

Jason missed the rest, because he went into the bathroom to beat off. When he next looked at the TV, that black guy, Link of *The Mod Squad*, wearing sunglasses, was looking down at some wounded "brother" on the ground, saying, "You see? *Violence* is not the answer. The Movement has no need for any more mother-fuckers like you."

Tiff came home around then, and Jason said, "What a trip, just like in a cartoon," and Tiff didn't know what he was talking about, there was some commercial on about buttmuscles and then they watched some band rock out. Tiff said, holding a beer, "I thought I was gonna choke on it at work. What a sucky business."

Jason didn't care. Michelle and Brian came home, and they were talking about *Twilight of the Idols*, which they were both trying to read. Everybody smoked a joint, got hungry, no one had very much money, and then the pizza solution occurred.

When Jason gets back with the pizza Ken is also hanging out, and some old Godflesh album is on. Jason wants to tell Ken about this idea he's had for a video, a short film about this SS officer who is haunted by his guilt and blows out his brains.

"It's been done," Ken says. He's just trying to bring Jason down, and Jason can't figure out why he wants to be like this. After some pizza, though, Ken says, What about making him a witch-hunter, putting it back in the Middle Ages? He could torture and burn witches, make them kiss the cross. You're right, that's better, Jason agrees. It was the female holocaust, puts in Michelle. Gooey cheese thread from the piece of pizza making it into her mouth. They burned, like, nine million women in a couple hundred years. Burned them at the stake. Use sepiatone, Ken says, to make it look old. Like you just found this film in some old church. Then Ken, who's very handsome, well sort of, tells them about some torture he's heard of. Brian tries to one-up, out-gross him, but he can't.

They're in a pink stucco bungalow, rented in Tiff's name. Her hair is bleached platinum-blonde, in a frizzoid cascading mane. Since she got off work, at the place where she does boring, endless data entry, she's put on dark ruby red lipstick, etc. She has her eye on dark-haired Ken, who's getting drunk.

Around them the other houses and court apartments are sky blue, yellow, tangerine, and salmon pink. There are palm trees, jacaranda, and a new red Coke machine. The setting sun turns the atmosphere bright bronze, shadows brown.

Ken gets onto his thing, helped out by Brian, about how white people are best. Ken says, "The descendants of Saxons, Goths, Danes, and Celts. Normans. I don't know about Slavs. Angles and Frisians, though. Franks. Romans and Greeks. The strength of the strong."

"That's where our culture has come from," Jason says. "Dominance, not submission. Not this kind of communal thing from Africa, where there isn't any progress, nothing ever changes."

Brian, with spiky painted black hair and glasses, agrees. "L.A.'s already pretty much like *Blade Runner*," he says. "The Hmongs, and the Salvadorans, the Islams . . . they don't even wanna learn English. They don't wanna blend in."

Ken agrees. He takes another sip of beer. The white race is doomed. It's outnumbered. What a tragic end to the history of the world. What a farce.

Some alcoholics live next door. The guy used to direct porno and a couple of ridiculous horror films, lowest of the low-budget, anyway Minski's got some kind of disability and he and his wife every so often have these amazing, bad-news fights, sometimes stabbing each other in the arm or something, the wife seems the really violent one though now and then she'll get a black eye. Anyway, they don't complain about the noise. Then there's some Salvadorans. They don't want any fucking thing to do with the police. It seems like there's about twenty of them living there, off and on.

Jason goes into the kitchen. It's really a mess. Michelle is trying to organize the dirty plates and stuff a little, but it doesn't seem like she's having much luck. She looks depressed. It seems hotter out since it got dark.

"Do you remember SMX?" she asks.

"Smacks," Jason replies, finishing off his warm beer. "Yeah. They were okay."

"I'd like to hear them again."

"Sure," he says. He works at a new and used record store. Used stuff, he brings home whatever he wants. "I'm almost positive we have their cassette. The first one, anyway. The second one sucks."

"Yeah," Michelle says. "Their guitar player got fucked up and left or something, right?"

"He got busted for heroin. Why is it that junkies always are the best musicians? Or, the best musicians become junkies. God, I saw Smacks at the Roxy, and they were awesome. You're making me nostalgic," Jason says. "There's nothing worse than nostalgia. I hate it," he says, just to make a statement of some sort. "It's counterproductive." But he's not sure.

TWENTY-SIX

When Justine comes out of her room, she finds the house full of music, and Keith is jazzed up, like he gets sometimes—every so often he'll have the urge to teach her something he suddenly thinks is important, or it's always been important only he hasn't been sufficiently inspired to see that she needs to know it until now. She likes it when he's like this. She'll listen, or watch, and try to understand.

He's taught her about TV, and TV news. Tabloids. Commercials. Movies about Vietnam. Lots and lots about music. Tonight he's on the blues.

Mostly they're just listening. Now and then he'll tell her an anecdote, or point out a part that he especially likes. This is the old time, acoustic blues. Lots of stuff with just a singer and a bottleneck guitar.

"This is Mississippi Fred McDowell."

Keith likes the names. Sleepy John Estes. Blind Willie McTell.

"Not much is known about Barbecue Bob."

Justine laughs. It's always cool when she gets his jokes.

"I would have liked to have been like that, to have been named Hambone Keith, or Switchblade Keith, something along those lines. Scholars would argue about whether I'd been killed in a knife fight or poisoned by some unknown jealous bitch."

"You'd like that, huh."

"Sure."

"I liked that one by Robert Johnson," Justine says. "How old was he when he sang it?"

"Twenty-six, back in 1937."

"He sounds like he could be fourteen, or a hundred and five."

"Yeah."

"I used to try to see old people, like over a hundred. I thought I could read something in their eyes."

As she says this, there's no way she looks much older than mid-twenties. Her skin is so soft and unlined. Nothing about her is old except sometimes her gaze.

"I also studied people when they were dead, a couple of times. It was hard though. One place, animals kept coming during the day. I tied it to a tree, but they really wanted it. The other time, I saw more, I understood more, but then this man I knew took her away. He thought it was a problem, having her around. I was really looking at her, though, it was like she was my sister, so it was too bad when she was gone."

'What did you think, when you looked at her?" Keith asks.

"I don't know. I felt like I understood who I was, what I am."

Keith is silent. They listen to Bessie Smith, singing with a piano player and an old-time clarinet.

"Do you feel like you need more blood tonight?" he suddenly asks. He's thinking about Tamara, who is still certainly under Justine's spell. Maybe, if she needs more, they can go out tonight and find someone else.

She's looking at him now like she reads his mind. His protective impulse might be just egging her on, making her want to cross his desire, to be perverse.

"Yes, I need some. Because of the wounds. Let's go out." She changes her clothes. Her immodesty in front of him has a careless quality about it, yet sometimes she looks at him differently, he doesn't know what she feels. She brushes her hair and puts on lipstick and blush, regards her face appraisingly in the mirror.

Out in public, she can get along very well. Her affect is often somewhat self-absorbed and remote, but she can also be carefree and flirtatious, she enjoys the interplay.

"How do I look?" she asks him, and he says nothing, gazing at her up and down, then he embraces her and lightly kisses her neck, making her squirm and laugh.

Los Angeles is a city of extras, of extra people, homeless and runaways, people without names. Or, they have names, but nobody knows or wants to know what these names are. Nameless people are not missed when they disappear or turn up dead.

"You pick up someone this time," Justine asks, and Keith figures this is his prize for them skipping an easy return visit to Tamara Rothschild, whom Justine could rouse and lead outside as she willed.

In a gay bar, a handsome blond man in his forties buys Keith a drink, and asks if he wants to see his museum.

"Yeah, I would. Is it all right with you if my sister comes along?"

"Your sister? That's fine. Where is she?"

"Listening to some music."

"Excuse me for asking, but I can't help but wonder, what happened to your hands?"

"I was a hit man," Keith says. "I fell in love with the guy I was supposed to kill."

It feels true as he says it, and he misses this long-lost imaginary love, real emotion comes through.

"My name's Dan," the other says.

Keith smiles, nods in acknowledgement. He doesn't offer his name in return. It's like it's slipped his mind. They leave behind the Shirley Bassey medley, and Keith does not resist when Dan massages the back of his neck. It feels good.

"Where are you parked?"

"That way."

Opposite directions, so it's determined Keith will follow the other's black Corvette. It's hard to tell what Dan thinks of this sister idea. He seems open-minded. Justine is amused when the subterfuge is explained to her.

"You're my brother?"

"Yeah. He's going to show us his collection."

When they get to the house, in Beverly Hills, Dan looks older than Keith thought. His hair is white instead of pale blond. His skin is tough-looking, as though he's been deeply tanned for too many years. Does he really believe that Keith is going to go to bed with him?

A bald-headed tall black servant lets them into the house. All of the large, strategically lit interior is open, like one big room, going up with three stories of landings and galleries, freestanding staircases, mirrored ceiling and walls at unexpected places, making the exact dimensions hard to calculate at first glance. The place is indeed like a museum, a museum of Mayan, Aztec, and Incan kitsch. Some of the exhibits may well be expensive, or rare, but the overwhelming impression is of hundreds of toys and small cheap colorful figures, touristy items, hung on wires stretched all over, dolls and suchlike, wires strung high up and diagonally, dark wood tables and stands in turn used to show off painted plaster figurines and pottery, gold and jade monkeys and jaguars and carved wooden gods. The obviously cheap mass-produced item from Mexico City next to what might be pre-Conquest, stolen from some tomb.

Justine and Keith follow Dan up the steps, which appear to be made of glass, as are the floors above, transparent but seemingly strong enough to bear all this weight.

There are little areas a half-level up, with their own little staircases, to confuse things further. There are potted plants all over, big green fronds and vines, stuffed parrots and taxidermied snakes. Painted standing screens, with Mayan hieroglyphs telling the histories of forgotten warriors and kings.

Up on the third level, they come to where Dan evidently sleeps. It's disorienting to look down through the glass floor.

"This is great," Keith says, with some honestly felt awe.

"I'll open the skylight." Dan sits down on his low, large bed and hits a switch.

He looks up at Justine now, really with interest for the first time. Then he cannot look away.

Keith feels like a pimp. He tries to freeze himself and just dig the utter strangeness of the surroundings, as well as what's going on. It's a secret, it's something no one knows about or believes in, way outside of any ordinary accounting of good and evil. Justine has her mouth on the guy's neck.

But only for a moment. She turns to Keith then, and he feels terror, it's involuntary, there is blood dripping from her fangs, her gaze is fixed and cruel. He doesn't move; in a moment the murder is out of her eyes.

She gasps.

"Tainted," she gets out. She wipes her mouth, spits blood mixed with saliva onto the floor. She's angry.

"The butler," Keith says. She needs it bad now, he can tell.

They go downstairs, leaving Dan dreaming, eyes open, mouth agape. The fillings in his teeth pick up the light.

The butler does not welcome Justine as she comes into the kitchen. He sees the fangs immediately, and throws a silver tea service at her, turning his head to avoid looking into her eyes. He tries to get a meat cleaver out of a drawer, "Get the fuck away from me, goddamnit," but Justine is undeterred.

She's so fast. Slams the man's hand in the drawer and then leaps up onto him, lithely, he's so much taller and more powerful but as soon as she's into the vein his knees buckle, he turns, falling, and she rides him on down to the tile floor.

Taking a walk in the opposite direction, Keith can't stand it, too much is pent up—he kicks up through a glass table, shattering it, sending shit flying noisily all around.

The butler, depleted, will survive.

TWENTY-SEVEN

There is an indigo ribbon in Tamara's brown hair, matching her indigo skirt. Otherwise she has on a white blouse and navy tights, black shoes, white lab coat, beeper, and stethoscope. They sit across from each other in the air-conditioned cafeteria of the hospital, at 4:30, an "off" hour, so there's hardly anyone else around.

"I still don't feel right," she says. She seems vulnerable, maybe a trace depressed. "I don't like to say this, but . . . did we do something else the other night besides drink?"

"You mean like some weird drug?" He's quoting Iggy Pop. He doesn't expect her to get it, and she does not.

"I don't know. It's just that this business of losing my memory has never happened to me before. Did you offer me a sleeping pill, maybe, is that possible at all?"

Keith thinks it over. He takes a bite of this stale croissant he got to go with his coffee, as some kind of a breakfast after broken, unsatisfactory sleep.

"Justine might have given you something, I don't know. Whatever it was, I'm sure it will be out of your system in another few days."

"How can you know that, if you don't know what it is?"

"You wouldn't believe me if I told you. You're not in any danger, I swear to you."

"Why should I be in danger?"

"You're not."

Tamara tries to figure this out, not looking at him.

"I live a very strange life," he says. "Everyone says that, I guess."

"Tell me more about how you live. You're with this woman, Justine, right? Where does the money come from?"

"She's rich. She inherited a house in Beverly Glen."

"If I wanted to visit you there, would that be all right?"

"Oh yeah. That would be great."

"Are you guys involved in selling drugs?"

"No." He shakes his head, smiles, amused. "Nothing like that." In a few minutes, she asks, "How are your hands?"

"They're okay."

He shows them to her. The bandages are a little bit dirty, not too bad.

"Who wraps them for you now?"

"Justine."

"She does a nice job."

Tamara moves her head sometimes sort of awkwardly, not like a confident young woman sure of her grace and appeal. More like someone who'd play an oboe or a bassoon.

Is she reassured? From the way she looks at him, it's plain that plenty of questions are being left unasked. But the longer they sit here, even if unspeaking, or talking about nothing, the more it feels like they're communicating, like they have an alliance somewhere offstage or offscreen. They're comfortable together. Neither of them means the other any harm.

TWENTY-EIGHT

There is a Macintosh computer in a room at the back of the house, a room with straw matting texturing the floor, another big geometric painting, rattan furniture, bookshelves filled with a disordered collection of books. There are some games within the computer, and Keith has found one that he likes to play. This is all he can do on the computer, is play this game. It's a Chinese tile game, subtle and hard. Peaceful. The object is to remove the decorated tiles, randomly stacked in a pyramid, until they are all removed and an illustration of a colorful Bengal tiger, or Chinese dragon, is completely revealed. Whereupon "cymbals" crash, and the computer plays a little song to celebrate your win. It is a difficult game.

Tonight, Keith wins twice in a row, so he stops. He goes out to the living room, where Justine reclines on the couch. He sits down, so that her bare feet are over his lap. She wears a slightly oversized white nightgown, or shift. He puts his hand up between her thighs, and she is warm. She does not seem to mind the hand. She squeezes it, in fact.

"I've never asked," he says. "How did you get this house?"

Justine collects her thoughts, then answers, taking her time, reciting the most coherent story she's ever managed to tell him heretofore.

"There was a man named Maximilian Durand, whose wife had died, and he lived here alone. His one child was some kind of a dancer, living in New York. They never talked. Max was very rich. He had been a backer of some films, and a producer, but he was tired of all that. His wife had died of cancer, and he had watched it kill her for over a year. So he was afraid of dying, very afraid. He became a vegetarian, and did yoga exercises, and traveled to India and Nepal. He had all kinds of adventures. He climbed a mountain in the Himalayas, and lived by himself in the forest up in Oregon for a year. Then, back here in Los Angeles, he met a woman one night. He became devoted to her. She had some special abilities, and he thought she could do something to extend his life beyond its natural span. They kept to themselves. They were married, in Las Vegas, in the middle of the night. They lived together in this house. It could have gone on for many years, but he wanted this thing from her. Well, he died, believing as he died that he would reawaken soon. The doctors called it 'pernicious anemia.' He left all of his wealth and property to this wife. A lawyer handled everything for her. The son in New York got some money, and there was no funeral to come to, because Max was cremated two days after his death. That's what his widow thought was best."

Keith bursts out laughing at this. When Justine smiles, just a little, Keith breaks off his laughter, and moves up so that his face is right in front of hers, he puts his right hand in her hair and says, in a low, barely controlled voice, "You shouldn't laugh at him."

Justine, taken by surprise, astonished by his audacity, replies, "I *didn't* laugh at him. You're the one who was laughing. It's not fair."

She sounds like she may start to cry. A tear wells out of Keith's left eye, as he stares at her, trembling.

"Did you go to bed with him?" he suddenly asks.

'What makes you think you can . . . ? No. He tried once, but it was no good. You're impossible. You don't understand anything! He was better off—No! What are you doing? Stop it!"

Keith kisses her on the mouth, mashing her lips as she pushes against him, he tries again and then gives up, a curious smile upon his face.

"I don't care about Max," he says after a while. "He was a sucker."

"What's wrong with you?" Justine says, provoked, an innocent child in her nightdress, long brown hair messed up. "Leave me alone."

"I don't want to leave you alone. I'll do what you tell me, though. If you want to be alone, I'll leave you alone."

There are actually tears in her eyes. She's still angry. Keith stands up and walks back into the computer room at the back of the house. After a while, he hears her bare feet, but she does not come in, nor does she speak to him. He listens intensely, he is intensely aware. He closes his eyes. What is he doing? He thinks of when he'd push the melted heroin, mixed with blood, into his vein. He'd push the plunger down, and the instantaneous rush would scare him, just for a microsecond, there was always the chance it would be bad stuff, or too strong and he'd O.D. His life was fucked up.

What is it now? He replays Dan, last night, and the butler, he sees the classic puncture wounds in both of the throats. How can he talk to her, this vampire, talk to her like she's a person he has come to know? It's insane.

It's like they're living on the moon. Things are different, when you're living on the moon.

TWENTY-NINE

It's an afternoon a few days later. Justine and Keith have hardly spoken, hardly interacted at all. No hunting, no blood. The bell rings. It's 3:00. Keith is awake, showered, wearing a white shirt and black jeans, black jeans he's had for five years. Since before the trouble, back when he still played guitar. He puts on gloves, walks out barefoot to the gate. Who will it be? If it was going to be the lawyer, Philip, he would call. He wouldn't just show up. The gardener came yesterday. The new maid starts next week.

Oh, it's the girl with the mohawk. Pouty and sulky-looking, moving around in a kind of olive green sleeveless dress with pockets, short enough to see most of her thighs. Black shoes and black anklets. Again, lots of slim chains as accessories, going down into the dress. A thick leather cuff buckled around her left wrist.

"Hi," he says, and opens the gate. She doesn't seem happy to be here, and where's the car? Keith doesn't remember her name.

"I don't think you gave me a phone number," she says, "so I'm just dropping in. It's probably inconvenient, but I was with a friend, and she just let me off. So, sorry, I don't have a ride home."

She seems to be challenging him to find her unwelcome. If he was to say, "Yeah, I don't know why you're here. Take a cab," it seems like she'd be somehow pleased, or if not pleased, *satisfied* in some way.

"I'm glad you're here," Keith says. "It's no problem, later on, to give you a ride."

They walk into the house. She wants to look around a bit more. She tries Justine's doors, which are locked, and gives him an interrogative look but says nothing. He puts on some music. The latest in Tunisian disco. It's great.

Her name comes back to him, and he says, "Michelle, can I get you something to drink?"

"What do you have?" she asks, and follows him out to the kitchen to see. The chains cause her to faintly tinkle as she moves. As she looks into the refrigerator, he can smell her perspiration, and perfume. She chooses a Beck's Dark bottle of beer. He takes one too.

They go to his room, and sit on the couch. She brings out, from her purse, the latest issue of the magazine, *The Darkest Night*. In the table of contents, he sees an interview with Vladimir, the video director, by Michelle Zwick.

"I haven't told anyone," she says seriously. "I'd like to do an interview with you, it would be great, but not if you're not ready. I think I can understand."

Keith has taken off the gloves, in order to leaf through the pages of the magazine. It's less cheaply done than he would have assumed. Michelle touches his shattered left hand, which, unbandaged, looks kind of bad.

"Slammed in car doors, you said."

"More or less. That's descriptive enough."

"You could do something with sampling and synthesizers, couldn't you? You could still do music, one finger at a time."

"I don't want to," he says. She's caressing, examining each of his hands now in turn, looking at his face now and then to see how he's taking it, being ultracareful to be gentle, not to hurt. He lets her.

One night several months ago Justine was very curious about his sexual history, she wanted to know if he remembered everyone he'd ever fucked. If he remembered all of their names. Then, had he ever fucked a black girl? Yes. A Japanese? Yes. Other Orientals? Vietnamese? One Vietnamese, yes. In Houston. Anyone much older than him? Yes. When he was sixteen, a woman in St. Louis, thirty-six. She liked young flesh. Michael did her first, and Keith never thought he would, but one night he was seduced. Had he ever had sex with someone fat? Yes. She had a sweet face, and he picked her out. What about experiences with other males? There was a time in New Orleans, with some very pretty transsexuals, and then in prison, every night Pascual would blow me, and I'd dream.

Now, at this moment, Keith wants to touch Michelle, wants to see and feel her big breasts, but he doesn't want to take the initiative, not with his fucked-up hands. He never masturbates, because of these hands. He hasn't fucked in four years. Not since Renata was alive. When he was a junkie, one time a stripper gave him head, but he couldn't maintain his erection, so they never went anywhere with that.

The taste of the beer seems stupid to him now. They both drink some more, in the blondish light, and he thinks of Dr. Rothschild, Justine, the concept of young prostitutes in Thailand training the muscles of their cunts so they can do tricks in Bangkok nightclubs, smoking a cigarette or writing with a pen, expelling ping pong balls across the room. He focuses on Michelle's painted, dark and glossy lips, the bare skin of most of her skull, and he says, "I'd really like it if you would give me a kiss."

She flashes just a half smile and puts her arms around him, and they kiss for a long time. It's something to do. They kiss and kiss. The beer on hot young breath. Tongues in each other's mouth. It seems huge, this one connected mouth. The tape ends, and he's glad. They continue to kiss, sometimes taking breaks.

"I like you," she says, at one point.

He kisses her in response, and draws her to him. She's mortal and warm, dumb and young and wise. Wise when she does not speak, when she's unknowing, when she doesn't try to know what's going on. Keith likes the soft hair of the mohawk cut, the way it brings into prominence these delicate hollows at the side and then the back of her skull. She sighs, and her eyes close, naked skull turned sideways, grazing his mouth. The bed is right over there. She stands up, stretches, pulls him along. She takes off her dress. The chains tinkle and sway.

THIRTY

Driving, avoiding the freeways, Keith copes with traffic. The radio is on Michelle's favorite station. He feels like he can touch her, she doesn't mind his touch. She looks as if she's in a bad mood, but it's just her mouth. They both wear sunglasses against the glare, the white sunlight reflecting off all these steel cars, shiny and dirty, old and new.

He's sort of talkative, though he's not talking fast, but by asking him about different bands on the radio, "Do you like these guys?" Michelle has got him to let out a few opinions here and there.

"Most bands, no matter how long they go on as entertainers, they only have—at most—ten or twelve good songs. One greatest hits album, and that's usually stretching it. Look at the Kinks. Thirty years, twenty-five albums or so, maybe five, six good songs. One or two for ZZ Top. None for the Dead. It's really hard. Because the form is so simple, you have to be naive, so the first stuff you do is always your best. As soon as you begin really learning how to play you start to lose it."

Michelle passes him a length of raspberry rope, rubbery candy from her purse. She's chewing on some, red against her white teeth. She thinks of the names of bands, and they argue or agree about how many good songs, if any, the band in question ever did.

Neil Young and the Rolling Stones did quite a few.

It's 7:30. Keith realizes he wants something to eat. Hamburgers? Sure. They stop and invade this kind of fifties retro pink-and-black Elvis Presley and Gene Vincent rockabilly café, with meat loaf and mashed potatoes and gravy on the menu, home cooking that Keith never had at home. He asks Michelle. No. Her mom was into wheatgrass tea and sprouts, tofu and carrot juice, she's a vegetarian—"I'm not," Michelle says, and brushes some atmospheric grit or ground glass from her nose. They order hamburgers, and Cokes, and split a side order of fries. Michelle puts catsup all over the fries. Red. The fries look yellow in this light.

Keith has explained (more lies, sort of) that he lives with this rich woman who takes care of him, she's very jealous but the main thing is that she just doesn't wanna know, as long as she's not directly confronted with someone else it can stay cool. She comes home late, Keith says. Michelle doesn't seem to judge him on this, or think less of him; it doesn't seem to cross her mind.

She lives in a house, she tells him, along with Jason, Tiff, and Brian. Brian is a student, with a part-time job at the library. Jason works in a record store, Tiff in a computer dungeon. Michelle had a job in an office, answering the phone, but she was fired for tardiness. Then she got her mohawk. So she's unemployed.

"Do you want to borrow some money?" Keith says, as she sucks Coke through a straw. It's funny that he should bring it up, because it occurred to him earlier that she might ask him for some; in fact, when he first saw her today, that's what he imagined was her goal.

"If it's okay," she says. She's a little hostile, perhaps out of shame.

"Here," he says. "Don't think about it. It doesn't mean anything," he says.

Nevertheless, infected by the exchange of money, they're not as free with each other the rest of the way.

In front of the pink stucco house, Michelle starts kissing him, at first just to say goodbye. Then as if she's trying to tell him something. Or just to do it.

As they sit side by side, she says, "Oh God. Do you see those guys there, sitting on the porch? I didn't notice them before. That's Fred, the bass player for Saint Agatha. The other one is Ken. I better go. I'll see you."

THIRTY-ONE

"Who is that guy you were making out with in the front of the Benz?" Jason asks, with a smirk.

The speakers are blasting rather frantic industrial Brit rap. "*Strap down! Get ready! Be refreshed!*"

"Why, is Fred really jealous?" asks Michelle, with a certain amount of pleasure, putting on fresh lipstick. She has changed her dress, and put on spiked heels and mesh tights. They're all going to the Invisible Club.

"You know he is. You choose to make him suffer," Jason says, like he's quoting something, putting his hand on her shoulder in the garish orange light.

"Where's Tiff?"

"She'll be there. Who is he?"

Strap down! Get ready! Be refreshed!

"Why doesn't Fred ask me himself?"

Jason leaves, and goes to find the extremely thin Fred, who suddenly tonight is tormented by love. Ordinarily morose, with a hyphenated last name, he believes in the music of Saint Agatha body and soul, it expresses all that he has never been able to say. Right now, he is out back with Ken, listening to Ken tell him some story about ass fucking, meant to shock and show off, that's just making him more unhappy. Fred is stunned, on vodka and MDA. He's not bad looking. Jason says something to him, and he comes back inside. When he sees Michelle, she ignores him, then gives him a demonic, infinitely knowing, mocking look that cuts through him like a laser beam. He's totally smitten. He'd like to beat her up with love. To be transfigured with pity and forgiveness while she crawled and wept, wept with all her heart. They all pile into cars, and whether or not by design he ends up next to Michelle in the backseat, pressed close to her thigh. Last weekend, he wasn't even thinking about her. She didn't seem that special. Now . . . she's an enigma. He has no idea at all what she thinks. She liked him once, but that seems a mirage.

THIRTY-TWO

Patrick doesn't understand exactly what's wrong with Tamara. She was sick this week, and she's been moody ever since. It's Friday night, and they're at a dinner party at the Malibu house of Orlando Newman, the head of the New Economic Policy Studies Institute, where it seems as though Patrick is going to be offered a job. He wants it, too. Although he's been a stock analyst and market strategist for several years, at heart he is a wonk. He truly believes that he is capable of formulating something new, something that might impact the entire globe in a positive way. What was it Thorstein Veblen said? *"To theorize with all the abandon that comes from a complete disregard for the facts."*

Carrying his glass of Liebfraumilch, Patrick slips away from the others, going back up the twisting, freestanding staircase, up into the "tower" room where their host has said he goes to think, to look at the sky. As he feared, he finds Tamara there. It's even worse than he imagined. She's been crying. She's sitting on the floor, face in her hands.

"What's wrong?" he asks her, sitting down next to her, speaking very softly, with real concern. If she wants to go home, he'll take her home. People understand these things, these human frailties, or they ought to. Patrick rubs Tamara's back, between her shoulder blades, trying to reassure.

"I'm sorry," she says. "I don't know what's going on. I had such a nightmare last night. It really scared me. I don't seem to be able to get over the impression it made. Patrick, I don't feel like being a doctor anymore. I'm tired of seeing patients, I can't face them. . . . "

"Maybe you should take a leave," he says. "You've worked too hard, you're emotionally exhausted. You identify with their problems—you're too hard on yourself."

"I don't know, Patrick. Maybe you're right." Anticipating her needs, he passes her a handkerchief, and she smiles, then uses it to blow her nose. "I'm sorry about this," she says.

"Don't be. I'll take you home."

"No, you don't have to. We have to eat, and I don't mind these people, they're all right. I'll put some makeup on."

Patrick's appearance is one of composure and reasonableness, not inelegant in his wire-rimmed glasses and short hair. He always appears serene, even a bit slow to react. At the moment, he probably shows nothing, but he's alarmed. He's paying attention, and he senses that Tamara is not telling him everything. She is so naturally candid, when there's a difference, he can detect it. And so he's torn. His inclination is to be direct, perhaps playful— sometimes it's a game of theirs, him asking questions, give him just a little bit of data and context and he's a good guesser—but in this case, somehow this is not the right move. He must be subtle, and watchful, patient, until she gives him some cues. They've been above this sort of deception—or kidding themselves.

They eat salad, asparagus, and red snapper, downstairs with the others, watch the sunset and listen to this German fellow discourse on manufacturing and changing investment opportunities in southern China. The German has been there. He speaks slowly, provisionally; one can't tell just what it is that he really thinks. He no sooner suggests a possibility than he postulates the downside, all the bad variables that might occur. A Japanese theorist named Hiroshi interjects.

Tamara gives Patrick a little smile, as if to say the stormy weather has passed, and he smiles back. He doesn't know what to do. A problem exists, but just what it is remains obscure. He's helpless before the revelation of his tenderness.

THIRTY-THREE

There is no one in the house. The doors to Justine's chambers are open. Keith can feel that she is not in here. It's dark out. He is drawn to her. He misses her. He wants to see her, out in the dark. It doesn't cross his mind for a second that she won't know Michelle was here, that they fucked.

His eyes get used to the darkness. There are outdoor lights, but of course she hasn't turned them on. They aren't necessary. She can see in the dark very well.

It takes a while, but he finds her. Justine is sitting, in a devout attitude, legs crossed in a half-lotus, under the bougainvillea and bamboo, in the dirt. Keith sits down facing her. Their clothes will be soiled, but that's not a concern. For the first time in a while, noticing what she is wearing, Keith experiences a pang as if she is his child. It's totally nonsense, but this emotion passes through him, he is protective, in wonderment . . . she looks at him, and he touches her cool hand. The air smells like flowers and moist, dark earth. Justine wears this short, light-colored print dress, with a white collar and short sleeves. It's like a child's dress. And then she has on tights, navy or black, and her shoes, shoes she can run in. There's this particular look she has, when she seems to look up, up, and up for no reason, her dark pupils run out of room, Keith has seen this occur when she's been very blank, or after she has fed, or when she's trying to remember something and cannot.

"I didn't know if you would come back," she says, and he can hear, as one can sometimes, a touch of her lost French.

"Don't be ridiculous," Keith says, after a few beats.

Justine seems to sigh then, and she turns sideways, to lie down in the dirt. There are traffic noises, hushed, over the hill.

"How could I leave you?" he says.

"I don't know," she answers after a while. "I wouldn't stop you." She watches her hand, close to her face, in the dirt. "There was a little boy I used to play with, Yves, we all played with him, I was no more than six or seven, he was younger, smaller . . . slow-witted. He didn't talk much, just smiled, and yet, when we were in the forest, he didn't seem so dumb. We caught birds." Justine picks up some of the dirt, smells it, seems to be contemplating it. "His older sister was ravished by the brigands, when they came through . . . Gascons, Bretons, Walloons. They robbed us. His sister gave birth to a bastard, and then went deep into the forest . . . she became a witch. She lived with Mother Jeanne, and then when Mother Jeanne died, she took her place. I saw her burned, tied to a ladder, on a rainy day. I remember how she screamed. It was as though she really did not expect it, and yet, as though she expected nothing else, she more than any of us perhaps understood that the world is merciless and cruel. Afterwards . . . little brother, Yves, ate dirt. That's all he would do, so sadly, I saw him . . . until he died."

Obeying some inchoate urge Keith pushes Justine over onto her side, onto her back. She does not resist. His hands are so clumsy, he needs two hands at once to unbutton her dress, but he fumbles and then slows down, he unbuttons it almost down to the waist, slides his right hand in, to feel the sleek, soft white skin, the small breasts.

"Your wounds are healed."

"That is because I am not really flesh. I am made of night-flesh, or dream-flesh . . . I am not real."

He lies down next to her. She shows her chaste pleasure in this by touching him, caressing him, running her hand over his back and up over his neck, resting her hand on his cheek.

"In those days, the forests were vast, they stretched forever . . . and I preyed on vagabonds, or brigands, travelers . . . during the day I took shelter in a cave."

"How were you . . . you've never told me anything about how you were bitten."

"I'm not sure," she says. "I think it was someone from the chateau. Someone of noble blood. The family was cursed."

Is she remembering more? Everything is so dark. Keith wishes he could see these memories through her eyes. But then, it is somehow familiar, as though he has had some glimpses in his dreams.

"I knew what was happening," she says now, "today, when you were with that girl."

"I thought of you while I did it to her."

"Don't say that. What are you trying to do to me?"

"I don't know," he says. Lying in the dirt with her, he moves so that his arms are around her, so that he can kiss her face.

"If you want me to, I can bring Tamara here," Justine says. "You could have her too."

"No," Keith says. "You're the only person I know anymore, in the whole world. A bad idea, isn't it?"

She sighs, trembling. "You are so painful, you cause me so much pain. I'm constantly—filled with you."

"Your breath is sweet," he says, and kisses her, lightly, on the cheek and then the lips. She embraces him all at once, very hard. She holds on, and breathes.

"You make me forget what I am. But then . . . I have to return, and it hurts."

"I'm sorry."

"No," she says. "It's all right. It's good."

They roll around together, kissing, embracing, there in the darkness, in the dirt.

After a while they both get up. Justine yawns and stretches out her arms. There are so many colors of blackness in the night. She smiles at Keith, a naive smile he's never seen.

Inside the house, she spins around, arms out, softly singing to herself as she proceeds down the hall. The lights swim together in Keith's eyes, red prisms and drifting, gold, liquescent, decomposing frames. Does Justine have wings? Does she have scars on her back, where they were cut off? She sings an old song in French, one she may remember from when she was a peasant child, so long ago, before concrete, electric lights, and cars.

PART TWO

PART TWO

THIRTY-FOUR

Sabrina is supposedly more practical than Chase, and she sees this house more in terms of what is wrong with it, what will need to be fixed, than in terms of its history and alleged romance.

Located in the Hollywood Hills, it's quite old by local standards, having been built in 1923. It combines Pueblo, Mission, and Italian motifs in a structure roofed in red tile and covered with pebbledash gray cement. The house has a rear-garden orientation. The kitchen is on the street side, near the entrance. The rear of the house, by contrast, looks out through oversized windows to the gardens, which are immediately accessible to the rear living room.

The gardens have gone to hell. All the fruit and nut trees, the flowering shrubs, the palms . . . everything is in sad shape. However, this is the sort of project, indeed, that Sabrina likes to oversee. She speaks Spanish fluently, having spent a great deal of time in Mexico and Latin America, and having lived in Costa Rica at one period for three years. So she can communicate with gardeners, and with the household staff. She's a benevolent tyrant, or so she believes.

Chase is more of a dreamer, and you can tell him anything, anything might take his fancy for a couple of days. He has at various times been quite taken with the notion of extraterrestrial visitations, or with deep hypnosis to explore past lives. He's an enthusiast, and not all of his enthusiasms just pass away with a "poof." One tends not to bring up these seemingly disavowed and forcefully forgotten crazes to him, but he still maintains the conviction, albeit only in private, that he was an adventurous merchant, traveling all over the world in a former life, maybe in 1200 or so. He has had certain dreams which have convinced him this is true.

For all his imagination and even seeming flakiness, Chase is a very hardheaded businessman, and secretive about his affairs. On first acquaintance, it may seem easy to get money out of him. But it is not. Some lawsuit is always pending, and he generally settles out of court, on his terms. His three children from his two former wives are all unhappy about this secrecy and tightfistedness. And yet, they don't find it wise to burn any bridges, for he may suddenly, out of nowhere, be extraordinarily generous, on a whim.

Sabrina is his third wife, and he is her third husband. She is a professional beauty, more or less. At forty-three, ten years younger than Chase, she looks wonderful. Maybe slightly over-trained, but she has an enigmatic, sensual face. It promises no end of interesting thought, or at least, interesting-looking poses to be struck. She deflates Chase's sudden enthusiasms. It's a game both of them enjoy.

The history of this house is as follows: it was built in 1923, for the real estate magnate William Howard Sturdevant (as distinct from the other William Sturdevant), who was a friend of Harry Culver, that is, a subdivider, much given to such sales gimmicks as free lunches, boys' boxcar races, beautiful baby contests, and a searchlight visible at night for more than thirty miles. Sturdevant had his army of salesmen doing calisthenics and chanting positive-thinking maxims before the busloads of prospective customers arrived, to be greeted by an all-female marching band. Sturdevant was also associated with Edgar Rice Burroughs, the creator of Tarzan, and of the Tarzana development. But Harriet, Mrs. Sturdevant, fell in love with a World War I veteran with a wooden leg, and Sturdevant, whether or not as a direct consequence, suffered a heart attack and died.

In 1928, the house was acquired by Lawrence "Cosmo" Wheeler, the pilot and aeronautical engineer who founded Aurora Aviation, which manufactured airplane motors and attempted to compete with Lockheed and Douglas in building monoplanes to carry the mail. Cosmo Wheeler married the silent film actress, Daphne Phoenix, and for a short period of time led a very active social life. But his airplane had wing design problems, and repeatedly crashed. Cosmo went broke, Daphne Phoenix left him, and he sold the house in 1932.

The next owner, Alfred Ulman, a half-Jewish movie producer, was reputedly homosexual. His wife, Minerva, often appeared in men's clothes, sporting a cigarette holder, sometimes a riding crop. Ulman's best friend, who lived at the house for a while, Laszlo Bloch, was later, retrospectively, thought to have been a Nazi agent. In any case, after a decade of extravagant masquerade parties and increasing alcoholism, Alfred Ulman shot himself in 1942. Minerva lingered on, in the company of her constant companion, the British poetess Jo Spurgeon, until 1954. Minerva died of asthma.

The house then remained on the market, empty, until 1958. The reclusive heiress Caroline Maria Severance purchased it, moving in with her lover, the classical pianist, Anton Roubatieff. Possibly they were married, a year or two earlier, in Mexico. Their daughter, Olga, was most likely born in 1956. Nothing much is known for several years, except that the couple was seldom seen. In 1967 or so, Roubatieff disappeared, or left. Caroline Severance was rumored to be a morphine addict who never ventured out during the day. She died in 1973, under somewhat mysterious circumstances. According to Olga and her hippie friends, Caroline committed suicide, intentionally overdosing, allegedly driven to it by untreatable pain resulting from a fall off a horse in her youth. She had degenerative disc disease, Olga said. Unfortunately, none of this could be verified, because Olga burned her mother's body, following, she said, instructions left her in the suicide note. She also, however, set fire to the note. Whatever the truth may have been, Olga's behavior apparently was bizarre, and she was committed to a psychiatric clinic for the next three years.

In the meantime, representatives of the Severance family, coming from Vermont, provided for Olga Roubatieff by selling the house, and establishing a trust.

In 1975, the house came into the possession of the painter Richard Fabian, who was always able to sell his critically despised landscapes and portraits, but who lived off the money of his wife, Cerise. Richard Fabian was fiercely right wing, a member for some time of a paramilitary unit of the Minutemen. He worried about racial purity, Communism, and the manipulations of American culture by the Jews. If the art world generally saw his work as beneath criticism, he met this indifference with a vitriolic hatred centered on the lack, as he saw it, of "good drawing skills." After Cerise died in a car wreck in 1984, Fabian turned solitary, and was bankrupt by the time he died in 1991. His long-estranged son Mark, working for NASA in Florida, married with two children, wanted nothing to do with the house or its contents. He gave it up for a song to Oswald Neff, the real estate agent, who's known Chase Blessington for many years.

Discovering all the strange antiques in the basement, Neff contacted Chase, thinking of the latter's longtime interest in American folk art. Neff, trying not to rub a skin cancer on the bridge of his nose, was shocked when Chase actually wanted to buy the whole thing. Neff is the one who took an interest in discovering what he could of the history of the place, intrigued by his memory of the Severance woman's death. He told Chase what he knew, just to pass the time of day, and the latter wanted more.

"This place has possibilities," Chase said, in the rear living room. "I feel something here."

He and Sabrina have had all of the rooms redecorated. Sabrina has a talent for this. The "junk" in the basement rooms has been left alone. Chase wants time to get used to it. All of the life-size figures, made of metal or wood, painted. Some seem ready to move. It seems as if Richard Fabian must have made them, in his last few years, when he was alone.

Chase says, "When I went to Georgia, I ate sliced ham, greens and navy beans, cornbread with honey. Drank moonshine out of a jar. I did business with a man named Turnipseed. In Atlanta I introduced Turnipseed to my friend Raymond Singh, from Bombay."

They are in the basement, cursorily examining the figures, some of which have tape recorders or radio speakers in their heads. Sabrina is somewhat bored.

"Size double-A batteries," Chase announces. "Then we'll find out what they have to say."

"I'm not sure I want to know. They give me the creeps."

Several of the figures have names. That is, engraved plaques either on the base or on little chains, hanging around their necks. "Lady Maude." "Felix." "Sam Bell." Others are archetypes, like The Tattooed Man. The Snake Lady. The Knife Thrower. The Old Black Man with a White Beard. Bikini Girl. Carved and painted wood with clothing and movable joints. The feet are often rudimentary, in one case actual wheels. (Spaceman.)

There are many canvases stacked against the walls. Fabian's son doesn't want them. He presumably has good reasons for his feelings about his dad.

Sabrina is looking at the paintings idly, with no particular interest, when Chase goes into the wine cellar. There are no real finds in there, but he has to check once more.

Some of these landscapes aren't so bad. Here's one that reminds Sabrina of rural Pennsylvania, where she's never actually been. There's something sort of ominous about these black-faced merino sheep. This isn't really a very friendly landscape. The acid yellow sun looks poisonous, with a bit of a halo, the yellow sun itself outlined in black. The sky is absolutely blue, light blue, but the day seems dark. Unmoving. These asymmetric trees look unnatural, created rather than grown. The only inhabitants are these two cream-colored big sheep, with black faces and feet, thick coats. Sabrina does not think that human beings are welcome in their world.

For some reason it brings to mind how Chase began, several weeks ago, to invoke "the late Tolstoy" as a model for his behavior. He would bring it up at dinners or with anyone, with people high in the U.S. government, with entertainment people, movie people, or with the Japanese. He would say, "When I want to see which way to go, what to do, I try to imagine what the late Tolstoy would have to say." Or: "When I'm faced with a difficult problem, I try to think of the late Tolstoy." Or, when told about someone's situation, maybe how that person had screwed up, Chase would put on a suitably serious expression, shake his head, and say, "It might have helped him if he'd stopped a moment and considered: What would the late Tolstoy have done?"

Chase would admit, if questioned, that he had never read much Tolstoy. He would explain that this did not disqualify him from having an *impression*, which he trusted, as to what was contained in his work and thought. Just to say "the late Tolstoy" conjured up an image, did it not? You didn't necessarily have to read the books. The few remembered biographical details, and the aura surrounding the closed books—a great deal could be transmitted in this way.

The explanation never failed to please. And the rare bibliophile who was intimately familiar with "the late Tolstoy" seemed to find the reference—just bringing up such a concept—sort of inspirational, or thought-provoking, and Chase knew when to keep his mouth shut, when it was better to simply raise an eyebrow, or nod, or say, "That's true."

Now, however, the late Tolstoy seems to have run his course. These sheep remind Sabrina of the old man, how he dressed like a peasant, raging about what he saw as various refusals to look at or tell the truth. If peasants and children did not appreciate Chopin, for instance, then there was something wrong with Chopin. Simplicity was all that mattered. Simplicity meant unmediated truth. And yes, Sabrina has read *Anna Karenina*, and most of *War and Peace*. (She skipped some of the battle scenes and movements of troops.) Tolstoy could be one of these silent, possibly malevolent, mysterious, immovable sheep.

"Sabrina, come in here!" Chase appears, just for a moment, a smudge of dirt on his forehead, like ashes, eyes shining. "I've found a secret passage!"

She immediately follows him, to see. He shows her how by turning—that is, revolving—this one seemingly stuck-in-place but uncorked and empty wine bottle, the wall behind him opens, almost silently. You might not even notice unless you were quick. If, after turning the bottle, you push it *in* . . . the wall stays open.

"I don't know, Chase. What if it closes on us after we go in?"

"We'll wedge something in here." He moves a box, and fetches a flashlight. Irrepressibly, he is delighted.

He goes in first, and when he finds a light switch, and it works—well, Sabrina's too curious, she can't resist.

This seems to be nothing more than a bare, cement-block walled passage, turning a corner, leading to a door. A big, carved wooden door. The single naked lightbulb behind them doesn't illuminate things very well over here. It's dim.

"Look, there's a key in the lock. Isn't this incredible?" Chase is almost whispering. Sabrina nods. She's excited, but part of this excitement arises with fear. She can see that Chase feels it too. He hesitates, then finally turns the key. He reaches for the door. The door opens, swinging inwards. They cautiously go in.

THIRTY-FIVE

No light switch is found in the secret room, but there is a large candelabra, with red candles halfway burned down, cobwebs connecting everything . . . Sabrina doesn't want to be left here alone, so she goes and returns with wooden matches. The candles are lit.

This room is filled with all kinds of things, but dominated by a very large fine dark wooden box, carved, like a puzzle-box somehow. It is, oddly, wrapped round with chains.

Chase laughs. "This is something, isn't it? What do you think is in there?"

"I don't know. I don't understand the chains." Sabrina doesn't like it, actually, yet the wavering glow of candlelight helps make the adventure inevitable, or unavoidable, and she is not without physical daring. A part of her is definitely enlivened by risk.

"I'm pretty good with locks," Chase says, and if he says so he probably is. He studies this padlock, takes out his wallet, brings forth an iron needle or pin.

Other boxes are all around. Sabrina sees, in the uncertain, untrustworthy light, many different items, one by one. An old, toy gas station, out of metal, with gas pumps and lift. A banjo with slack strings. A set of wooden bowling pins, paint peeling off. A framed, brown photograph of Berlin in 1932. In another box, she picks up some old magazines, one of a nudist colony . . . seeing this sickens her, she doesn't know why. The woman standing there, naked, full frontal, in maybe 1953.

She opens, cautiously, a big trunk, and discovers costumes, they smell ancient, but someone left a sachet in here. The extravagant fabrics feel as if she ought not touch them, they come from another world, a lost world.

Yet there seems no going back.

Costume jewelry, necklace upon necklace of faux-pearls, shiny silver beads, more delicate stuff, gold filigree. One red piece of glass catches the light and seems alive, red like she's never conceived of red before. Sabrina is beguiled, and slowed, dulled, made old. But she is fascinated.

"Chase, look." She points out that on the wall above him, an outsize ragged black cross has been painted, or traced with a burning torch.

"I've got it," he says, and opens the padlock. He pauses, looking straight at her. She comes to him, and they begin unwinding the chain. It makes a noise hitting the floor, it rattles and clanks.

The box itself—it's hard to see how it opens. It's carved in such a way, it's hard to see a clear line that might be a break, indicating a lid. They touch it, run their hands over it, driven now to solve this, exchanging not a word.

Chase presses on some little tab, it gives, and he now thinks he sees how it works. He pulls up, and pushes, and Sabrina helps him. After the first little bit, it moves easily, without creaking.

Within, lying on his back. There reclines a man. He opens his eyes.

"No!" Sabrina exclaims, and starts to retreat. But her legs feel heavy, her will is too weak. She turns to look, to see Chase, to exhort him, and the vampire catches her eye. She knows, it's like she knew this was coming as soon as they came into this room. She tries to say, "Please," and he knows what she's thinking, and smiles. Not without mercy, perhaps. Chase, meanwhile, is going nowhere. As soon as he had the chance, he looked down deep into those black, bottomless eyes.

"I've been dreaming about you for a long time," the man says, standing by the side of his box. "I want to know all about you. I haven't had anyone to talk to for such a long time. I've slept, they put me to sleep, but now I've been blessed, you've awakened me from my lonely sleep. You cannot believe how much I love you for this. You saved me. Now I will save you."

THIRTY-SIX

The sunlight was of course a prime factor in Biograph and other early studios locating themselves in Los Angeles—another important reason was that it was close to Mexico, and so if one wished to flee subpoena servers, detectives, or saboteurs hired by Thomas Alva Edison's Trust, heading across the border was an option easily and frequently used.

David Henry Reid was drawn here from New York, where he had appeared with no particular distinction on the stage. There had been trouble, complications, and David had been glad to escape, to have some reason to come to California. As it turned out, he was much more effective on film than he had ever been on stage. He did not work with D. W. Griffith, but instead acted for Colonel John Bascombe, appearing as the lead in a number of features between 1910 and 1912. *The Devil's Eye*, *Blind Love* (in which he played a blind man), *The Sultan's Spell*, *Thread of Fate*, *The Final Sin*, and lastly, *Rapture of the Night*, after which he disappeared. Given the nature of actors, no one worried about or missed him too much. There were plenty more young men with pretensions to take his place.

David had met a woman, someone who enchanted him, appearing only at night, refusing to talk about herself or where she came from. They walked together, late, past the Mission San Gabriel. Up Spring Street. David talked to her about his days in the theater, exaggerating, claiming to have played Hamlet to much acclaim. He quoted poetry to her while they gazed upwards at the stars. He spoke about the new cinema, and how different it was. He waxed enthusiastic about the films he had been in. Justine, he was disappointed to understand, had not seen one.

What he suspected, after several such meetings, was that she was the mistress of some rich older man. She had become bored with being a cloistered flower, and in David she sought, with a certain licentiousness, someone better looking, more her own age, who would not expect matrimony. David found this all reasonable, and highly worthy of his time.

Finally, she asked to visit his lodgings. He felt sure that tonight they would consummate the affair. It was lucky, too, because instead of staying in that wretched boarding house, for the last week he had been watching over a friend's bungalow, while the friend and his wife traveled to Santa Fe.

The orange and lemon trees outside, the avocados and date palms—these David showed off, in the moonlight, quite as if they were his own. Justine did not seem especially impressed, and it suddenly occurred to him, because of her accent, that she was a Countess, exiled from France, to Martinique, and now here. An adulterous passion had ruined her. This accounted for her air of melancholy—perhaps she took opium to quench her sorrows, to forget! David found this conjured-up fallen woman terrifically exciting. Once inside the bungalow, he sought to kiss Justine, only to find that his passion . . . swirled around him, it was as if he was falling from a great height while yet standing upright. It was a sweet pain, such a sweet pain, with sharp fangs biting ever more deeply into what felt like a huge, gaping dark wound. He didn't understand, and he dreamed, he saw himself standing on the battlements of a castle, in winter, in Russia or someplace more strange. Down below was a river, covered with a thin sheet of ice. The day was heavy and cold, there was snow, and David was perhaps a hundred feet above the water, debating *when* (not whether or not, but just when) to dive into this river, feet first, breaking through the ice like glass, splintering shards of blue and gold and silver, purple and gray. The air was absolutely hushed, unearthly it was so still.

If the maids had come as usual the next day, they would have found David's dead body, but they had left town because their mother was sick. They had explained this to David, but his Spanish was not so good as he pretended, he had nodded without understanding, and so had not engaged anyone to take their place.

Colonel Bascombe assumed he was drunk, or had woman trouble; David had struck Bascombe as rather that sort. So the corpse lay undisturbed for three days and three nights. When it awakened, gradually, it did not know what it had become. It did not know that word. Everything was different, however. The new vampire was wracked with painful appetites: he kept vomiting, but nothing came up. Then he looked out the window, and he could see so far into the night, so far, so many things that had been invisible before.

When Justine came in, it was as if he was saved, he had been forsaken and lost and now all would come clear. She would help him, together they would find a way.

She said, "I am too late," and he saw that she carried a knife. Somehow he knew at once that she had meant to kill him, to save him from this torment, this in-between state of the soul.

She wanted nothing to do with him now. She left, he could not stop her, and he did not see her again for many years. In the meantime, on his own, he learned to survive.

When he saw Justine, in a nightclub, in 1939, he found himself transfixed with love. She recognized him, of course, though he had changed. He spoke to her. He said, "Why don't we go out, as we once did, and look at the stars?"

Her eyes appraised him. It was heartbreaking. He meant nothing to her, he saw. She was not even curious about him. There was nothing to do, in such a public place, but watch her leave with her "date."

One other time, he caught a glimpse of her, in the sixties, in a turbulent mob scene, but he could not reach her. He is sure that she thinks of him sometimes. He is sure that she is still around. He will find her, and they will be united.

He has done terrible things, and suffered the accidental fate of being confined for twenty years. He went into a coma, he was as if dead, he became desiccated, and ugly, but he is alive. He would probably have starved to death in there pretty soon. That stupid Olga. If she's alive, she will pay.

But now, he needs to bathe in blood.

THIRTY-SEVEN

The writer says, "I appreciate your talking to me. Michael Stein,

Keith's friend, said that he doesn't know what has happened to Keith in the last year or so, but that he thought you might have some idea, if anyone would."

"I see," Tamara says. "Now explain it to me again: you're writing an article about Renata Spengler, something like that?"

"I have a contract for a book, with a substantial advance. I'm pretty far into it. I got a lot of good information for instance from Renata's roommate at Syracuse. But as you can imagine, it's really crucial that I talk to Keith."

'Well, I don't know where he is, but as a matter of fact I did see him a little while back. I'm not sure it would be that good for him to rake over all that stuff again, you know—it pretty much ruined his life."

"I can understand that," the writer says. "But on the other hand, it might be good for him, a *purging*. Plus I think I need to hear his side of it. Gilberto Reyes has been saying recently that it wasn't suicide, that he thinks Keith killed her after one of their fights."

"That's so completely ridiculous. Reyes is crazy."

"Well, I don't especially believe him, but I feel like I need to get something from Keith."

Tamara thinks it over. She's in her office, charts piled up, white jacket on. She looks at the writer and says, "I'll call him and tell him about you. But I don't think he'll want to talk to you, so don't get your hopes up."

"You know his phone number? Why don't I call him myself? Maybe we could just talk a little over the phone?"

"No," Tamara says. "I won't be a party to any ambush."

"I'm sorry if it sounds like that. But I'm awfully far into the process, I have a lot of material, and without something from him there'll be this big hole at the middle."

"I'll tell him about it. Why did you decide to write a book about Renata anyway?"

"I had met her, several times, and interviewed her. When she died I was . . . it just seemed so tragic. Everyone who knew her still thinks about her. I mentioned it to my editor, and before I knew it . . . I think it's going to be the best thing I've ever done."

"I'll tell Keith. I'm sorry, but I go through so many names—"

"Eric Zimmerman."

Tamara doesn't like him, and he senses this. A thirty-six-year-old guy, successful without being well known, who's into any new fashion, anything new in music, and who is also a relative expert on serial killers and bizarre crime. There could be a movie deal connected to this book, so nothing is going to stop him from finding this washed-up guitar player, nothing. Whatever it takes. Lord knows he has his ways.

One reason Tamara doesn't like him is that he's left his sunglasses on while here in the domain of the hospital, this seems to her especially affected and vain.

THIRTY-EIGHT

Michelle has the van this afternoon. She dropped Jason off at the record store, and now she's come up here. She presses the buzzer. It's funny. She didn't necessarily think she was coming here to fuck, but now, as she sees Keith walk into view, she feels a warmth, and she suddenly wants to very much.

"Let me in," she says.

"No," he replies. "I don't want to see you today."

Taken aback, it takes her a moment to rejoin, "Why not?"

"I don't think it's a good idea. If you still want to, maybe you can come back some other time."

"Asshole," she says, as he walks back up the drive and into the house. She's quite angry at him. It doesn't occur to her till she's driven some miles that maybe he thinks he can treat her like this because he loaned her some money. Oh, she's furious now. She drives over to the Saint Agatha house, listening to a Skinny Puppy tape. The singer says, "*Torture*." That's the only word she hears, the only word she understands.

Crying a little has made her mascara run. She tries to fix it, contemplatively, taking her time in the rearview mirror. Then she goes in the Saint Agatha house, and since Fred isn't there, she acts seductive around Tim, the programmer-synthesizer whiz. He offers her a hit from a joint. She drinks a Coke, and Tim plays her some of the band's unmixed tapes. She listens to him talk about this and that. The atmosphere isn't sexual, not now. The music, in its unfinished state, is more interesting to her than when they doll it up. The robotic chunka-chunka is so loud it functions as a drug.

And when Fred arrives, his obvious suffering cheers her up. She likes him like this.

THIRTY-NINE

Two young women, naked, lie on the tile floor, deeply entranced, ugly raw bites on their necks. Their eyes show nothing. They wait to be bitten again.

The light coming in here makes the flesh look yellowish, ochre where there's some tan. One of the young women is Japanese. It is daylight. David sleeps.

Sabrina comes in, desultorily kneels, and begins to scrub blood off the floor. She too is in a kind of trance, but she can think. Slowly. It takes an effort. She is not able to form any thoughts counter to David's freshly imposed will. It's like she's on strong tranquilizers or anti-psychotic drugs. Numb, yes, but not a peaceful or pleasant numbness.

She scrubs for about an hour, and then stops. She does not notice the big stain she has missed. She gets up, and begins picking up these people's clothing, which has all been thrown over against one wall. It does not occur to her to look in wallets for money, nor does she feel any curiosity about checking I.D. to find out names. The Japanese woman says something, but Sabrina does not listen or try to understand. She needs to burn the clothes. And then, spend a couple hours making herself up, preparing for David and the night.

The household staff and gardeners have all been dismissed. New servants have not yet been engaged. David wants to put on plays here, stage private spectacles, like he did in this house in the past. He has been a presence here, it seems, for some time.

Chase is functioning better than she is, though David orders him about with more contempt. Chase is able to carry on more or less normally, at least on the telephone. He welcomes what David brings, as he understands it, or chooses to see it. David brings everlasting life. Things just need to be properly managed and arranged, and Chase need never die.

The spell, or venom injected, affects Sabrina differently. At first it made her very sick. She fights it, Chase tells her. Why not go with it? He will make us like him. We don't have to die. Sabrina has always feared aging, hated it, but she doesn't know if she so fears death itself. Maybe she does. She doesn't know.

David has had intercourse with her, when he's been hot, glutted with blood. David is capable of some kind of inward orgasm, intromission, without ejaculating. He strips everyone, once they are in here, secure.

He needed a great quantity of blood the first few days. His skin needed to soak in it. He washed his face with it. The victims—he calls them his "children"—are beheaded when they are of no further use. There is a Confederate officer's sword, finely balanced, out of the theatrical props found in the secret room. This is what David uses. He has them kneel, and becomes angry if he cannot separate head from body with a single stroke. One such person he hacked at savagely for some time. It was so nearly bled dry, the fellow's new, severe lacerations did not bleed. The flaps of skin tore back. The cuts just seeped clear fluid.

David picks up some of the heads and talks to them, smoothing out their hair, addressing them fondly, once even with tears in his voice. "Look how pretty she is," he said to Sabrina. "I think I love her best of all." Sabrina gazed into the vacant eyes of the young Hispanic woman, and agreed, "You're right. She is the best so far."

Chase is out buying a boat. Then, at night, the bodies and heads, in black plastic, can be taken aboard. And then, weighted down, dropped off out at sea. No trace left. Sharks will have something to eat. Killers. Swim.

The pace has slowed in recent days. David is reinvigorated. He looks younger, better. He hints that he may be terrifically old, that he was alive when the Romans fed Christians to the lions before bloodthirsty crowds.

"I can remember, times long in the past . . . I see them as clearly as if they are in a film. That is what I see, those scenes, all during the day when I am at rest."

FORTY

The secret room was built in the 1920s, for William Howard Sturdevant, to hide bootleg liquor. He planned to sell Canadian whiskey, but his plans came to naught. It wasn't worth it. The competition with gangsters was too fierce.

Although David entered the house in 1938 or so, and had some disciples there, he did not know about the secret room until 1966, when he came back and moved in. For several years, little changed. There were all kinds of runaways around, more than ever, and after disposing of the pianist, Anton Roubatieff, he toyed with mother and daughter, having them perform acts on each other for his edification. He eventually made Caroline Severance a vampire, and together they put on midnight plays, or "happenings," spectacles utilizing hippie kids that Olga recruited, giving acid to them, as she operated under David's lightest spell.

Some of these hippies came to feel great reverence for David, and he enjoyed this. His hypnotic powers, sans bite, were quite profound. Visions were experienced that were as much a revelation to him as anyone else.

But he grew careless. He might not have injected his serum often enough into Olga, he didn't pay enough attention to her. His spell waned. There were other things going on, black masses for instance, and he allowed too many strangers around. Caroline Severance killed some boy Olga thought herself in love with, and a few days later, Olga and some of the hippies exposed Caroline to the sun, hideously burning her to death. David was chained within his oblong box.

Olga had been taking so much acid, besides constantly, every day, smoking pot, that she was unable to give a good account of herself to the authorities. That much seems to be clear. Does she now, wherever she is, really believe in what happened, or did they blank out her brain with electroshock, Librium, and Stelazine? Where is she now?

Chase, agreeably, has hired a detective to track her down. If she is not close by, she's safe. Otherwise, David will see. Maybe he could spare her, in spite of everything, like a Christ.

Chase talks to Sabrina as if he will master all systems of philosophy, as if living for hundreds of years must eventually bring perfect wisdom, as if he'll be a living Buddha, a prophet, sustained by his fellow man's blood. As though eventually, as one of the living dead, he will transcend his body, his flesh, his very form. He will become God. All he needs is more time. Unlimited time.

David has driven around several nights, exploring, seeing how people live these days. You can only learn so much from TV. It's interesting to spy without being seen, even when there's no suitable prey. He is curious. In the shadows, he watches people live, talk, fight, go out, undress, go to bed, and he has no desire to interfere, he just wants to completely disappear. To be less than a fly. A spot of dirt. At such times he loses his will, and is languid, almost unable to force himself out of the light before dawn. Arriving panting at his box, intentionally having stretched it out to the last minute, taunting the risk of burning, David wonders how Justine stands it, how she does it, what she thinks about during the blank, utterly blank, endless night. Where is she? He knows she is somewhere not far.

A vast sadness settles over his crypt like a gigantic moon made of lead. He stares all day, unblinking, at the unseeing face of this lead moon.

FORTY-ONE

"Do you remember when you first met me?" Justine asks.

"Sure. You asked me if I had a light, and when you smoked I noticed you didn't inhale. You waited for me to do something, and then you offered to buy me a drink."

"And you said, okay, but you had to meet someone at your apartment in fifteen minutes. Then you looked into my eyes and said, Do you want to come with me? It won't take very long. I said, All right, and then . . . you warned me that it was a drug deal, if that bothered me."

"You smiled," Keith says, "and shook your head."

She smiles now, a slow-developing, seraphic smile. They are watching a vampire movie on late night TV. Keith has his arm around her, she rests her head on his shoulder, looking up into his face from time to time.

This man and his daughter visit the castle of the Count. The man is a philosopher, a scientist, a scholar, and he talks with the Count in front of a roaring fire in the fireplace. He seems to understand what the Count is, but to believe that he will not be harmed. The sacredness of the guest. But he is wrong. Servants come in the early morning hours and murder him with an axe.

They then throw his body into an adjacent, deep blue lake.

The daughter, who seems about sixteen, is now naked upon her bed. She is dead. The Count turns to the camera, panting. The whites of his eyes have gone red.

During the commercial, Justine says, "I tried to starve myself. I thought I could starve myself to death. That way, I would avoid further mortal sin. I stayed in my cave, and every night was a torment, the pain and the hunger were so awful, I couldn't stand it. I would tell myself, just one more night. I was too weak." Keith kisses her forehead, as though in absolution. She says, "I lasted forty-nine days. Then, one night, it was raining, and I found these two soldiers, sleeping by a fire near the entrance. So I bit them both, I killed them. Another time, I tried to linger in the morning sunlight, but it hurt too much. I couldn't make it anywhere near true dawn."

The movie is dubbed, presumably from German, much of it evidently shot in a real, very impressive castle. The son comes looking for his father and sister, and finds that the local officials, the nineteenth-century police, are in the pay of the Count. The son's best friend is attacked with an axe, his arm cut off at the shoulder. It's a violent film. The sister, Natasha, appears, a vampire herself. Her brother tries to talk to her. Incestuously seductive, she is sweet, but then breaks the spell and shows her fangs. He drives a stake through her heart.

Justine watches intently. The evil servant who wielded the axe is killed, stabbed what seems about twenty times, over and over, each stab wound making an audible thwunk, as he gasps blood.

The Count, of course, will not escape. He is transpierced on a giant spike, writhing, the spike coming out through his chest in the area of his heart. Then he crumbles away, gradually, in dated special effects, until he is a skeleton, with red eyes and gaping jaw. And he dissolves into bluish dust.

The last scene is of the sister, at peace now in death, a wreath of garlic around her neck. The coffin is closed and nailed shut, lowered into the grave. Dirt falls into the hole, covering red roses, rose petals. Then we see the brother, mourning, and his friend, who lost his arm. The music is still ominous as the credits begin.

"That's sad," Justine says. "Ludwig loved his sister. It seems to me she was his one true love. He will never be happy again."

"No," Keith says. They agree.

"Why don't you invite Tamara to come visit?" Justine says, after a while. The doctor had called, earlier, about 9:00. Keith told Justine about this Eric Zimmerman, and that Tamara wants to see for herself how he lives. Justine at that time had shrugged, and said, "I am doing nothing to her. It's been long enough—I have no power over her by this time."

Now when she repeats this idea, having her visit, Keith decides, why not? If Justine has ulterior motives, he might as well see what they are. He truly does not believe she will bite Dr. Rothschild again. It's almost more like she wants to play at being "normal" for one evening.

Earlier today, Keith had a dream. He tells it to Justine. He had an appointment in an office building, and when he went in, he saw all the people he'd gone to high school with. They all worked there, in this office, in the government, bureaucrats or something. Civil servants. Most of them seemed happy, at their desks or walking around. Keith went down one long aisle, turned left, then came back toward the entrance, glass doors against the endless dark. He saw faces he had not thought of for years. Faces he remembered well. As he walked amongst them, however, he came to realize that he was invisible. Or at any rate, no one could see him. He saw Craig Enloe laughing with Melissa Kent. He experienced such an anguish, a nostalgia, as he saw that he was no longer someone who could exist within their world.

"Come here," Justine says, and he returns to the couch, where she holds him. His face is luminous as, after he kisses her, he suddenly bites her on the neck, rather hard.

"Do that again," she says. Instead, he pulls down the thin

straps of her lacy white slip, and he bites one bared breast.

"Harder," she says. The new feeling is a revelation to her. Keith bites her left nipple, hard. She likes it. The seraphic expression melts into something more carnal; her mouth is open, and she groans.

How did he know that this would work, biting her like this? Justine's face dissolves. He knows enough not to go on biting again and again. No, but that insight, or tease, serves the purpose of gaining her body's attention, and there is a radiance, a warming from within.

FORTY-TWO

She takes great care with her appearance, with her makeup and clothes. In recent years, she has come to take more and more pleasure in new clothes. With money, places will let you come in at midnight—anything's possible when you have money. Before inheriting, "legally," a fortune from Max Durand, she variously robbed people as she needed to get by, putting them under her spell so that they were happy to go to the bank and come back with some cash.

In front of the mirror, a bad memory strikes her, so that she clutches at the pearl necklace she was about to put on. Always, a woman alone, wandering around at night, is a target for criminals, or perverts, rapists, and murderers. Usually, Justine is well protected; in several cases she has taken care of such attacks with little problem. One time, however, a gang of drunken cowboys caught her, and she was so outnumbered, she thought it would be stupid to show her fangs.

They overpowered her, and several of them raped her; then, feeling the need to move on before morning, outlaws on the run, they stabbed her ten or twelve times and left her for dead. This was in maybe 1883, something like that. 1892.

They hung her up, in her torn dress, in the branches of a tree.

Justine now has a look as if she has been turned to stone. She rocks a bit, side to side, and dares glance at herself, and begins with resolve to brush her hair. She can see Keith, reflected in the mirror. He is reading a magazine. Some music is playing, some guitars.

She is conscious, as if at a great distance, of such delight with him, and at the same time, such dread. Keith is striking to her, not merely because of his good looks, but because of his grace, imbued in all his movements, spoiled only by the tragic feature of the mangled hands.

Still, it is not the physical qualities that she sees in him that arouse her passion—it is the spiritual side, his soul. It has thawed her, dangerously, she's frightened of what is happening, she's afraid it may turn out very badly for them both.

To be in a situation where he was indifferent enough to life to find it acceptable to spend time with her, to go out with her on her rounds, he had to have been more or less killed first, a great disaster had befallen him, he didn't care if he lived or died.

She goes to him.

"When I died," she says, "whatever happened to me, it was a terrible thing. Either my soul left me, and I have existed all these years as a soulless being—which is how I can stand the things I do—or else my soul is still inside me, somewhere, hidden, shrunken down, doubly damned. I don't think I have a soul. That's what makes me so horrible."

"I feel a soul in you," Keith says, affected by her distress. "It's in there. You wouldn't even worry about it if your soul had disappeared. I feel it in you."

"Are you sure? Then I am damned."

"You don't know that. What you've done, it's been necessary for you to survive. You haven't gratuitously murdered children, or poisoned the water, or spread the plague. Have you?"

"No," she says, but she is not secure. Melancholy overcomes

her, as she recollects some of her deeds. She clings to Keith, and she tries to think, to understand. He is all she has, and she knows that if she stays with him, she will be the ruin of him, her evil will infect him. But maybe he has been brought to her for a purpose. Their intersection will save both of them somehow. This seems flatly impossible to her, she can only imagine that they've come together by neutral chance; therefore they must get all they can out of what is possible in the fleshly here and now. She is afraid to try to imagine anything more.

FORTY-THREE

Everything Keith has done so far in relation to Justine he has done because it has come naturally, it has felt right. He has examined his behavior from time to time, to the extent that he is capable of rational thought at this point, and it all seems to make sense, given the unreal circumstance he has come to inhabit as his life.

The sexual attraction to Justine has been slow in coming, although from the first he was curious about her in this way. There's a certain wantonness she possesses, almost unconsciously, but he does not wish to respond to this. She has exerted power over people so easily, put them under a spell, that Keith from the start has wanted to differentiate himself from one of *them*, even if this means forever maintaining his distance, turning himself down to match her liquid nitrogen cool. He can do it. They get along well, though, and the very fact that he doesn't *want* something from her helped them become closer as time has gone on.

If he has touched her, it has been in a way to test himself, as well as to test her. He needed to touch her to keep faith in her corporeality, to *find her* . . . beyond this, he is not intelligible to himself.

When she says that she has wondered whether or not she still has a soul, he feels a great emotion well up inside of him, at the same time that he thinks this is a false question. She may truly believe that she is damned, quite literally damned, but he is so sure he experiences the light from her soul he cannot believe she really imagines seriously that she is soulless.

It is not a modern question, this consideration of the soul. He leaves behind in an *instant* the nervous irreverence with which one might ordinarily banter about such an unknowable, metaphysical concept—he finds within himself an uneasy but hard-core reverence that he can connect to Justine like a sticky tentacle, answering her need.

He loves her, or he loves the part of her he recognizes, and he can stand the other part, he can expose himself to it, collaborate with it, even if in so doing he is playing catch with death. He forgives himself for his morbid bravado, if that's what it is. What interests him in Justine is precisely that which is alive, that which is vulnerable, reachable, that which he can be with as another human being, a lost soul maybe, a tiny blink of light that does not want to be forever alone. All the fantastic stuff around them— that she is a vampire, and once died, and has been alive for so very long—he tries not to dwell on any of this, or only to think about it as he must from night to night.

Life is essentially mysterious, and he seeks to accept this. When he and Justine are fucking, the alchemy of their joining creates a new dark world that is something no one else ever can have possibly known, a world like a mesmerizing jungle that has never seen the sun, a jungle of huge pulpy molten metal fruits and flowers of dripping steel, blind insects that fill up the night and then fly away forever, animals copulating in squishy jewel-like trees, bleeding penises curling as snakes around and around the tendons and bone-branches into the blue-black nerve-ending pools of shining liquid, down into the living maze one never tires of exploring, running into convulsing glittery walls and back and round the turn into a canal that bursts into color where there can be no color, where everything is slippery wet black mirror fragments that come together and then fall apart, come together and fall apart in moonlit rooms.

FORTY-FOUR

Chase talks to these kids, in science-fiction glaring white sunlight, next to a chicken-wire fence with a big hole ripped in it, leading into dried-up dirt and broken glass.

"We're making a movie about teen life in the streets. Living in squats. That kind of thing. We'll pay one hundred dollars each."

"For what, man?"

"The initial interview. Then it depends on the director, how much we use you. If we use you at all. But the hundred dollars, that's yours, unless you act like a jerk."

There are five of them, all dressed in quasi-stylish rags. Chase likes them, in his new fashion. He sees them as pawns. He has always been inclined to be manipulative, and he's been clever enough at it that he's usually gotten his way. He is under David's spell, true, but he wants this bargain, he cooperates with all of his will. A few years ago, he had an episode, his heart beat irregularly, they kept watch on him in a coronary care unit—he hated that feeling of helplessness, helplessness and terrible fear. If he had died then, he would have died like a sheep, as most men die, unknowing and weak. This fantastic, bizarre opportunity—why of course he jumps at it. Meeting David is like getting a chance to meet God. God or the Devil, but a supernatural being who can grant one supernatural gifts.

Sabrina, by contrast, seems to possess an insufficient fervor to live. Chase thinks . . . *she* has to take care of herself. If she comes along, he wants her, he will treasure her companionship, but he is prepared to be hardheaded, to cut his losses if he must. After all, she is his third wife. She no doubt married him with the expectation in the back of her mind that she would outlive him, and inherit, and that would have suited her fine. Well, maybe it will be Chase who survives, albeit on another plane of existence, by extraordinary means.

In the evening, Chase and David come to the squat. It's an abandoned apartment building, partially burned and then boarded up for several years.

There were five kids this afternoon. Now there are seven. One of the new ones, a male with a baseball cap on sideways, insists on the money being paid up front.

"I think you're fags."

"We'll interview you first," David says.

There's no electricity, no water. The room for the interviews has candles, and a battery lamp.

"What's your name?" Chase asks.

"Flip. Flipper to you guys."

David laughs, achieves eye contact. He puts the boy under. As each one comes in, he has them stand there, in a line. The last two, Ruby and Mark, are entranced but left seated in the other room.

"Undress," David says to the five kids in the line. "Take everything off."

Chase, without being asked, picks up the clothes as they are dropped, piles them into a corner, stinky, moist with sweat.

David sucks on the neck of a fat girl, then takes some from Flip. This seems to Chase to go on for a very long time. Chase lingers uneasily.

When David is done sucking Flip, he turns and looks at Chase, with a very odd look on his face. He looks like he doesn't know where he is. He staggers, then turns back to the naked kids in the line. A knife is in his hand.

The kids see the knife, it gleams in the dim golden light. They stay docile, almost with little half-smiles. David puts his hands over his ears, as if against some tremendous noise, mouth open, eyes closed. Then recollects himself, and begins cutting throats, standing behind each figure, grinning lacerations ear to ear, holding up the head by the hair if the body goes down too suddenly, too heavy and slack.

Chase watches from the doorway, not quite nauseous, not recognizing the emotion that fills him up like ink.

One of the children moans, another gasps, a whistle sound at the end of each breath. It's interesting, the attitudes into which they have fallen. David hesitates, nudging aside an ankle with his shoe. He slashes the face of a boy. Crouching down, he castrates Flip, and places the product of this operation in the fat girl's mouth. He cuts the eyes out of a blonde girl, and puts them where Flip's penis and testes once lived, in the gashed-open red wound, which is something like a cunt.

He wipes off the knife, and his bloody hands, on a t-shirt he's picked up.

They leave the building, leading out Ruby and Mark, who seem oblivious to what happened to their friends. There was a little winding river of blood beginning to flow out of the killing room; it seemed as if the floor was not quite level, from earthquake or shoddy construction. The river was slowly heading for the stairs.

Chase is managing to refrain from any judgment of David's behavior. He is unfit to think anything bad about the manifestation of Death. The rules have changed.

A minimum of blood on him, David sits in the backseat with Ruby, fondling her, as the low-key, skinny Mark sits up in front. "You're so pretty," David murmurs. He kisses Ruby on the forehead. She's not especially good-looking. She has a ring in one nostril, the letter S tattooed on her left shoulder. Brown hair with some green and pink.

Ruby lets out a long sigh, nestling her head against David's chest, as he holds her close.

"I feel your heart beating," he says. "You're sweet." He kisses her cheek, and holds her all the way home.

Despite what his brain tells him, Chase has some difficulty driving, his legs are shaking so much it's hard to give the car gas smoothly, and his foot seems to want to slam on the brakes. He does not know if David notices or not.

FORTY-FIVE

It was Flip's blood. At the first surge of it into David's fangs, everything radically changed, universes of colors and microscopic flamy atoms swirling in mathematically determined irregular nebulae, atoms that might be planets or the interior constellations of all reality, all bodies, all matter, these cheap plasterboard walls and this flesh, the water vapor suspended mixed with chemicals in the desolate air, the hamburgers and tacos on these teenagers' breaths— David was suddenly on acid, Flip was on acid, David knew what it was from Olga back in 1969.

The fat girl's earlier blood diluted the effect somewhat, but he was determined to go through it, to ride the experience and see where it went. Before he had bit Flip he had had a terrible headache from putting out the energy for so much control. His hypnotic powers are not infinite; he had overextended himself. The fortunate thing is, so many people, once entranced, stop fighting it, and never try to fight it again, even as the spell may greatly weaken and wane.

All this landscapeless floating, black dots over mountains of skulls. The ugly jolt-buzz of the same primitive, childish note hit again and again, flat lives of sticky concrete TV screens and the penis, penis again and again into the mouth, the other holes, the neck.

In the backseat of the car, he sees all these buildings on fire, cherry-pink fires in the artificial electric night. Dead bodies moaning on the side of the road, crawling, skeletons burned black as if coated with oil.

This breast belongs to a thirteen-year-old girl. No, it is an old crone. The rest of her body is crumbling, red and purple, rotting away. David stays outwardly calm. He was an actor. The easiest acting in the world is keeping a straight face.

All he can remember of daylight is some scenes from over-exposed, early silent films. Black and white, but really gray. White as if the earth is colliding with the sun.

That night, that night. He believes he had an erection when he died. Justine came so close, so dark it was as if she was made of the darkness herself. He breathed out, he breathed in. Justine, in a white gown against a stormy sky, the sky rushing, fast-motion dark clouds against a sky of orange-red.

The mountain of skulls. He tries to climb the mountain of gray-blue and ivory, sometimes bloody skulls. He's dressed in a black suit, climbing the skulls as best he can, slipping, hurting his hands, panting, the skulls tumbling, no matter how long he climbs he cannot see the top of the ridge. Some of these faces are familiar. He tramples them, he is triumphant, he climbs up to a sterile garden, dark blue with a black sky and white moon. The sky comes right down so that David can reach up and touch it if he likes. It's not enough.

He gets out of the car and goes into the house, his arm around Ruby's shoulders. Then he puts his hand in between her shoulder blades, pushes her in.

FORTY-SIX

What Keith often does is go driving, listening to loud music in the car. He stops someplace where he can either eat in the car, sit outside and eat, or take something portable home. These expeditions take him an hour or two, sometimes longer, depending on how far he roams.

Justine likes to accompany him, after it gets dark. In any case, whether or not she is with him, he always orders for two or three. Then he eats the same thing the next day, at home. Or goes out again, and these untouched portions begin to pile up. Justine enjoys watching him eat. She likes feeling like a citizen of this urban sprawl, slightly sweaty, making an entrance, looking around at the other denizens of this restaurant, *cabanita*, bar and grill.

Keith generally favors little self-contained units, like blackbean burritos, Northern Indian vegetable or lamb samosas, individual gourmet pizzas, Jimmy's famous hamburger and fries, a grilled half-chicken Jamaican-style, or a Syrian lamb schwarma sandwich, with pickles and baba ghanoush. When Justine is with him, she likes to smell things, and so far she hasn't had any ill effects from just *tasting* such delicacies as mango ice cream.

Tonight they go to get Indian takeout. Keith puts the white sacks next to him on the front seat, and Justine goes into the back. The samosas and pakoras and mint chutney smell good, even with the windows down. They're both kind of dressed up. It's Friday night. Keith wears a linen suit, pale cream, a plum-colored shirt, and black gloves over his bandaged hands. Justine, in the backseat, playing a part, wears a short apricot-colored dress, gold earrings, a gold necklace and bracelet, and raspberry-hued stockings and shoes.

They cruise the boy hustlers, until Justine sees one she likes. As she opens the back door, her skirt rides up, intentionally, to show soft pale inner thigh. A garter belt, this means. The blond boy wears a baseball cap on backwards. He feels lucky. It's possible he's no older than fourteen. Tall for his age, and tan.

"What's your name?" Justine asks.

"Dree." He is smiling, wondering what is expected of him. He has a hard-on, and Justine touches it through his jeans. He sighs, and it takes a moment to get him to hold her gaze.

She sucks the crook of his arm. They lift him out of the car, and leave him in an alley, seated next to a dumpster, leave him to sleep for an hour or two. Justine gets in the front seat, and Keith eats a samosa as he drives them home.

Tamara and her boyfriend are coming over later on. Justine is

119

hot and restless. She wants to be next to Keith. She's excited. Nothing that ever happened in the past seems to matter as much as her eroticized relation to this man right now.

Once home, they realize there's forty-five minutes or so until the guests arrive. This new thing they have, the sex—what else is there to do? They don't really have to get undressed. The blood beats black. Keith bites her, his breath spicy, ecstatic, bites her vulnerable neck.

It feels to her like his cock rearranges her vagina, taking it in new directions, moving around whatever there is in her that might correspond to a living, human female's womb. Justine is violently moved, and her secret passages tautly grip and twist and contort, but it leads to such a saturation of peace, a liquid peace, the wet suction in inner blackness leads to unspeakable bliss. What is like a cunt squeezes, convulses. She can't embrace Keith tightly enough. She wants them to literally *merge*, their flesh to melt together, there to expire in a pool of shiny ruby blood, or what's left after blood.

Devoutly, Keith works at building the friction, never allowing himself to be frightened by how much some momentary spiky spasm may jolt him with pain. Sometimes it feels as though his penis is being drawn up through her body, like it's been stretched to four feet long, or like it's bisected, right and left devils, each surging up into separate new worlds. Everything outside them is being obliterated by this blinding love.

They join themselves in devotion on the floor in his bedroom. Afterwards, she doesn't want him to pull out. "Oh no, *no*," but he must withdraw. Soon she follows him to the bathroom, where he attempts to wash his penis of this black, sticky, tingling, burning substance. But it will not wash off.

"It dries, and then seems to disappear while I'm asleep."

Justine puts one foot up on the toilet seat, trying to see her vulva in the mirror. "Is it on me too?"

"No," he says, examining the vestibule of her genital. "It

comes from deep inside you. I can feel it, I think I can, when it begins to gush. I like it," he says, and she is pleased. Her fangs come out as she smiles.

The bell rings, from the speaker-button at the front gate.

"Oh no," she says, and pretends to be afraid.

"I'll protect you," he says, taking her in his arms, and she allows herself to be, in play, soothed.

FORTY-SEVEN

Because Tamara cannot—she does not want to—keep anything from Patrick for long, she has told him all about the evening she ran into Keith and Justine, with its strange aftermath, and the subsequent meeting with Keith.

Now, a week or so after hearing about this, he remains suspicious, and skeptical of Keith's alleged good will. When Keith called and invited Tamara over, naturally she asked if Patrick might come along. Keith said yes, of course.

They have been at a party, in Laurel Canyon, so it's actually quite convenient to stop here on the way home.

It is Justine who lets them in, who greets them at the door. Patrick and Tamara are dressed up, Patrick in a navy blue blazer and black silk shirt. There may be just a hint of mousse in his hair. Wire-rimmed glasses. A new wave wonk.

Tamara has on a rather sexy aqua dress. Scoop-necked, leaving her arms bare. Her brown hair down. A few freckles. They sit down together.

Justine brings in four glasses, a bottle of champagne. It's a wonderful room, in what seems like a devastating house.

Keith comes in, greets them, sits down.

'Who is that by?" asks Patrick, gesturing toward the painting taking up most of the wall to his right, the hexagon radials.

"I don't know," Justine says. "Do you like it?"

"Yes. It looks like it's a Balthasar Cady."

"My dead husband bought it," she replies. "There are some others, by this same artist, in some of the other rooms. Shall we drink?"

"Yes," Tamara says. "To friendship, and truth."

They clink glasses, and sip.

Patrick is fascinated by the lovers. They go together wonderfully, he thinks, just as complementary types. They're both so good-looking. He leaves aside all other questions, just trying to absorb the impression that they make.

Tamara talks to Keith about the writer, and Keith thanks her for withholding the phone number.

"I really wish there wasn't someone trying to do a book like this," he says. "I guess it's inevitable, but it's too bad. I wish I could stop him."

"You look very pretty," Justine says to Tamara. Justine doesn't seem to have any eye makeup on, but her lips are terribly red.

"Thank you. I like your dress."

"Do you really? You're very kind. Keith has told me how nice you are, and I see it now, in your eyes. But when I first met you, I'm afraid I thought you were, ah, stuck-up."

"Did you?" Tamara rejoins, after a beat.

"Yes. I was mistaken. I'm very sorry for what happened to you that night."

"What did you do to me?" Tamara asks, not judgmentally, leaning back, black pump dangling on her right foot. She takes a good-sized sip of champagne. Patrick takes one too, as if he must. It tastes good. He feels a certain sympathy in common with Keith, and he realizes that Tamara was right. The situation is by no means black and white.

"Did you give me some drug? If you did, what was it?"

Justine puts down her glass, and smiles in a way that seems to mean she will not answer, that she is lost. Keith finishes his glass, calmly, and pours everyone but Justine some more, the bottle in his black–gloved hand.

"Why do you care?" Justine answers at last.

"I don't like mysteries," Tamara states.

"Is that why you said 'and truth'?"

"Yes. I want you to tell me the truth."

"I want to know too," Patrick says, and Justine turns his way, the sandblasted–glass coffee table in between them, a porcelain vase there like an elliptical egg standing on end, white with a map of a thousand rivers or crossing streets in blue. It's hard not to follow her gaze.

"I am a vampire," Justine says. "I put you under my spell, and took some blood from the back of one knee."

These words are so unexpected, and absurd, if not insane, that Patrick and Tamara are simply frozen, in shock. Tamara just stares. Patrick wants to laugh, but it suddenly crosses his mind that one does not lightly laugh at mad people in their own homes.

Justine's head goes down, as if in thought, then when it comes up, she shows her fangs.

"Maybe these are not real," she says, and then stands, and hesitating for just a moment, she walks up the wall, into the corner of the high ceiling, gravity baring her thighs. Tamara turns to Patrick, amazed, to check if he sees what she sees.

Justine vaults down, lands light as a cat. When she comes as though to sit down next to Tamara, Tamara pulls away, making a helpless little cry.

"I am not going to harm you," Justine says. "But it's tiresome . . . you both wish to believe this is some kind of trick. Let's see. I don't know what else to do. Do you want to stab me, and see that I do not die?"

"No," Patrick says. "Let's not have any stabbing."

"It could be a retractable blade, with fake blood," Keith offers, and Justine smiles at him. She would never have thought of such a thing.

"I remember . . . I had a scab behind my knee," Tamara says.

Obviously, however, she doesn't know what to think of this. Her eyes reveal to Patrick that she is badly troubled—as he is—by the vision of Justine going up the wall like that, so effortlessly. That was just too weird.

Justine has given up. She sits down on Keith's lap, turning sideways, her arms around his neck. Wordless, they are in communion.

"What about you?" Patrick asks of Keith.

He doesn't answer, though perhaps he begins to. Patrick finds himself unsettled by the lack of calculation or guile within the look Keith gives him.

"Let's go," he says quietly, to Tamara, and she allows herself to be led outside, the smell of jasmine on the warm night breeze. Tamara is so docile, suddenly exhausted. It's certainly not a night he's going to leave her to sleep alone. Patrick keeps thinking of Justine in Keith's arms, not even looking up as they left.

124

FORTY-EIGHT

Jason's show, *The Darkest Night*, is in this version enlivened not only by the usual Russ Meyer clips—46D babes frugging to sixties surf guitar—plus various moments from assorted Italian horror movies, or black-and-white porn films just for a micro-second, or three good-looking women taking off their skirts, standing there in corsets and stockings, suddenly revealing penises—in the midst of all of this, we see, "live," Michelle with a delirious smile on her face, shaving cream rubbed into her mohawk, that and five days' stubble shorn off, a hand with a safety razor belonging to Ken.

Videos of various bands. Jason, on his own initiative, plays the rarely seen twenty-minute SMX "Doorcloser," a song that builds and builds and builds, leading to crescendo upon crescendo feedback-drenched, mind-bending crescendo.

Michelle watches closely, on the monitors, extremely stoned, her newly bald head distracting her, new sort of heavy earrings hanging from her ears. There is some sort of a vague narrative to the video, maybe. The filmmaker has scratched the negative and multiplied the fast cuts wherever he shows the band. Scribbly white lines all over everything. There's Keith, looking like he knows what he's doing, smiling privately, as his guitar thickly wails and moans and blurs.

"I fucked him," Michelle announces, to Jason and Ken. Tiff is in the bathroom, or she'd hear too.

"Who?" Ken asks.

"That guy. Wait. There. The guitar player."

Jason says, bitchy for some reason, "What was it like?"

"Oh," Michelle answers, "he's just a guy. His hands are all fucked up now, you know. They slammed his hands in car doors . . . that's why he got on heroin. That's why he can't play the guitar."

Tiff returns to the control room. She's laughing about something one of the technicians said. After they finish here, they're all going out. It's 2:00 A.M.

FORTY-NINE

"If vampires then why not witches?" Patrick says, over coffee, in his breakfast nook.

"Well then, why not?" Tamara replies, wet hair, in her terrycloth robe.

"Sure," he says. "And UFOs, telepathy, astrology, werewolves . . . here, wait a second and I'll get Dial-a-Psychic on the line." Patrick rolls his eyes and squeezes lime juice onto his papaya half. "It's all a trick," he says. "I'm amazed you'd even think twice about such a business."

"I have an open mind."

"All we really saw that's hard to explain," Patrick avers, "is how she went up the wall. If it hadn't been, you know, kind of *theatrical*, we would have examined that wall for hidden footholds. That's what it must have been. She's a performance artist-gymnast with magic-shop fangs."

"I know," Tamara admits. "That's what it has to be. Only— why? Just as a joke, I guess."

"Just as some kind of weird, alternative rock joke, from the girlfriend of a guy who used to be in a weird, alternative rock band. Remember, they did that song, 'See Me Nowhere'? It's like that."

"I sort of liked them, though," Tamara says.

"I liked them too. If we prove we can take a joke, maybe they can be our alternative friends."

FIFTY

Out on the boat, dropping black plastic wrapped parcels weighed down with chains and cement blocks, slippery heavy torsos or legs going up into the hip, the buttock through black plastic, just drop them into the water as the boat rides the swells, up and down, there's no pretense after a while of any spell on anyone. Chase steers the boat, the radio playing music, golden oldies, "The Lion Sleeps Tonight" and Jim Morrison's "*mojo rising ... There's a mojo rising*," as Mark with a headband around bleached white Clorox hair dumps the last one with a kersplash! over the side. Chase offers him some coffee out of the thermos, it's cold out here, and Mark puts in two packs of powdered creme and three, no four lumps of sugar, he's got some kind of ring on his finger that came out of a cereal box or something, Chase thinks "Cracker Jacks" but doesn't say it, it dates him, he doesn't know if they have Cracker Jacks anymore.

Mark is shivering, sniffling, sitting there as they head back in to shore. It's like he looks to Chase for something, just because Chase is an older male. Like the fathers he's been hustling and fucking since he was twelve. Is he crying? Is it possible that he's crying? No, it's just salt in his eyes, and he's shivering, his nose is running from the unexpected Pacific cold. Seagulls barking, dirty birds.

It's another mission accomplished, and Chase has already begun to forget what they have done. The underside of the little death-factory that is immortal life.

"There are some donuts," he says to Mark. The boy eats one, with more coffee, not looking at Chase, as if he knows. The father-figure would sacrifice him in an instant, for the promise of more life.

"I went down in one of those cages once," Chase suddenly says. "You know, like on National Geographic specials about sharks?"

"Oh yeah?" Mark says. "Really? Was there a shark?"

"A big one, banging his snout against the bars, trying to get in. He could see me, I could see that he saw me, he knew I was there. I thought he was gonna break open the bars."

'What kind of a shark was he, man? Like I've seen those hammerhead guys, they're fucking ugly, if one of those got you it would be incredibly gross."

"This was a big white shark. He wanted me, there for a while. He was aware of my existence, as food. I used to have dreams afterwards, that he could just swim right through the air, he'd come down the street on a sunny day, about six feet off the ground."

Mark laughs, a new donut in his mouth.

"Sounds like a pretty bad dream."

"Yeah, it was."

The radio plays some other song.

Back at the house, days go by and Mark isn't bitten. Ruby, meanwhile, has her skinny bony body wounded all over. Chase wonders at this. Mark is just hanging out.

They all sit at a big table and eat nearly raw, bloody, just-seared-black steaks. David is still abed.

Mark says, "Man, I'm used to having my meat, you know, kinda, uh, cooked first, before I chomp it down."

"Put some salt on it," Sabrina says.

"Do you have any catsup?"

"Yeah," Chase says. "Minh, get him some catsup."

Minh is the almost pretty, seventeen- or eighteen-year-old latest addition to the household. She's David's pet. She is a superior violinist, he said once, but no one here has seen or heard her play. There's no violin. She seldom speaks.

"And some Tabasco, or Heinz 57," Mark adds. He is from Kansas, he told Chase. He and his mom just couldn't communicate anymore. That's four years ago. He went back once. He's now sixteen.

In the garden, where Chase has found Ruby, she's lying on her face, and Chase is checking her for signs of life—yes, she is alive—Mark comes up slowly, even shyly, as if he doesn't want to interfere, and then says, without a great deal of conviction, "I'd like to leave now."

"You can't. I mean, I'd let you. I'd give you a couple hundred dollars and a bus ticket to Wichita, but . . . "

"I understand. You don't think David would dig it. That's cool," Mark says, very low-key about the whole thing, his premature jerked-out-of-boyhood version of serious reflection and acceptance of life's irrationality, something like that. Chase feels badly, he suffers a bit, pulling Ruby up to her feet to drag her inside. David is almost through with this one.

"How old do you think he is?" Mark asks, helping with the drooling, nearly comatose Ruby, who seems to respond to his touch more than to Chase's, if she can perceive who he is at this point.

"We don't know."

They arrange Ruby very nicely on a couch. It's late afternoon. The sun will be going down soon.

Mark could escape, he could leave, there've been many times he could have just walked away before now. Chase doesn't know what he's thinking, or what he imagines David is thinking. Maybe they have some communication Chase doesn't know about, but he doesn't believe this to be true. David seems barely aware that Mark exists. To the extent that he acknowledges the boy's continued presence, he seems to accept it as perfectly natural that he should function as a kind of unskilled, not strictly necessary assistant for Chase. It seems to be, to David, a faintly amusing situation, one that reflects somehow on Chase. As though he should know what to do, instinctively, and does not, and has not done what should be done.

It's uncanny how, at the moment David comes fully awake, everyone in the house *feels* it, feels him as he rises and prepares for the activity of the night.

Tonight he spends a long time in Sabrina's room. What are they doing? Or rather: what is he doing to her? Perhaps they are having a philosophical conversation. It has happened before. Or else something depraved may be going on. There are different ways for David to use each of them. Nothing holds him back.

'Well, well." David is suddenly there, in the living room, looking at poor Ruby. "She doesn't look half good, does she? She looks all used up. What do you think, Chase?"

"You're right."

"Am I?"

"She looks all used up."

"Thank you for confirming my observation. Let's take her someplace quiet, where she can rest. Mark, come help us, won't you? Ruby was a friend of yours, wasn't she?"

"No, not really. I knew her, that's all."

"Did you like her?"

"She's sort of a backstabber. You know, talks about you behind your back and stuff."

"We've all known those kind of people, unfortunately. But

then, don't you think, there's a little of the backstabber in all of us? In you, and me, even Chase?"

"Sure. Everybody's mostly fucked up."

David is enjoying this colloquy. They take Ruby into the killing room, where there's a drain in the floor, a hose connected to a faucet over a big sink.

"Everybody has to die sometime," David says, in a mock-philosophical tone, pleased with himself either over simply his own relative longevity or immortality or, more ominously, by some secret he has on his mind that Chase senses he's about to share. "The leaf on the tree turns golden brown, or red, and flutters to the ground. Four out of five lion cubs starve to death or die from disease. They take it pretty well. What you should do, if it troubles you, is focus on all the time before you were born. You were happy then, you were at peace. There was no pain, and you knew the entire universe, you knew it from the inside out."

This discourse, Chase realizes, has been directed to Mark, and Mark understands. David pats Mark on the shoulders, and says, "Take off your clothes." Mark nods his head and complies. Without anything being said, he gets down on his hands and knees. In a position of submission, expectant, skinny frail tattooed body and bleached lusterless dead hair.

David holds, horizontal, on his fingertips, like an Egyptian offering at a sacred ceremony, his precious sword. His sharp, finely balanced, Confederate officer's sword.

Chase accepts it from him, hefts it. This is a test. He remembers David explaining to him once that when the Ku Klux Klan first started, they wore the white sheets "to frighten the Negroes, who were very superstitious at that time." The white sheets and hoods transformed the night riders into the ghosts of the Confederate dead. Yet David says he had nothing against blacks, and that in fact he has never spent any time in the deep South.

The part that bothers Chase the most is Mark's voluntary, passive acquiescence in all this. Proving himself as a predator is one thing, he knows he has to do it, to rise to the occasion, but what is Mark doing? How can he . . . commit suicide, at his age, in this way?

Mark is a sacrifice. Chase, trembling, takes a deep breath, and prays for whatever athletic prowess and strength he still possesses to guide him through, in glory, like Rameses or Thutmose, a warrior-pharaoh, the incarnation of the god.

Thwunk! Oh no, it's not going to come off with one stroke, there must be a trick to it, a vertebra to aim at, he was supposed to just naturally know. Tunk! He's already tired, and Mark has rolled onto his side, his position isn't so ideal, but Chase now hates him, he brings up all his frenzy to win, to live, to survive, and the head rolls free—blood flying up everywhere, Chase finds it all over his face, his hands, soaked through his shirt.

Now Ruby. David pulls up her hair, to expose the nape of her neck, as she kneels, wobbly, weak. Some forgotten info-bit—oh yeah, in the French Revolution, the guillotine, the hair would dull the blade. Chase does much better this time.

"Kiss her," David says, holding up the severed head by the hair, and Chase is ready to, David laughs and Chase finds himself fondling Ruby's head in his own two hands, it's fascinating, he feels an interest and attraction that he never felt when she was alive, he is suffused with the fearlessness and lust of a demon, or of Satan, as he kisses the dead mouth and touches his own living hot tongue to the dead piece of interestingly foul meat between her lips. He loves this head.

Sabrina must never know. When he becomes a vampire, he will not do such things, but these are his initiation rites, and he must seize this power beyond all human understanding, seize it or forever fall, and he is finding it in him to dare the transfiguration, his fear he will discard forevermore.

Later on, putting Mark and Ruby into black plastic bags, his breathing troubles him, his heart seems to beat like each muscle-clench will be the last one. He has to stop for a while, he knows it's just nerves, there's no way he's going to have a heart attack and drop dead before the change.

He breathes regularly, he calms himself, he is okay. He takes a break and has a cup of tea before coming back down to finish his job.

The sun comes up and hurts his eyes as he loads up the trunk of the car. Inside, Sabrina says, "Where are you going? What happened to your little pal?"

She knows, Chase thinks. And what has *she* been doing? David fucks her, and she likes it. If she cannot stand where this is going, then commit suicide, he thinks. She's weak. She does not comprehend.

His hands are shaking, but this will pass. The blood is washed off, but Chase is not and never will be clean again.

FIFTY-ONE

She wants him to do everything to her. She doesn't want to miss any possibility of indulgence in the flesh. These nights, they are in a mood of constant excitation, their genitals respond to the momentary expression on a face, the tone of a voice. Every nuance between them is sexual. The music Keith has on when she wakes up, the way he turns his head to gaze at her as she comes into his room—pure sex.

Justine is jealous of his body, she wants him to do things with her he never did with Renata or anyone else. She has never known a male this intimately, and it fascinates her, there is a mad intoxication in it, a joy in being wanton, of being, to her mind, his whore.

After all, she has long been accustomed to regarding herself as evil, as living in a state of continuous sin. Yes, undoubtedly, at times there has been a perverse pleasure in this. And there have been times when she has lain with mortal men, for often they have been very attracted to her, in a sexual way, perhaps even the more so when they know what she is.

But never before has she so wanted to play the whore, and to so indulge herself in a man's body, to know him everywhere, to have him enter her and discharge in every hole, she swallows his seed as though, like they used to say of the weasel, she might conceive via the mouth.

She entertains the dark fantasy that she will pierce her flesh with a knife, forming wounds which he might thrust into and then heal with his semen, she could give birth to who knows what writhing demons, slick wet glistening red and blue-black.

However, even as she has become sensitized to pleasure, so too has she become liable to pain. She tries to cut herself, and it hurts, sharply, it takes an effort on her part to unfocus it, and it seems that the wound closes more slowly than it would have shortly before. She is changing, unknowably, and she dares hope, with unbelievable foolishness, for some sort of a crazy miracle, she does not allow herself to think it through.

But then, the next night, upon rising, she tries an experiment. Coldly, apart from Keith, she drives a knife right through her hand. She feels it, it hurts, but it's not nearly as severe as it ought to be, were she human, were this mortal flesh.

"What did you do to yourself?" he asks, and she shrugs, she does not respond to him as she has.

She wills herself to feel nothing for him, to see him as ordinary, banal. She pictures him dead. An hour passes, though, and somehow it comes back, some small movement on his part sparks it, the way he looks at her then, so calm, and she thinks, "How beautiful he is." Her pierced hand begins to throb, and freshly bleed, as she puts her arms around his neck.

They fit their bodies together, familiarly, as if it is the most natural thing in the world.

She wears him out. If his cock is not inside of her, she is touching it, or sucking it, coaxing it, reddened and chafed, to rise once more before dawn. It sometimes seems to her that the cock has its own personality, its will, separate from Keith.

"Black is my true love's heart," he says, with a little smile, and he has some of her mysterious black substance on his finger, holding it up for her to see before he sucks it off. Nothing of hers is unlovable to him, he seems to have said. She embraces him as hard as she can, rolling on top of him, kissing him tongue to knowing tongue.

FIFTY-TWO

On an impulse, Keith calls long distance, to New York. Pacific Time, it's 3:30 P.M. Part of it is he'd like to let Michael know that he's all right. They haven't spoken since Keith was in rehab, more than a year ago. Before he got out, went back on heroin, because he *wanted to*, and then a month or two later ran into Justine.

He flexes his fingers. It's hard to understand, but they don't seem to be as bad.

"Yeah?"

"Michael, this is Keith."

"Jesus. So I guess you're not dead then, right?"

"Not yet."

They're laughing together, the old rapport immediately there. Michael can read his voice.

"What're you doing? Shit. Are you still in L.A.?"

"Yeah. I'm in this relationship. It's kind of different, a different scene."

"Rumor has had it, motherfucker, that you'd snuffed this mortal coil. A guy came around, a writer—have you heard about this? He's doing Renata's biography, and he's been trying to track you down."

"Yeah," Keith says, noncommittally. "I don't want to have anything to do with the guy."

"Really? Why not?"

"I don't want him to write his fucking book."

"Oh." Michael pauses. "Listen, I gave him the name of that doctor you saw. Does she know where you live?"

"I don't think so," Keith lies. To change the subject, he says, "What are you up to? What's the latest project? It's been a while since I've read any of the alternative press. Though actually, now that I think of it, I know a girl who writes for *The Darkest Night*."

"Goth-death shit, right?"

"That's what she led me to believe."

"Actually, man, I'm working for a publisher now. Designing book covers. I take the subway and wear a tie."

"No shit?"

"Yeah, Shawn's brother knew the guy, and he liked the artwork for our CDs and a couple of others I did."

"How is Shawn?"

"She's great. We're married now, you know."

This is the first Keith's heard. More on this subject, and he feels increasingly removed, although he doesn't want to, after the initial brotherly recognition.

"Also," Michael says, "I'm going to be working on an album for Ghost, you remember them? I'd love it if you'd come and help me out. They just said they want it to be sort of like Pink Floyd. Spacey, slow buildups. You could twirl knobs and program some stuff, if that sounds cool. I'm supposed to go into the studio in about a month. Any ideas you've had floating around . . . well, this is a small label, but for some reason they seem inclined to let people do whatever they want."

"I'll think about it," Keith says.

"Tell me about this relationship," Michael says, in a little while. "What's her name?"

"Justine."

"Is she French?"

"Yeah. But she's been in America for a long time."

"Do you live together?"

"Yeah, we do. She's in the other room right now, asleep." Keith is uneasy and restless when he gets off the phone. He is not sure Justine will understand. But he will tell her, he knows, even if it makes her jealous and unhappy. Does he want to make her unhappy? He doesn't know. It's impossible to know if one's own motives are pure.

FIFTY-THREE

Chase talks to Sabrina, in her bedroom. It's funny how all the rooms have changed their appearance, how the commonplace has turned untrustworthy, unreal. Somehow, more out of the old habit of disputation than from genuine conviction, leaving unsaid all that lies so heavy on them both, he has ended up talking about Raskolnikov, though on any kind of close examination his situation and Raskolnikov's do not match up well at all.

"Of course you remember—how Raskolnikov pondered the hypothetical problem of how if the killing of one despicable old woman stood in the way of a Napoleon seizing his destiny, why then, is not the potentially great man called upon to act, to do it, sweep the obstacle out of his way?"

"That didn't work out so well then for Raskolnikov, did it? He was paralyzed afterwards. He found himself simply an axe-murderer, hiding in an attic room, afraid to get out of bed. Not so glorious, that."

"Yes, I know. But he had to try. And remember, even the late Tolstoy was frightened of death. Near the end he said, 'What does it matter, what I have accomplished, if it all has to end in death?' "

Sabrina replies, "Everyone has their moments of weakness. Tolstoy was human, all too human, and he was an open book, he hid nothing. He freely admitted his natural fear of the unknown. But . . . what if someone said to you, you will live, but the price of your continued life will be that a hundred Chinese people on the other side of the world will be tortured to death. Would you say, 'Yes, kill them, I want to live'? What if it was a hundred children, here in America, and you had to stare into the face of each one? Would it be worth it? Would that be acceptable to you?"

Chase cannot answer, cannot speak.

Sabrina's hand is shaking as she brings a filtered cigarette up to her mouth. She has started smoking again, after having quit for fifteen years. She looks good, a sort of dark glamour exuding from her eyes, even if she is feeling the strain.

In the oversized living room, the carpenters are working on constructing a stage to David's specifications. The wooden life-size figures have been brought up from the basement, even if they have no function as of yet. They stand about haphazardly, staring witlessly, seeming at times curiously animate, as if containing some unknown form of intelligence, or consciousness, as though at the proper moment, yes, they can move.

Chase and Sabrina survey the work, and study the figures, neither of them exactly sure how it will all look when done.

She tries to comfort Chase, who seems tormented, but she cannot bring herself to offer him much affection right now. If she could say, "It's all right," or "I understand," but either of these seems false, and they are becoming, every day, more and more, strangers moving apart.

Idly, as a way of avoiding everything else, they speculate, not for the first time, as to how old David really is. Like "tourists," which they are not. They are far from that.

David has given conflicting accounts. Once, in front of both of them, he said that he had been a druid, a Celtic ceremonial priest. Another time, however, he alleged that he had seen the Egyptian pyramids when they were first built, and had worshipped Amun-Re. Now Sabrina reveals that he told her he was first bitten in Romania, as a traveler, in 1695.

And, supposedly, he was an actor in silent films. The truth may well be something never alluded to or discussed. They cannot tell.

The workers are putting up painted scenery. Several different backdrops, to be slid into place by means of a lever and some machinery.

Sabrina and Chase run out of things to say to each other, and each, separately, for a few long moments, apprehends the sadness of this. The lack of words. Words for which there are no use.

FIFTY-FOUR

The air is metallic and worn out, old air recirculated in the warm city's endless strips. Police helicopters hover, ominous. Eric looks up, then gazes around him, at all these beautiful or semi-beautiful, self-conscious, lightly clad bodies. He finishes the Thai lunch, extremely hot coconut curry shrimp. Devlin, his buddy the detective, has furnished him with the telephone numbers, the addresses, and since one of them is known to be Dr. Rothschild's boyfriend, the other one, J. Durand, looks like the best shot. Devlin says he called it, a man answered. Yeah, it sounded the right age and so forth.

Devlin smokes a cigarette now, dropping the ashes on his dirty plate. He's telling some story about when he used to be a cop. After five years on the force, his blond good looks led him to try acting. Now he's more or less unemployed. The detective business is in a slump.

Eric's hardly listening. A black car pulls up to the curb, like a hit man's car. The Hispanic guy looks like a hit man, like gazing into his shades would be the last thing you'd ever see. Lost in his own introspections, Eric only responds when Devlin reaches the end of his story, the conclusion being: "I told myself, I looked at myself in the mirror and said, Get a grip. It's not the first time, it won't be the last."

"Sound advice."

"Yeah. All you can do is hope for the best. Last night I stopped for a car crash, on the exit ramp from the Santa Monica freeway. Everybody was kind of high on it, you know? Shit, this black guy and this Vietnamese family, they had blood on them, but no one was hurt too bad. The radio was playing, and the lighting was good, it looked good— everybody was taken out of their ordinary existence. They were so considerate of each other, so thoughtful, waiting for the police."

"Yeah," Eric says. "It was a social event."

Nearby, where he parked, there's this abandoned children's playground, surrounded by chain-link fence, a locked gate, cement. All these brightly painted saguaro cacti, made out of iron, or steel, in different sizes so you could climb on them, hang, play. Painted green, red, yellow, the paint now partly scuffed off to show silver, the remaining color dull, blackened in spots.

As he drives, patient, past palm trees and thronged cars, parking lots of malls, a dull day that somewhere else you'd say it's about to rain, Eric is thinking about Renata, it's like once again she's slipped away. He can't imagine her. Sometimes she seems very real to him, not only when staring at her pictures, but at other times, he'll suddenly feel like he knows how she felt, or how she would feel about something if she was here.

It's no surprise to anyone that he should feel haunted by her, or in love, obsessed, building a composite picture from all these tantalizing, ultimately mysterious pieces of the story of her life. He spends hours replaying one of her commercials, or going over and over some footage of her that was never cut, Renata topless, wearing only a kind of g-string swimsuit bottom, her face going through real emotions, there as she thinks about whatever was in her mind as the sun shone down on the Canary Island beach. As some woman fixed her hair, painted her lips.

It's been a year since Eric and Julie stopped seeing each other. Once in a while they still talk on the phone, but there are no plans to get together again, not even to share a meal. Traveling as he does, Eric has a number of "phone-pals," male and female, whom he very rarely if ever actually sees. It can seem like an intimate friendship, because he can say anything to them, and vice versa, or it can seem lonely and forlorn, as if the voices exist only in his head.

For several months, it's seemed more and more like it's him and Renata, like they're bound together in some way. It seems more pure, since he can never have her; he feels virtuous, as though he is devoted to her spirit in an unselfish, unsullied way. If he has masturbated while studying images of her naked body, this is only human. He means it as an homage. Could he have the opportunity, he would worship her, he would adore her, kiss her feet and lick her ass, he would be her servant, if she wished to she could pee in his mouth, he'd drink it down. He's never worshipped anyone in this fashion in real life, but he wishes he could.

And so, if he is jealous of Keith, and thinks Keith was unworthy of Renata, he didn't love her enough, on another level Eric wants to somehow get close to him, to have Keith like him, because he wants to know the flavor of Keith's affection, to experience him in ways inaccessible without intimacy, without some quality of momentary "love." This will allow him to feel closer to Renata, to understand her more.

Eric takes off his sunglasses, puts them in his shirt pocket. He has a tiny tape recorder on his body, a tiny camera he might use if he gets a chance. The latest in Japanese technology, perfect for industrial espionage. Eric wears a khaki shirt with several pockets, loose khaki pants, red-and-black Air Jordans, a Rolex, a cross on a chain around his neck, nestled down amongst his black chest hairs. He rings the buzzer, and no one says anything to him. He waits a long, suspended five minutes, and presses the button again. He's prepared to go into a Zen mode and stay here like this for a while, whether or not it gets any results.

But no, that won't be necessary. Here comes Keith. Eric recognizes him at once. He feels an upsurge of affection for him, he smiles and is sure Keith will like him in return. They already have a bond, a connection. An affinity. Keith will sense this, and be unable to resist.

FIFTY-FIVE

Keith feels bad, like something bad is going to happen, he's polite to this Eric Zimmerman but the whole situation is making him nervous. The thing is: he very strongly thinks that he doesn't want this book to be written at all. So the fact that Eric has found him—it's like Keith is in shock, he doesn't know what to do. He needs more time to think, but it's impossible. He shouldn't have called Michael, he thinks. Keith is in a spot. Some kind of a decision is about to be made. He says edgier things than he intends, though it doesn't really matter what he tells him; Keith's voice functions as informationless noise.

"So," Keith says, as they walk in the garden, "this is going to be one of those books like the Dorothy Stratten story, *Portrait of a Centerfold*, something like that."

"Well, hopefully on sort of a higher level. Maybe more like that book a few years ago about Edie Sedgwick."

"I don't know who that is."

"She was this poor little rich girl, model, ran around with Andy Warhol and eventually O.D.'d. Pretty famous for a few seconds at the time."

After they walk further, look at some flowers without speaking, Keith says, "I really wish you wouldn't do this. It serves no purpose in the world, other than to make money by exploiting Renata's memory. I think she's better left in her grave. She had enough cheap publicity during her life."

"I'm sorry you feel like this," Eric says. "I mean, I'm dismayed. But . . . the book's going to be finished, and published. It will probably be a lot less 'cheap,' as you put it, if you help me understand some of what you know. Both because you can put Renata in a different light than anyone else can, and because Gilberto Reyes has been saying all sorts of shit about you, shit you ought to reply to, for your own good."

"I don't care what he says about me," Keith responds. "I know I've got nothing to say about him."

"What about the idea that when you and Renata went to Venezuela, there at the end, you were down there to score heroin, because your habit was getting out of hand? That's something that sort of has to be listened to, at least, since you were busted for heroin after the funeral, and then spent time in rehab back here in the States."

"Why do you ask me something like that?" Keith says. "Are you taping this? You are, aren't you? Motherfucker."

"I always do, as a backup," Eric says. He doesn't like being discovered, however, one can tell.

It starts to rain, softly, silvery and brown. The air feels sticky, and smells like slightly rotten fruit and distant smoke.

"Do you want some iced tea, or a beer?" Keith asks, polite, as if all tension between them has washed away.

Eric requests a beer. Keith comes back with two Beck's Dark, a couple of apples, some cheese, a big knife to cut these things up. They can sit in bamboo chairs under the bougainvillea canopy, where there are also some grapevines. Here they are mostly out of the rain.

"Tell me," Keith says, "have you ever come across this one photograph, it looks like it was taken a long time ago, in which Renata is standing, it's a nude, and a hand is coming out of her cunt?"

"Oh yeah. That's by Toulon. It's in his latest book."

Keith nods. Now that he knows it exists, he's not really curious to see it, to compare it to what has been in his head. He feels tranquil, the tranquility of one who has accepted his fate. Sentenced to death. To be shot by a firing squad, or hanged. You cannot choose. There's nothing you can do. You simply must compose yourself, and accept what is to come.

"What I would like to do," Eric says, gamely, "is spend some time with you, maybe a couple of days, and go over that last year month by month. I already have a lot of data. I've talked with the members of your band, and I have the tour schedule, and Renata's calendar from her agency, so a lot of the basic stuff about who was where, when, is already nailed down. I've talked to models and photographers who were with her on the last few shoots, and so as we go over some of this I would imagine your memory will be jogged, and we can really see how her mood changed due to what was going on between you guys."

"You've put a lot of work into this," Keith observes. "Do you have expenses paid by the publisher?"

"There is some money there, yeah."

Keith gestures. "So that's a rental car. Where are you staying?"

The rain falls harder. Eric seems to feel like he's won, and he's loose. He talks about a screenplay he once did.

"Should we go inside?" Keith says.

"Sure."

They stand up. Eric takes a few steps, turns to see what Keith is doing, and he sees what is coming but cannot accept it, cannot believe. Keith plunges the knife into Eric's chest, a thrust aimed at the heart. Stabbing someone in the stomach or the back is no good, it's uncertain, while cutting the throat entails close contact, a fight. Or so it seems. If this doesn't work, he'll see.

But it goes well. He gets blood on his hand, that's all. Eric dies lying on his back, rain falling down from the sky onto his face, beading up and running off, absorbed into the thirsty, greedy lawn.

FIFTY-SIX

While she sleeps, Justine fears that she is hideous to look at, eyes filmy, like a corpse, some dark blood perhaps drooling from her mouth. Rising, she washes, and slowly dresses, for she knows that something has occurred. Keith is safe, she can sense this, but something has happened, and she is sorrowful. She dresses in black.

It is raining out, softly. She finds Keith still sitting under the vines, contemplating the man on the lawn whom he has killed. Justine feels a trembling, which is nudity, and she weeps, she has moisture, she cries, clinging to him. Whatever divinity Keith possessed is gone now, he has fallen, and she mourns this. He is like her. She has poisoned him. The unhealed wound, the dirt of the flesh, the inner blackness that they share. He holds her, and when he tries to console her, she says, You would never have done this if you had not met me. I am corruption. We are doomed.

Later, she says, more calmly, I don't want to live without you. He buries his face on her breast. It is clear that he understands.

What will they do?

FIFTY-SEVEN

It is Justine who returns the rental car. Together, they go into the hotel, up into Eric's room. They pack his bags. There is a nice ghetto blaster, all kinds of cassettes. Sony headphones. His laptop. They take everything, leaving the key on the table, for the maid.

Keith experiences fear, but then, once they're in the Mercedes, he lets out a big sigh of relief. He starts up the car. Nobody stops them.

He says to Justine, "Renata is dead to me. You know this. I

never think of her."

"Let's stop someplace," Justine suggests.

Keith says okay. He pulls her over to him, and she licks his neck, her tongue rough, like a cat's. Not very wet right at this moment, or hot.

He takes them to a nightclub he remembers in West Hollywood, a place where he used to score drugs. They sit at a table where they can watch the dancers, out on the dance floor, same-sex couples mostly, here and there some males and females mixed. Blue and hot orange lights. Vermilion, then for a long time shades of pink.

Justine takes a small sip of her drink. Keith slugs his down, orders another. He thinks of when she said, "We are doomed." It feels true, but he wonders exactly what she meant. If they are doomed, is it his fault? He supposes that if someone really begins to look hard at Eric's "disappearance," the trail will lead to him. Since Eric found him, another surely can. It won't be a secret that Eric wanted to talk to him.

Justine, as if reading his mind, touches his hand. He grasps her fingers in his bandaged grip. Yes, on a much higher level than whether or not he is arrested for some crime, they are doomed. It is hopeless.

He doesn't care. There's nothing to think about. The worst has already occurred. All the precious moments are a gift.

These drinks are really watered down. Justine finishes hers. Keith wants to kiss her, to forget everything else. The body of Eric still lies out on the lawn, all wet, in the dark. They'll figure out something to do with him, to get him out of the way.

At a break in the music, they leave. This might be a good place to come, some other time, to seek someone to provide nourishment to Justine. There are a lot of dark corners, where people are now kissing; she could almost do it right here in the club. Two women with short haircuts up against a pillar break apart. One smiling, the other panting, provoked into more desire than perhaps she anticipated. To Keith's disappointment, they do not kiss again. The one full of desire stares at Justine. Then, her eyes unreadable, her gaze passes over Keith. Keith and Justine walk by them. He holds her cool hand, guiding her through the jostling, sex and alcohol intoxicated crowd. The sleazy, fuck-me ambiance has its appeal.

They go someplace else, quieter, a blues club, where they can talk. Some blues guy plays the electric guitar. Keith orders two hamburgers, and Justine smiles when the waitress puts hers down in front of her.

"I almost forgot," she says. "I think if I could, I'd put a lot of catsup on mine."

This strikes Keith as funny, and he laughs for some time, as the blues guy continues playing his guitar and everyone smokes cigarettes. Justine laughs too.

Keith teases her by holding up a french fry, dipped in catsup, mutely, with an innocent expression of "Want one?" on his face. She shakes her head, laughs, pushes her hair out of her face.

On the way home, the lights everywhere reflect off the wet black glistening streets. When they arrive, they decide they better do something about Eric's body before morning comes. It's a tiresome chore.

FIFTY-EIGHT

Justine's hair is wet, like she's just out of the shower; all she has on is a blue silk kimono, with a big red sunburst on the back. Her skin is marvelously clear and pale. Tamara senses some faint disharmony in the air, and Justine, though amiable enough, seems dejected underneath. Keith, by contrast, struck Tamara as fretful, and inattentive, when he let her in.

Patrick is out of town, and this seemed a good idea earlier on. Tamara is repaying the joke with one of her own. She has come over to examine Justine, to call her bluff. The two females sequester themselves in Keith's room, closing the door. It's 10:00.

She takes Justine's blood pressure first. Pumps up the cuff and tries a second time. It's impossibly low. Tamara frowns.

There is no discernible heartbeat. No pulse. She puts the stethoscope on again, and listens forever. Finally, yeah, she thinks she hears a beat.

"How old are you?" she asks, gathering her composure.

"I don't know," Justine says. When Tamara looks at her, Justine continues, slowly, "When I was young, we were a long way from Paris, and the abbot didn't speak of such things as what year. I might have heard a number, but I don't remember it. Then, I lived like an animal for a very long time."

Tamara says, in a few moments, gently, "Can I ask you some dumb questions?"

"Sure."

"Do crosses bother you?"

"No."

"Garlic?"

"No."

"But the sun . . . ?"

"The sunlight would kill me. Yes."

"I wonder why that is. Maybe the ultraviolet rays. Have you ever been around a sunlamp?"

"No. Please, no experiments."

Tamara recognizes a joke, and smiles. They smile together.

"How much blood do you need?"

"I need to take some once or twice a week. Maybe less, sometimes."

"Do you kill someone, each time?"

"No. That's not necessary. Only once in a while."

"Have you ever tried bloodbank products, packed red blood cells, that kind of thing?"

"Yes. A few years ago. It doesn't work. It has to be living blood, from somebody alive."

"Animals?"

"No. A human being."

"And you hypnotize this person, beforehand?"

"Yes. I try to make it as painless as I can. I usually disguise the wound, and leave them without memory of anything strange."

"How did you meet Keith? Did you bite him?"

"Yes, but he was on heroin, so I couldn't use any of his blood. We liked each other, for some reason. I don't know why. I noticed something in him, I think."

"And now you're very close."

"Yes."

"Does he have any desire to become a vampire?"

"No. He says he doesn't want to."

"But if you took his blood . . . "

"Until he died. Then he would rise, after three days, if his body was not disturbed."

"Why does it change? Why isn't it just like someone bleeding to death?"

"Oh, when I bite them, I inject them with my substance."

Justine shows her fangs.

"Can I take a closer look?" Tamara asks, zeal for knowledge overcoming reflexive fear.

Justine's eyes dilate, but she allows Tamara to examine her deadly mouth. It's very interesting. Justine demonstrates how she can squirt some of this clear viscous fluid, like a snake.

Tamara would love to have some of this to analyze in the lab, but she doesn't think it is a good idea to ask. She feels that Justine likes her, but this could all turn around if Justine perceived her as a threat. Already, by revealing herself in this way, she must feel she's taking a tremendous risk. Tamara doesn't want to abuse the act of faith.

This is all too much to take in. She trembles. The world is much more wondrous and wildly strange than most people will ever know. She cannot begin to imagine what it would be like to ever try to bring up the subject of vampirism to any of her colleagues. It changes the whole world.

"Do you want to see how I do it?" Justine asks, and it takes a moment before Tamara realizes what she must mean.

"Yes."

"All right. I need to go out tonight anyway. I'll ask Keith if he cares if you come along."

He doesn't, or says he doesn't. Justine gets dressed, and the whole enterprise seems to be amusing her, or that's Tamara's impression anyway.

"How many people like you are there?" Tamara asks, in the car.

"How many vampires? I don't know," Justine says, blithely. "Not very many, I don't think. Los Angeles is a good place, the conditions are ideal . . . and I've only come across a few."

"Where are we going? Are you just going to be looking for someone on the street?"

"No." Justine laughs.

"There's a women-only nightclub," Keith explains, "where Justine's very popular."

"Every few months," she says, smiling. "It's a sure thing, and it's fast."

She becomes thoughtful then, staring out the window at the nighttime scenery of blackness and lights. Tamara is nervous.

There is no easy parking near this club, so they let Justine out at the curb. Keith says they'll make a circuit, and come by every five minutes or so.

Justine nods and turns to go. She is wearing a light cotton red jacket over a black bra, a blue mini-skirt, her stomach bare. Some makeup, and a necklace of pierced gold coins.

"This is really happening, isn't it?" Tamara says to Keith, after a few minutes of driving around, making right turns.

"It's real." Then: "I don't have to say to you . . . "

"You can trust me," she interjects.

"I know that," he replies, after a moment. "I'm sorry to make you feel like you have to say it, but I'm glad you did. I don't completely understand what she's doing, why she showed herself to Patrick and you. It's so completely against her way of life, how careful she is about everything."

"I won't betray her. My first reaction, already, is that it must be some sort of blood disease."

"A blood disease that keeps her young forever, but that makes her unable to face daylight without death?"

"Sure. Where does the blood go, by the way?"

"Some of it comes out again, but most of it disappears inside her body, as far as I know."

"There might be some way to treat it," Tamara says. "I'd like to analyze a tube of her blood, see what it does."

Justine is walking down the sidewalk, with another woman, short black hair, a crewcut, black leather tight jacket and pants, boots with little silver chains.

They get in the backseat. The woman smells of alcohol and musk.

"This is my new friend Sal."

Sal says nothing. She blinks her eyes, but seems to be in a lugubrious trance. Keith drives them away. Tamara turns around in the front seat to look at the action in the back.

"Watch."

Justine's fangs are out. She turns Sal's face toward her, as if for a kiss. She slowly presses onto the vein, then bites, so that the skin tears, and some blood runs down—until the fangs are fully engaged.

Keith pulls over the car and parks it, turns off the lights.

Sal moans.

"Usually," Keith says, "it wouldn't be the throat. Less conspicuous places—"

"Like behind my knee."

"Right."

"And she won't remember any of this."

"I don't think so," he says, quietly. Is he sad? Tamara cannot tell. He appears serene.

When Justine is done, she slumps for a moment, her forehead against Sal's nose and lips. She wipes off her mouth on the lesbian's black t-shirt.

"She asked me if I needed discipline," Justine says, in a slightly hoarse, low voice. "What does that mean?"

"What did you tell her? Did you say yes?" Keith is amused.

"She was very serious, so I was serious too. She wanted me to say yes, so I said yes."

"Is that the first thing she said to you?"

"No. She asked me if I had come in there before, and I said yes, but it had been a while. Tell me what she meant by saying 'discipline' like that."

Justine's fangs are retracted, Tamara notes. Keith explains what Sal probably had in mind.

"The club seemed different," Justine says, thinking back. "What should we do with her?"

"We should take her back to where you got her. She won't wake up for a while, will she?"

"No. Don't you want to just let her off somewhere?"

"I think you guys should take her back," Keith says, "at least to the front door. Say that she's too drunk, she passed out. They'll know what to do with her."

"Wait a minute," Tamara says.

"I'd do it," Keith says, "but I'm a male, and they'd suspect the worst. Especially since she's bleeding from the neck."

"I don't want to go back there," Justine states, and Tamara turns and complains that she's here as an observer, it's not her job to get involved. She doesn't want to.

"What if we dump her someplace and she gets raped and killed?" he says.

"You can find a safe place if you want to," Justine notes, and

Tamara realizes this whole problem is something between the lovers, friction for the sake of friction. Justine says, "What about Griffith Park?" and Keith just says no, that's not good tonight.

Meanwhile, he is driving them inexorably back to the damn club.

"You *bastard*," Justine says, as he stops the car.

Tamara and Justine prop up the tall, muscularly heavy Sal between them, and walk her to the door of the club, just as some new arrivals are going in.

"What did you do to her?" the fat doorwoman says, light mustache and tattoos, and they bring Sal in as Tamara replies, with amazing composure, "We played vampire, and she fainted at the first sight of blood."

"Yeah," Justine adds, deadpan, "she's no fun. What a pussy."

They sit her down on a chair just inside the door, in dim reddish light, and Sal opens her eyes.

Justine kisses her on the cheek, and she and Tamara go back outside, Tamara laughing to herself in her blue jeans, ponytail, and long-sleeved white shirt.

It seems quite funny now, driving away in the car. The madder one was at Keith, the more unwilling, the funnier it seems.

PART THREE

FIFTY-NINE

It is the same face as before, but it is different. She used to have faint shadows under her eyes; these are now gone. It is the same face, and yet it is as if it formerly was wearing a mask, which has now disappeared, dissolved. This unselfconscious smile—she would never have allowed her face to be so open, back in 1912. He cannot believe she is this vulnerable. He simply needs more time to study her act.

David looks closely, also, at her companions, who do not seem to have received the baptism of blood. No, as far as he can tell, they are free agents, they are with Justine by their own choice. She appears to feel safe enough, though, as he watches her. No, she does not think she is invulnerable, and her face is not so constantly accessible as all that. But she looks younger than he remembers. Slender, mobile, quite in contrast to the languid, unknowable vamp.

He hates her like this. He hates what seeing her like this does to him. There is too much mystery, too much he doesn't want to think about, but he must. The situation is a problem for him to solve. It may be mathematical in nature. The answer may be found through subtraction, or division, taking something away or separating what is now joined.

The man, for instance. Obviously, he is a candidate as some sort of a love object for Justine. David prefers to suppose otherwise, but the longer he watches them together the more he notices that they seem to be familiar with each other, physically, in that love object kind of way. She is playing a strange game, a masquerade. David cannot guess her reasons. Maybe there is some great sum of money to be had by romancing this fellow. Maybe she doesn't want to bite him because he has AIDS.

This is one of many possible scenarios. The brown-haired

woman may be the man's sister, presumably a lesbian. She sits with the man and Justine, in a booth in the bar. They are talking about something. David cannot hear. He wonders about the tall woman who went into the lesbian nightclub.

It was at that moment, as the three women were on the sidewalk, that he had first noticed Justine.

Her incandescent face.

His first thought was: She bears an uncanny resemblance to Justine. How interesting. I will pursue her.

Then he realized, by the other women near the entrance to the club, that he would be conspicuous if he went in.

She came out again with this other one, they got into the waiting car. He was glad he had not parked. He followed them, and they came to this bar.

David has written down the license number, not knowing if this will be worth anything. Since it is fairly crowded, he has dared to come inside. Justine does not appear to be properly wary. He is memorizing her new look, her expressions, what she is wearing. It's disturbing to view her with only this strapless bra on, she has taken off the red jacket, bare shoulders and arms and stomach, hand moving her hair out of her face.

When they leave he follows them.

The brown-haired woman drives back out the gate, in a different car. Get her license number. There. The most important actors are here. David lingers, although there's no place to park and get out. He drives around and around, slowly, thinking of what he has seen.

He wishes he could see her again, to make sure this is real. He'll have to come back another night.

He doesn't know what he's going to do.

SIXTY

"Why don't you go after Tamara? It wouldn't take much," Justine says, in her white nightgown, in the dark.

"She has Patrick."

"So? You could take her away from him."

"I don't want to."

"You admit that you could, though, don't you?"

"No, I don't think so. Why are you jealous?"

"I can't help it. What if I suddenly grew old overnight, if I aged a hundred years? You'd be disgusted by me."

"Maybe. How can I know? What do you want me to say? It goes the other way, too. What if the Venezuelan gangsters had burned my face with cigarettes, and I was disfigured? It's all so hypothetical."

"I would still love you."

Keith laughs at her.

"You would never have gotten to know me in the first place. I've never yet seen you pick someone ugly or fucked up."

"But if you were burned *now*, I'd take care of you. I'd bite you, and make you like me, and the skin would all heal."

"If I was a vampire," Keith says, "we would bore each other ridiculously. I'd like it better, just to try it, if I was one, and you weren't."

"What a dream," she says, unamused.

"Why don't I read some more to you?"

"It's late." Some nights, he reads aloud to her, lately from Virginia Woolf's *Orlando*, which she especially likes. Keith discovered, some time ago, that Justine is virtually illiterate. She's embarrassed by this.

They are silent. Then Keith says, out of nowhere, as if they've still been talking all along, "Besides, I killed any possibility of that when I took care of Eric Zimmerman. I knew what I was doing, too."

"What if we were both Chinese, on the other side of the world? If we were normal people, and we met in school."

"We'd be in Chinese prison," Keith announces. "Chinese jail."

"Good," she says, with a little smile, bringing his fingers up to her lips. The gesture has a ceremonial feel.

SIXTY-ONE

He doesn't want to get too close. Maybe he doesn't get close enough. But he doesn't want Justine to sense him lurking.

The notion that he doesn't get close enough makes him want to get closer, and so he does. He sees things. He sees them doing things. One night he actually comes into the house. Then he runs away.

These aren't streets an automobile can just park on, generally speaking, so he instructs Minh to drive in a large circuit, coming around every so often, and he can recognize the sound of the engine of this particular car. If Minh is arrested, through some fluke and an inability to satisfactorily explain herself, David thinks he could make it home before sunrise. He avoids cutting the time too close.

He thinks of these spying expeditions as "scientific." Yes, he is studying Justine's behavior, as if she is a rare bird, say a hummingbird that only drinks nectar from a specific, rare, exotic flower, poison to all others in the wild.

SIXTY-TWO

They used to play this song called "Doorcloser," for twenty minutes, to end the show. Keith wakes up after having dreamed about playing it, only incidentally onstage. He wasn't aware of an audience for a long time.

It's 1:30 P.M. He's restless. He wants some fresh-squeezed orange juice; he decides to go get some, driving the car.

Sometimes he used to think of the term "Doorcloser" as an answer to the Doors calling themselves the Doors. Jim Morrison claiming to open the doors of perception—well, it was a joke, but Keith conceived of some cartoon superhero–character, Door-closer, and that was his magic, that he would close the Big Door. He could close it on anyone. Was he a manifestation of Death? No. He just closed the door. Think of it any way you like.

Sometimes the door must be closed to keep evil outside. To keep out the cold. Wild animals. To make sure the children are safe.

He goes to the music store. Dissatisfied, he buys nothing, and goes on, abstracted, to the musical equipment store. It makes him deeply uneasy to go in, but he does. He looks down at his hands. They seem blurry, and not so misshapen as they have been. It is as if he sees them in hyperfast motion, they are blurry because they vibrate with new life.

This part of the store is so hi-tech it's like a sci-fi interior of the future, all clean lines and Italianate elegance. He goes downstairs, and downstairs again, into the deserted warehouselike showroom where all the grand pianos and organs and harpsi-chords are crowded together, you almost cannot find space to walk between the furniture-pianos and all the potted ferns and palms. It's dead quiet down here, and the air is cool and old.

He sits down at a piano, thinking of Justine. The black gunk that comes out of her vagina, upon orgasm—he believes that this substance is absorbed, that it is feeding him in some way. It is healing his hands.

Although he never had any lessons, he was always convinced that, in his own way, he knew how to play the piano. It wasn't a matter of technique.

Great. He plays a chord. Softly.

The black substance does not have any sort of foul smell or taste. It is like deep, dark earth. Bitter, unsweetened chocolate. Chocolate that has been scorched.

Keith depresses the keys again, so faintly that only the last note sounds of the broken chord. A-flat. It means something to him, this note. He's suddenly full of anguish, he could cry as he remembers how they came to him, in the cell, smelling of alcohol and sweat, it was so hot, and they held him. At first he didn't know what they wanted to do. Rape him? Beat him up? The one in charge—Keith looked up into his shining brown face, big red lips.

Not hard, he puts his fist down, a tone-cluster, dissonant chord. There's a way of pressing down all adjacent notes, like playing with a ruler, or a book, that creates what he's always thought of as a rainbow effect.

When he goes upstairs to leave, a black man he vaguely recognizes smiles and says hello.

"Alonzo Pendergraph. I was in the Survival Network. We opened for you in Minneapolis." He pauses a beat, dreadlocks, café au lait skin. "You don't remember any of this, do you?"

His manner charms Keith, who shakes his head.

"I don't even remember being in Minneapolis. I think I had a cold."

They walk outside together.

"Jesus, you've got a Mercedes? I mean, excuse me for saying this, but I didn't think you guys made that much money."

"It's my girlfriend's," Keith says, smiling. "I don't even own an instrument. If it wasn't for her, I'd be on the street."

"No guitar? Serious?"

"I haven't touched one in five years. Four."

"That's bad. That's real bad. Excuse me, you know, for making a public service announcement, but don't you ever think about the people who bought your album, mmm, your true audience?

They'd like to hear what you're up to, man. I know I would. Even if you only, say, had fifty thousand hard-core, one out of ten, that's fifty thousand, waiting to hear your sound. Those are the ones who're really listening, trying to understand, not just showing up because you're fashionable, the flavor of the month."

"I'd have to learn to play all over again," Keith says.

"That's either a problem or an opportunity."

"Yeah." Then Keith says, "I'd like to play, like, *one note*. One note."

"Come over to my house. I've turned the garage into a rehearsal shed. One note. I understand."

SIXTY-THREE

"You've heard of 'universal donors'? People who can give blood to anyone, regardless of type."

"Yes," Patrick says, though he doesn't sound too sure.

"Well, Justine is a 'universal receiver.' She can receive anything, any type blood. I went to med school with this guy named Jay Culligan, who's a hematologist—I'd like to consult him, if I could do it in some nonobvious way. There exist diseases where you damage your own red cells, immunoglobulin deficiencies, G6PD deficiency, where you're treated by transfusion, that's the only thing to do. There's a lot about her that doesn't make any sense to me at all . . . like the business about having to stay out of the sunlight. The ultraviolet light must have some sort of exaggerated effect. And this aging thing: I'm not sure whether to believe it or not. I'd like to look at a smear of her blood, see if there's anything happening that's completely off-the-wall."

They're talking on the telephone. Ordinarily, if they're not together, they at least talk on the phone. Patrick doesn't want to believe any of this supernatural business is true, but Tamara seems convinced. He'll go along with her, he trusts her, but he wishes this all would go away.

On the television screen he locates a temporarily pleasing image, the sound off, he sees two four-women teams playing beach volleyball, in bikinis. Black seems to be triumphing over jungle print. What nice tans. Bare feet, long legs. One beautiful young woman wears blue-shaded wraparound plastic sunglasses and a backwards baseball cap. She leaps and spikes the ball.

Patrick says, "You're probably right."

SIXTY-FOUR

The light and sign-filled vacancy, palm trees and stoplights, automobiles everywhere, the horizontal, broken geometries of this city—David's senses are acute, he tastes the chemicals in the smoky, ancient air, he sees a tiny shard of broken glass catch the orangey black artificial light two blocks away.

He and Chase get out of the car, on this woebegone strip, and go into the office of the detective who's been hired to run down some pertinent facts. He has stayed late, and as if to demonstrate that it's unusual for him to be receiving callers at this time of night, he has turned on only one small desk lamp, so that for the most part the messy room is dark. The detective is a fat man. He's perspiring.

"Here," he says. Chase picks up the piece of paper, scrutinizing it, hoping that his master will be pleased.

David sits with his right buttock on the edge of the desk, facing, looking down at the man, who looks affronted, but does not protest.

"What about your files? You do keep files?"

"Naturally."

David slowly shakes his head. "There shouldn't be any record of this transaction. Not even in your head," he says, touching a forefinger to his own temple, as the fat man meets his eyes.

In a few moments, David unfurls, and comes down to carefully bite into a wrist. He injects some venom, then pulls the sleeve down to cover the wound.

"He won't remember?" Chase inquires, and David says, "No."

The fat man is left, slumped in his chair, free to go on with his fat man life.

SIXTY-FIVE

She knows that he is not here. The house is dark. Nevertheless, after looking out at the grounds, she finds herself going into his room. Slowly, scarcely seeing what is before her eyes, wearing her long white nightgown, bare feet, she presses her face up against the cool glass of the mirror, half-expecting her face to go through, but it does not. She closes her eyes and sees a black swirl, some blue dots that outline something she cannot make out. She sees a white ladder on its side, some orange paper flames, and there is Lucifer, horns and a tail, dark, you cannot look at him too closely, your eyes want to squirm away. She saw this in her sleep, she realizes. It's familiar to her. A screen, and beyond the screen a deathbed. Keith lies on the deathbed, his head propped up by pillows, not happy, no he's not happy, but he's calm. He sees the Devil and he can look him in the face. He is not without fear. It would be foolish to be without fear.

Justine presses her cheek against the glass and opens her eyes. Smeary, floating, dark shapes linger in her vision for a while, descending, replaying themselves as she blinks. She goes out of the room. She glides down the hall.

She takes a bath. The water makes a noise.

In the bathtub, she soaks for nearly an hour. When she gets out, the water makes another kind of noise, an orderly splashing as her body's volume creates an empty space, now filled. She turns on the light, and, once dry, gets dressed. She thinks of Keith while she dresses, wondering if what she puts on will please him.

It's odd to her, just for a moment, that there is this person whom she thinks of, with whom she is more or less sharing existence. There has never been someone like this before. Not like this. It makes her uneasy, wondering where he is, where he has gone. It's a mystery to her.

She used to see all these people, and she did not know them. There was no possibility she would ever get to know them. She would see them coming and going, and there was no way for her to understand what was in their souls. She might be a few inches away, and yet know nothing of how someone really lived. She didn't want to know. She was indifferent, or insensitive—she did not know how to understand what was right in front of her, because she saw them only in terms of danger, or of satisfying her need.

She faked things. She acted. She lied.

All the people out there now, she's seduced by them through Keith. Tamara, the doctor. All the people they come in contact with at restaurants, gas stations, bars. They're all so full of life. Even in the electric lighting of the night, their flesh glows, golden and warm and red.

Oh, she presses her fingers to her closed eyes, pressing on her eyeballs through the lids. She seeks forgiveness. Is it not as God willed it? If there is mercy, let there be mercy. It is so hard, so painful, to understand and accept the will of God.

SIXTY-SIX

It's after 1:00 A.M. when he comes in. He finds the house full of music, a solemn chorus, Heinrich Schütz's *Mass for the Victims of the Black Death*, from 1499.

Keith comes to her on the couch, and tells her about his evening with Alonzo. The vegetarian dinner cooked by Alonzo's girlfriend, Bridget. How Keith played, with concentration, one eternal note on the electric guitar.

"Do you know what a wah wah pedal is?"

She shakes her head.

"I used to be the wah wah pedal king," he says, smiling, and she joins his smile. "There was once this band called the Reverb Motherfuckers," he continues. "They didn't live up to their name. But if they had, that's the kind of music I would like to make. I'd be a Reverb Motherfucker . . . in the highest, truest sense."

Does she get it? What image can this possibly form for her? He kisses her. He strokes her hair, the nape of her neck. The chorus stops.

"What are you thinking?" he asks. "Did anything happen tonight?"

"No. But . . . there was someone here the night before last. I heard someone."

"Are you serious?"

"Yes."

"Why didn't you say something?"

"I thought maybe I was wrong. I didn't want you to stop what you were doing to me right then."

"Someone here, in the house?"

"Yes."

"I don't understand."

"It's simple enough. It was a creature, able to move silently, a creature of the night. Like me."

"Oh." He waits. She is quiet for a long time.

"I'm feeling very psychological," she finally says. "I didn't want to recognize it that night, but my powers have not deserted me. I knew what was happening. I knew he was here. And then he went away."

"You know this person?"

She shakes her head, slowly. "I don't think so. I'm not sure."

None of this sounds good to Keith. It's like she doesn't want to think about it, doesn't want to know about it, but if someone came into the house this leaves, to his mind, a distinct flavor of danger in the air.

"You see," she says, thoughtfully, "I wanted nothing. All I needed was for the nights to begin and end. I was without desire, or hatred, or revulsion against my fate. I wasted my time. There was nothing special for me to do.

"I was alone. I forgot, and I even forgot how I had learned how to forget. I never expected to recognize anyone. I would look at people's faces, and I never expected to know anyone, I wasn't looking for anyone in particular. Do you see? I was transparent, I was a shadow, and I told myself I wanted it like this. I was superior, I possessed wisdom, but I forgot what this wisdom was.

"Whoever this *creature* is," she says, "he knows me, he thinks he knows me. I felt this. I don't know who it might be. Maybe it saw and heard enough, and it will stay away."

"Somebody from the past," Keith says, and she shrugs. Yes. He wants to know more, but he doesn't want to have to ask. It's all so impossible, anyway. Everything.

"I was imagining, on the long ride home in the car, our life together," he says later on, soothingly, and she curls up even closer to him, in his embrace, interested, and he goes on. "You were saved, and we went to all the beaches in the world. We would lie in the sun and swim and laugh. Nothing could go wrong. At parties we got a little drunk, we laughed at special in-jokes and went back to the hotel and threw off our clothes.

"Here in the U.S., we drive across country, through Arizona and New Mexico, Texas, Louisiana, stopping to eat in roadside diners, to sleep in cheap motels. We are hypnotized by the vast open spaces," he says, touching her, "we become connoisseurs of the subtle differences in the sky. We learn the back roads of Maryland and Georgia and North Carolina, we see rivers and forests and big trucks, factories and new cars, hold-ups, different police uniforms . . . and we sit on a picnic table in the shade, kissing each other, tasting french fries and catsup and salt. We run out of money. It's okay. We get dumb jobs."

When he is silent for a while, Justine murmurs, "More," in a voluptuous, drugged sort of voice.

"We get off the plane in New York," he says. "The sky is cloudy and gray. We take a cab to midtown Manhattan, and check into a hotel. It's old. I tip the boy two dollars, and as soon as he's gone we take off our clothes and get into the bed. Out the window we can hear cars honking, people shouting, gunshots . . ."

"Yes," Justine says. "We're all alone. We could be in the desert, in a tent. Or on a boat."

SIXTY-SEVEN

It's Wednesday afternoon. 2:00. Keith is asleep. Someone rings, at the front gate. He feels irritable. Too many people are showing up these days. It's fucked.

"Yes. Who is it?"

"Devlin Spanswick. I want to ask some questions about Eric Zimmerman."

"You're with the police?" Keith thinks: This is it. He remembers where the guns are from the three Hispanic thieves.

"No. I'm a private detective. Can I come in?"

"Just a minute," Keith says. He throws on jeans and a shirt, fetches one of the handguns, the most appealing, the simplest—then he leaves it, and strolls out to the gate.

The guy on the other side looks like an actor, with his tan and his white-blond hair. But then, lots of people look like that around here.

"What do you want?"

"You don't want to let me in," Devlin states. "Why not?"

"Fuck yourself," Keith says, not in a real unfriendly manner.

He and this fellow understand each other. "I was asleep. So what do you want to know?"

"Well, my friend Eric said he was going to talk to you, he was looking forward to it, and then suddenly he checks out of his hotel, leaves for parts unknown, no word to anyone. . . . This is all very unlike him, you see. Eric likes to let his friends know what he's doing, every step of the way. If he isn't writing, he's on the phone. So I want to know: did he see you? Did he get an interview?"

"Yeah. We talked. I thought, actually, we were gonna talk some more."

"Do you have any idea where he might have gone?"

"Venezuela? I don't know. There seemed to be a lot of stuff he wanted to cover with Gilberto Reyes. Other than that, I have no idea."

"Did he say that to you? That he was going to see Reyes?"

"I don't know. I don't remember."

It doesn't feel to Keith like he murdered someone. It doesn't even feel like he's lying, right now. He yawns.

"Up late last night?" Devlin inquires, with a grin.

"Always."

"Well, this is my card." Keith takes it from him. "If you think of anything, or if he contacts you, I'd appreciate it if you give me a call. The service will take a message twenty-four hours a day."

"Okay."

And there the matter is left. Keith recognizes, in the sunny day, a portent of doom. Nevertheless, doom-laden, he is able to relax and fall back asleep.

SIXTY-EIGHT

Chase and Sabrina sit together, facing the stage. Several of the life-size wooden figures stand there, in their glory, mute. It is late afternoon. David sleeps. The Knife Thrower. Spaceman. Bikini Girl.

"He has told me it's not going to be long," Chase says. "He asked me this morning if I really wanted it, and I said yes. Immortality. He said that word. What about you? Come with me, please." He turns to Sabrina. "I'm frightened. He said there are one or two more tests, then that'll be it."

"I don't know," she says. "I've been having the weirdest dreams. He still takes blood from me, he took some the other night. I'm numb."

There is only one "guest" these days. It is Minh, the Vietnamese girl. She appears now, in a chauffeur's uniform. Long black hair pinned up under the cap. She changes the scenery on the stage to a dark purple sky with blue stylized clouds, an oversized emphatic pale yellow moon. She activates one of the figures, as a test.

The Knife Thrower says, "Red sky at night, unhappy in love."

Anguished, Chase says, quietly, "You must."

"Don't you think," Sabrina says, "that sometimes David is bigger or smaller, different times? Taller, shorter, thinner or more solid, strong. His body changes."

Does Chase understand? Did she speak aloud? She looks at his face but cannot tell.

SIXTY-NINE

In *Orlando*, Virginia Woolf remarks about Time: "An hour, once it lodges in the queer element of the human spirit, may be stretched to fifty or a hundred times its clock length; on the other hand, an hour may be accurately represented on the timepiece of the mind by one second." And: "Some weeks added a century to his age, others no more than three seconds at most."

Justine is keenly struck by this.

It feels like there are secrets between her and Keith, because of the matter of the "visitor." He doesn't seem to accept this as matter-of-factly as she has. It is a sign, she thinks, a sign of something else. It's not important in and of itself, the fact that another vampire is nearby, aware of them.

She persuades Keith to tell her more about this new friend, the musician, Alonzo. She is fascinated that he is a Negro.

"I had black friends in St. Louis," he says, when he recognizes the focus of her curiosity.

While he was over there, he met the next-door neighbors, out in the backyard. There was a blind guy, also black, who recited a Dodgers game, the radio broadcast, so that it was hard to tell if he was really remembering it, or just making it up.

"Hershiser lays down a perfect sacrifice bunt. There is only one play—to first."

This guy's companion was a gaunt white guy in a wheelchair, who never said anything, who seemed insensible until he suddenly reached out and snagged a baseball the blind man tossed in his direction, illustrating a catch an outfielder made.

An old woman took care of them, Alonzo said. Justine wants to hear more about Alonzo's girlfriend. What does she look like? She's pretty. Oh.

Keith drives them downtown. They find a suitable candidate, a drunken man who's dropped his keys. The alcohol in the blood makes Justine sleepy. She would rather have skipped this one. Coming back to the car, in her short skirt, dazed, she feels ashamed before Keith. Ashamed of what she is.

He's kind. He wipes her mouth. She leans against him, and he pulls her in. The guy is still lying in the doorway.

"I feel sick," she says, as they drive away. "No, I'm okay. I'll be okay."

SEVENTY

"No," Olga says. "Please." She is weeping, standing there in her shabby, stuffy little apartment. She's put on flesh since she was a teenage girl.

"You locked me up for twenty years," David says. "I was buried there, inside that box."

"José wanted to kill you, like we did Mother," Olga says. "I talked him into leaving you alone. The only way he'd do it was if we chained you in. I thought you'd just sleep, that you would shut down."

"I was kind to you," David says.

"You had me go down on my own mother!" Olga exclaims. Then she relapses into helpless sobs. "Oh God, please."

Chase is uncomfortable. He stands as a witness, a right-hand man. A stooge. He looks impassive, studying Olga, who is divorced, working retail, behind on all of her bills. Her ex-husband has custody of their two kids. She has been a Scientologist, and spent time with a Tibetan guru, in an ashram in the Rocky Mountains.

"I want you to say you are sorry, for all those years I was locked in a closed box. That's all I want, Olga; I want to know that you're sorry, you have regrets."

"I'm sorry. Please. I'm so sorry."

"Write it down. Here. Write it down. 'I'm sorry.' And sign your name."

Sniffling, her face red, Olga writes *I'm sorry*, in blue ink on a yellow piece of note paper. She signs her name. Olga Roubatieff. Uncertainly, she puts down the pen.

"Now eat it," David says. "So that it's part of your body, how sorry you are."

Unhesitatingly, Olga wads up the yellow paper and chews it,

once it's wet it comes apart, torn by her teeth. She swallows the scraps down.

"There. Say 'I'm sorry' once more."

She begins to mouth the words, as David catches her eyes full in his, her voice becomes inaudible; he reaches forward and pulls her head back by the hair, pulling her up straight. He unbuttons her pink blouse, just the lower buttons, below the bra. He snaps his fingers at Chase, and Chase steps in, bravely, the butcher knife there in his hand.

David caresses Olga's cheek as Chase opens her belly, making an incision and gashing her open to find the actual stomach, there amidst everything else. Chase cuts open the stomach-organ to find, there in brine and semi-solids, the chewed-up pieces of yellow paper, by now much the worse for wear.

"Yes, I believe you. You *are* sorry, aren't you?"

He holds her up by the hair until she is dead. The tip of her tongue protrudes between her lips. Then he allows her to drop.

"This blood is no good to me," he says to Chase. "Come on now, move. Let's go."

SEVENTY-ONE

As soon as Michelle's mother gives her the money, Michelle conceives of paying fifty dollars back to Keith. She knows he doesn't expect it, it will mean nothing to him, but it's a gesture that has some appeal.

She's had a bad week. She had a yeast infection, then got in a thing with Tiff. It's still going on. She spilled beer on Tiff, in front of some guys, later they called each other sluts, and now they're cold to each other. It's stupid really, but they haven't yet made up.

Michelle's period was unaccountably late, by seven days. That's always good for a laugh. Jesus. What a bunch of shit to have to think about, just when she's probably been drinking too much and taking too many drugs. Not good.

At least, since her head's been shaved, it can grow out some other way. The mohawk was getting old.

Visiting her mom is mostly a drag, but this time it really paid off. She had just gotten some extra tax money, and she felt rich enough to give some to Michelle. Michelle paid all her overdue bills, and she still has a couple hundred dollars left.

It's ridiculous to throw some of it away trying to impress Keith, but she doesn't like the idea that he thinks poorly of her. Why this should bother her she doesn't know. Well, since he turned her away that time, she supposes she could just show up again, but then he'd really have the upper hand. It would be weak.

This is much better. He'll notice this.

Also, Jason will enjoy it. He's been wanting to see where Keith lives, just to know. It's a night when there's nothing special to do.

Ken comes along. It's a long drive. Ken is telling them about some book he's read. *Diary of a Slave*, or something like that. No, it's from the dominatrix's point of view.

"Anyone can become a sex slave," he says. "You get to like it. You start to dig the pain."

Michelle is not so sure, though she thinks it's true that anyone's will can be broken. If it's done with enough skill. They smoke a spliff. Jason drives. He drives well when stoned. Careful and safe.

Saint Agatha are off on a mini-tour, so Michelle hasn't seen Fred for a couple of weeks. They're just going up to San Francisco, Eugene, Portland, and Seattle, then coming back down.

Fred sent her a postcard, from Portland, with a picture of a skull. It just said, "So far, so good. See you. Fred." She likes him more when he's away. The others refer to him as her boyfriend, and it's okay, 'cause he's not here to get in the way. There's no pressure or anything.

Tonight, she wants to see the woman Keith lives with, to check her out. Michelle imagines this person as someone who may be embarrassingly old. That will be good. She'll see, and know, and Keith will know that she knows.

Even if it's some beautiful movie star, Michelle looks forward to discomfiting him a bit. He'll have to explain himself, after she's gone.

There is no problem getting in the gate.

"Come inside," Keith says, as they get out of the van. He greets them, friendly enough.

They all go in for a beer. Keith introduces Justine. She is not what Michelle expected. Michelle introduces Jason and Ken. Beers are produced.

Jason goes on about how much he admired Keith's work with SMX. He tells Keith that he would love to have him be a guest or guest host on his cable show, *The Darkest Night*.

Ken catches Michelle's eye, and smiles. She wonders if he is about to say something to offend everyone, for that is his way. He needs to draw attention to himself. Lately he's been known to bring up the Holocaust, how the six-million figure is all wrong, it's way too high. That's just a start.

Michelle drinks some more of the bottled beer, then remembers what she came for. Even though it feels awkward, she breaks in.

"I want to pay you back this money," she says, and hands Keith the fifty bucks.

He says, "Thanks," and puts it in his pocket. Michelle feels ridiculous, but it's all right.

When they leave, once they're outside the gate, someone waves them down. It's a man.

"I want to help you," he says, into the driver's window, to Jason, and Jason lets him into the van. The man accompanies them home. A car follows, with another man and a Vietnamese girl.

David speaks to the goth kids, one by one. He comes into their house. He intends to take them with him, to populate his set. It's nice that they don't mind when he kills Brian, who is up with his computer. They all want to be vampires themselves, they think.

Brian's head is removed from his body. He's put into a trunk, on top of his papers and stuff. This is just like they've always thought the world works, and now it does. Sacrifice and mystery, ancient magical beings in the night. The primitive, holy truth of the blood.

The spell. The sky and the earth. Severed limbs and transformation. Transubstantiation. It's here. Despite whatever smothered misgivings they may fleetingly experience, whatever disquiet, it's here.

It's come.

SEVENTY-TWO

As soon as Michelle would start to cry, when she was a child, she would go to a mirror to watch herself. At first, and for a long time, she couldn't look into her own eyes, and hold it, without being freaked out, but gradually she trained herself to hold the reflection of the gaze as though it was a stranger's. She would talk to herself, and she didn't like to watch her mouth, until it came to seem as though the girl in the mirror spoke, she could dissociate herself from the image, from the words.

She was a burden on her mother, an only child . . . she was unwanted, it seemed, and her mere existence made it harder for her mom to get dates. Michelle learned to be quiet, to stay in her room all by herself. The last thing she wanted was to be in the way. No matter how she effaced herself, however, she ruined things for Brenda. She made the boyfriends uncomfortable, she didn't like them enough, they never thought she was an affectionate child.

When she was twelve or so, these really strange feelings would come over her, and when Brenda would go out on a date, leaving her alone, Michelle would hold ceremonies, she lit candles and painted her face with white clown paint and black lipstick, runic symbols from *Elf Quest* comic books, drawn on herself with black and red grease crayons from the Magic Shoppe.

She walked out on the street like this a few times, and people would cross the street to avoid her. She felt like she had powers, but mostly she sat on the floor in front of the mirror and talked to herself, she would feel like she was evil and strange.

Any powers she possessed worked only at night. During the day, in school or whatever, it was like she was always putting on a major act. People only really saw you, your real face, if you wanted them to. Otherwise they just knew this mask.

There began to be open discord at home. She got in trouble for cutting school, and flunking out, and it just went on from there. She was in rehab for a while. It was stupid. You just said what they wanted you to say. You broke down and cried, on cue.

She never thought that much about being a vampire, though she loved Anne Rice. Clive Barker was better, though he was so gross. She liked that feeling of being shocked, seized, of there being no way to deny that you were at the scene of the crime.

In this one *Tales from the Crypt* comic, this guy was like a vampire, only instead of blood he had to have this gland from bodies that were young and fresh. Only, as time went by, he needed it more and more often, so at the end he called for a pizza, figuring a pizza delivery boy would be about as young and fresh as could be, coming right to your door.

How weird to find out that Keith was living with a vampire! He was totally, David said, her slave. David said, Do you want to do it? and she knew what he meant, it sort of surprised her that he'd pick her, but she nodded, sure, she might as well. Somebody once said to her that doing heroin was like committing suicide, you got the feeling, without actually having to die. Michelle has thought about suicide and death a great deal, and she's convinced she's not afraid, as long as it doesn't hurt.

"You'll wake up in three days," he says. "Like Jesus Christ."

She nods to him, in the dark, heart beating, but staying cool, a blank face, like she knows. It's important not to show weakness, and if she shows vulnerability, inevitably, and fear, she doesn't know.

She takes a deep breath, and lets it out, and is staring at the ceiling where it's textured like the surface of the moon. Like a close-up of the pores of the skin, the skin of someone old, all ugly and rough. Someone like that, breathing, in an old folks' home, forgotten and alone. It's dark, and everyone working there is on drugs, shooting up in the hall closets, the call-lights disconnected and turned off. Low laughter. They're just waiting for you to die. They don't care. They don't even know your name.

It's like there are bandages everywhere, you're covered in bandages, your face, no that's not you it's someone else.

SEVENTY-THREE

"You see," David reveals, "I have finally located her. The one who made me what I am."

He looks at Sabrina.

"If you think I am so evil—she is a thousand times more evil than I am."

"She is a monster," Sabrina says. This response pleases: it's an example of why he likes having her around. She will say things to him.

"Yes, truly a monster. What should I do?"

"Destroy her."

Up on the stage, Minh shows Ken a chalk mark on the floor. He is dressed as an SS officer, in black, an armband with a swastika, one of those caps. He looks quite severe. Jason is fiddling with his video camcorder. Tiff is hanging around. Michelle is elsewhere, dead.

"Do you still love Chase?" David asks.

Sabrina does not answer at once. Then she says, "The things he's done, you've made him do them."

"Maybe. Or maybe I've simply allowed him to satisfy his deepest desires."

"I don't believe that."

Sabrina is lovely, visibly tortured by these thoughts.

"Do you still love him?"

"Yes."

"I believe you," he says, as though he does not. He brings her fingers up to his lips. A gesture. A kiss.

Sabrina trembles. She feels weak. To fight this feeling, she says, "Will you do it?"

"Will I do what?"

"Will you destroy her? This monster, this other vampire—I suppose she must be thousands of years old."

David looks at her. He thinks then, in a moment, of Justine. What could he do, to make her turn her head away? She's too evil. It fills him up like molten silver turned to lead. Crucify her, make her watch as her lover is castrated. He could cut her violently into pieces, for hours, and never get the answer why. Head over here, legs over there, torso, arms thrown over there. Would she have the same unintelligible look in her eyes as all the rest?

Then he would know. Or . . . it would be the worst deception, the worst trick of all time. He can't think. It's too huge.

He gets to his feet and goes up onto the stage, to Minh, his golden-skinned pet. She's sensitive to his mood.

SEVENTY-FOUR

1969. "So, what you're telling me is: you don't know where Suzie is, she's been gone for three days, all you know is that she's probably somewhere with Alison, right? Am I following you so far?"

"Yeah."

"So what's the problem?" Steve asked.

"What's the problem? Wow. That's truly cosmic. You know Alison, right? You've met her?" ·

"Once or twice," Steve says, unwilling just as a matter of principle to play into his little brother's scene.

Jon says, "And so, your wised-up, Peace Corps, fucked-up, world-weary, seen-it-all opinion is, like, Alison is a rational person?"

"I didn't say that." Steve lights a cigarette, looking out the window. "But . . . so Suzie went off with Alison, what are the diremost possibilities? They're probably romping naked in a pig farm pigfuckers' commune somewhere in Sonoma or Cucamonga or something. They're singing backup vocals to some lunatic even as we speak. So what?"

Jon, crazy curling hair falling into his face as he hunts in the ashtray for that roach he just knows awaits discovery, he finds it, aha, knowing he has big brother Steve's attention now, says, "Plausible scenario, man. Undeniable. Except the truth is more, uh, *sinister* or something than that."

"Sinister, no less. Explain yourself, Watson. What is significant about the dog that didn't bark? Ah, exactly that. *Why* didn't the dog bark? That's the key to the whole case."

Steve is bullshitting, but hooked. Ever since he returned from the Peace Corps, down in Guatemala, he's been so serious, so political, trying to write a book that will topple the evil empire.

"Well put, *kemo sabe*," Jon drawls, and takes a hit from the roach. This is its best part. Steve accepts the roach clip, inhales. It might be, probably is, nothing, but Jon is sincerely worried. "I checked with Alison's roommates, down in Venice, and they said she and Suzie were going to try to be in this vampire flick some weirdos are shooting up in Laurel Canyon. Karen said that these people are really into it, it's like some motherfuckers out of the Devil House in Haight-Ashbury. Some bikers are in it, Satan's slaves . . . that part I don't like, I don't like the idea—which I can visualize all too fucking clearly—Alison saying sure, we'll go topless, why not, everything is everything, and Suzie is loaded and goes along, and these bikers get a little bored between tokes and go for a little gang bang out behind the swimming pool or something, I don't know, it's supposed to be sort of a mansion . . . I just think Suzie might be amongst foul and treacherous companions, that's it."

"In a nutshell?" his brother asks, teasingly.

"In a nutshell, yeah," Jon says.

"Like a little *squirrel*," Steve muses. Then he comes back, in a few moments, with: "Look, Suzie's not stupid. She doesn't do everything Alison does. She didn't think she had to get arrested for shoplifting, just because Alison did, in order to fully check out that scene. And . . . she didn't work as a topless go-go dancer, just 'cause Alison did, right? And didn't you once allude to the fact that Alison has taken acid some number of times over fifty, that's five-oh, and Suzie hasn't blown her mind anything like that. Etcetera. Suzie didn't fuck the drummer of Iron Butterfly or try to climb in a sixth-floor hotel window to fuck Jim Morrison— that's all Alison's trip."

"Yeah Steve, check check and doublecheck. But there's an attraction factor here you haven't reckoned into your otherwise sterling calculations."

"And what's that?"

"Suzie's in the drama department at UCLA. She harbors thespic ambitions. Ophelia, *Hamlet*. Mina Harker, *Dracula's Revenge*. Suzie Breck, her name in lights. She could go for that."

"You might be onto something. So how does anyone find out where this alleged shit is taking place?"

"There's this crashpad ... Karen said she thinks some extras have been recruited, or, like, chosen there. Somebody there should know where to find the set of *Dracula's Revenge*."

"Is that what it's really called?" Steve asks.

"I don't know," Jon admits, with a smile. "*Dracula '69*"?

"Okay. You've convinced me. Let's book."

Steve is taller, darker hair, strictly speaking better looking, but his hair is shorter, he's much less hip than Jon. Steve is twenty-seven, Jon twenty-one.

Steve drives, while Jon flicks a Zippo lighter on and off, telling him where to go, talking more about Suzie and her friend Alison. Suzie is Jon's girlfriend, since their sophomore year in high school. She's pretty, unaffected, maybe a little impressionable or innocent, open to be burned, but not really to the point where it's like she just fell off a turnip truck, she can surprise you . . . it's just that it's fun to be open, ready to be amazed, and there still seem, somehow, so many never before known possibilities in the air.

It's late afternoon. The day is peach-colored, then burnt apricot and mashed raspberry-bronze, light reflecting off a million cars' glass windshields and rearview mirrors and chrome, sunglasses on sunglasses off, buy a Coke, smells like bodies frying in a special huge frying pan, fleshy parts mixed with crashed automobiles and smog-spice and desert bones of a destroyed forgotten pre-Aztec city, sweat and nerves and fuck-sweat and dead bright green birds, they might be parrots starring in movies, bright green and crimson and marigold and cerise.

The day is dying. In the crashpad they're playing the Stones' "Gimme Shelter." Who is *this* guy? His name's Ray. He says, "I don't know, I don't know. Really man, I don't know anything about it. Talk to Olga, if she comes round. Olga knows, I think."

"Where's Olga?" Steve asks, not pushing it too hard, almost as if he feels some affection for Ray. Ray's a creepy guy with a beard and darty eyes, some half-assed Southern felon accent. The jailbait teenyboppers are an unattractive, jumpy, cross-eyed lot. Jon's checking them out, giving away a few cigarettes, while Mick Jagger starts to sing some song Jon doesn't recognize, it's strange that he's never heard this one before. Maybe it just sounds different in here. Or it's on the wrong speed.

"Olga doesn't come by every night, man. Sometimes, I mean, to look for new talent and like that, but we might not see her for, I don't know, a week or two." This from a lank-haired bone-thin young man in a fading paisley shirt, gold lamé scarf and magenta velveteen bell-bottoms, sandals and dirty feet. He keeps pushing his greasy hair out of his eyes. "Uh," he says, privately to Jon, "I know where she lives. I'm lonesome, though—you ever hear that? Robert Johnson, the blues-player, he called up his record company guy one night and said I'm lonesome—hey, I'm lonesome about twenty bucks. *Comprende?*"

"Yeah, man. You know where Olga lives."

"Sure do," he says, smiling.

"Okay," Jon says. "Twenty bucks when we meet her. What's your name?"

"Mine? Dodge. Dodge City. You know, like out West."

Jon reveals the plan to Steve, who's not crazy about giving money to this asshole. Especially since: is it a sure thing that Olga knows where this vampire movie is being made?

"You'll see for yourself, dude."

In the confines of the car, even with the windows rolled down, it becomes apparent, if they missed it before, that Dodge stinks. Steve makes him for a speedfreak ex-con. Dodge keeps drumming his fingers and diddy-bopping and twitching and babbling along with the AM car radio, bubblegum shit like Tommy James and the Shondells, Dodge asking them if they can think of any other names that start with the letter Z.

"Zorro, I know a guy named Zorro, Zenon, that's for real, Zed, that means zero in England I'm not kidding . . . "

"Zora," Steve says, and Dodge is puzzled, shut up by this for a moment or two. "Zora Neale Hurston," Steve elucidates, but this elucidation fails to convince.

They drive on. It's dark now. The air is sticky and purple and lavenderish and shades of brown. Atmospheric smut on everything that lives.

"You sure you got twenty bucks? You wouldn't try to burn me, would you? You look too Christian for that kind of shit, brother, but these days beauty is barely skin deep—ugliness cuts all the way to the bone. Man, you wouldn't believe some of the ugliness I seen."

"I'll believe anything," Steve says.

"No you won't," Dodge says, with a kind of mean leer, "You won't believe Count Dracula if he decides to drink your tomato juice straight out of the can."

"He does that, huh?" Jon says.

"Fuckin' A."

It's a mansion, sure to God, and Dodge says this isn't where Olga lives. I jumped ahead in time and space, he says. This is the actual movie location. Security is kinda lax. But this is what you want, dig?

Out of the car, approach the mansion.

"Who is it?" says someone.

"Jeremy," says Dodge. "It's Jeremy and some friends. What's happening?"

"I don't know," the young woman's jaded voice says, without interest. "Nobody's here yet. You bring anything to smoke?"

"Jeremy" smiles, produces one bent yellow joint. Inside the mansion, all kinds of big klieg lights have been temporarily installed, the floor is a bungle in the jungle of crisscrossed cords.

Steve and Jon poke around, not knowing what they're looking for exactly, not knowing if they're engaged in productive behavior or not. Where's Suzie? Secondarily, whither Alison?

At about midnight, a few more people show up, and Jon questions some of them discreetly. They're wary, a little suspicious of Steve, of narcs and undercover pigs as a general concept, a hit or two of halfway decent pot and this fades away, Jon is likable enough, yes they think Suzie has been here, sure, Susan Breck, like the shampoo.

The *stars* arrive, and Suzie is clinging to the arm of the

handsome devil who is undoubtedly the leader of this pack. Steve thinks if she doesn't want to leave with Jon he himself is going to abstain from further involvement however tangential and just split. He's tired of this scene, the mystery is solved. Suzie's a free woman, she can do whatever she likes.

"Heard you're making a movie?"

"Yeah, you might say that." Suzie seems oddly somnolent on this guy's arm, spaced, completely aloof to the cats she used to know in a previous life.

Jon says, "Hey, Earth to Suzie. You tripping or what?"

The leader of the pack guy says, "Are you fellows actors?"

"No," Steve says, a little distance away, drawing attention now. 'We're not actors."

"We're, like, reporters," Jon says.

"Yeah?" David says. "Freelance? Well, we don't want any publicity. We're having some technical problems that we need to work out."

"Like what?" says Steve, and David smiles at him, he's really noticing both brothers now.

"Some stuff doesn't show up too well on film. Twenty-five or thirty-five frames per second, whatever it is, it's not fast enough to contain a certain *vibration*, I guess that's what you'd call it . . . it just shows up as a kind of indistinct blur."

"Special effects?"

"Who are you guys? Why are you here? I don't really like having unauthorized visitors to the set."

"Yeah," says this other girl, really zoned out but somehow feral, caressing Suzie's hair, a slightly overweight, sluttish, Slavic-cheekboned chick in a short black dress. Her bare white fleshy legs gleam, her thighs seem damp and hot, Steve is turned on and repulsed at the same time.

"Are you Olga?" he asks.

"I was a few minutes ago," she says. "Ask David now: he's God. He's Lucifer and Krishna and Osiris and Mick Jagger in an unmarked grave. We love you."

"What did you give Suzie?" Jon asks David, still trying to get Suzie's attention, failing, concerned.

"She's meditating," David says. "I've been biting her cunt for two nights now—she can't get over how come it hurts so good."

The words stun like sudden bee-stings or lashes from an invisible whip. Jon is rendered speechless—he's so used to non-violence, he's absorbed it from high school on, he's not ready for an ugly confrontation, he stares at David but he doesn't know what to do. He looks at Suzie.

Steve breaks in, "Where's Alison?"

"Deader'n a doorknob," utters Olga, with malice aforethought and the pleasure of a mean joke. She's a mean girl.

'Watch this," says David now, pale blue eyes on Steve's. Suzie stands up—Olga helps her pull her cotton mini-dress over her head, so she stands nude. She steps away from Olga, and smiles. "Suzie—bleed for me." All these heretofore unseeable cuts on her belly and breasts and thighs, hands, even her face, like ultrafine razor wounds—blood cascades for one swift cranberry red fading swiftly to pinkish couple of seconds, something's wrong with the blood, it's thick but the color fades out in the light instead of darkening, clotting, turning mulberry-ish brownish like normal blood. Eighteen, nineteen, or twenty cuts. No swelling around wound sites. Little droplets soon ebb and disappear. It's like the warm wind licks the drops away, too fast. What happened to the cuts?

"I can do anything to you," David says, and he's still a human being, or has the appearance of one, he plays at this for a few moments more. Then he says, "You guys are unlucky. You shouldn't have come," and his fangs come out, he's excited by the prospect of fresh, unique vibrations of cruelty and hell on earth.

He freezes Jon with his eyes and then Jon watches as his brother Steve is overwhelmed, Jeremy and others overpower him and bring him down. It's mostly girls, rushing out of the darkness, but there are too many, and it all happens too fast. After Steve is held fast, David bites him on the wrist, injects him so that he goes sleepy and lethargic. . . . Steve is stripped then, and bound with bandages, yes like a mummy, Steve's eyes show his terror—at the last moment, before his mouth is covered, one of the girls pulls out his tongue, using a silver, gleaming, delicate clamp . . . and with an incredibly sharp big scissors a fat girl snips the pink tongue off. Then they complete the mummification, and drag him away.

"They'll drive him to Death Valley," David tells Jon. "It'll only take a couple of hours. Then they'll dump him into a gully. . . . It all looks so flat from a little distance, but there are hundreds of washes and gullies, dry runoffs, it's quite a maze. If he makes it through the heat of the day, maybe a coyote will find him tomorrow night. But he probably won't last much past noon. Do you remember that line, *'The sun's not yellow, it's chicken'*? Your brother will have plenty of time to think, plenty of time to gather his thoughts."

Suzie, rather anemic already before her demonstration of picturesque martyrdom, has crumpled, she has lain down on the grass to rest, her mood flickering wildly if in slow motion, unsure if Jon Spelvin, her beloved Jon, is really here or if he's a David-willed phantom, a dream, another hallucination.

"Fuck her," David says in Jon's ear, his arm around his shoulders in a friendly fashion. "You can do it. Look at her ass, it's like a pre-Raphaelite, the way her nether lips peek out there, she's like a Burne-Jones. I'll give you half an hour, no tricks. Your cock is very heavy now, isn't it? This is all there is left for you."

David walks away. Olga is inside the house. David finds her. He is restless. This house is not where he lives, it's an ex-movie star's house. Didn't Barbara LaMarr live here once, a long time ago? She was a silent movie star, a vamp, who died of an overdose of cocaine. Not Hedy Lamarr, there's no relation. Barbara LaMarr was languid, men blew out their brains at her feet and she remained unmoved, she consciously sought to ruin men's lives. Those were her lives on film.

He finds Olga near the grand piano, on a gold-flocked beat-up couch, being fucked by some rapacious lead guitarist from Huntington Beach, long frizzy brunette hair and pretty, girlish foxy face. Pucca shell necklace. David twists his neck and kills him. Pulls him off Olga, whose cunt pulsates and throbs, swollen and red. He replaces the guitarist, member thrusting up into her belly, her head twists from side to side as he experiences her cervix, ovaries, fallopian tubes like waving palish fleshy plants on the bottom of the ocean, he fills her, she moans like an actress playing a dying tigress impaled by pharaoh's spear, David feels the most extraordinary sensations like his cock has taken root inside her and it no longer exists, it's a memory, that's all he is now too, a thought, a dark mental fragment torn off and left under a bush, a bush in an artificial landscape built in a box. Olga comes, and he feels the waves, like he's a shark trying to get back out to sea from the blackest coral beach, he struggles over each wave, he earlier saw the tall brother's perverse desire and it pricked him like a thorn in his red brain. Sex is partly ugly it is mayhem.

He thinks of Justine—it's not really thought, it's not a mechanically rendered verdict like a sought-out cinematic moving 3-D postcard it's a dark enigma it's more than the stupid vampire bitch herself it's something more it looms it's everything sexual and dirty and mysterious, just beyond reach like the end of a cunt even if you put your hand in and pull out the insides it's never there always escapes you cannot grab it. Olga looks nothing like Justine there's no resemblance he pulls out and it hurts her she screams like she often does.

It's been sort of a paranoid phase for David lately and nobody knows where he sleeps most days, he doesn't ever stay at Barbara LaMarr's old decaying mansion rarely at Olga's with that bunch there even though it has the attraction of a secret room no mostly he stays at another place he keeps it secret the old woman living there has no visitors no relatives friends.

Jon and his sweetheart are yet feebly coupling on the lawn. Or at least he's lying on her, sort of, while she languishes and fades, trance-ridden abandoned it won't take much before her heart stops beating whump whump . . . *whump*.

The cameraman is shooting heroin behind the dried-out ornamental fountain with the electrician and a thirteen-year-old runaway from Encino.

There'll be no film.

Lying half atop Suzie his dead girlfriend Jon has this weird sense of defective clairvoyance, of defective telepathy, or of defective clairvoyance and telepathy both at the same time. Tears flow from Jon's eyes onto the cool soft skin of his true love's face, her eyelashes seem so beautiful and vulnerable and this very vulnerability her helplessness her death seems somehow defiant, like she knows all and will help him when he makes the adjustment, the flicker into non-whatness, off-the-air, man down, all systems quiet blank green-gray screens no power full stop. He can perceive in a quick-flash movie his brother suffering grotesquely in the desert, rendered a cruel and hideous joke, mummy with severed tongue, black hole mouth.

"See no evil, hear no evil, and, um, speak no evil," David says, pulling Jon up and gazing into his eyes. He gazes deeper and deeper, he who has lived in darkness for so long sends the stored-up memory of the sun or something like it, red and yellow and then floating concentric overlapping nebulae of green, Jon has no idea the process has ended because his maculae have been burned out, he's blind, he keeps seeing the same colors, as Olga and Melvin, the electrician, with great seeming thoughtfulness and kindness lead him away. He feels no pain. He doesn't understand. They will drive him back downtown and put him out. He will never be able to rationally explain. Drug misadventure is assumed. The others all just disappear. Maybe they went to Mexico and started new lives, or went on a boat out to an island that didn't exist, they were operating under an illusion, and they drowned. Jon goes to blind college and learns braille. He plays the flute. Whatever he once was, he's not that now.

See no evil. He listens to the television. "*Yipes, Stripes, Beechnut's got 'em. Yipes, Stripes, Fruit-Stripe gum.*" He likes to eat more now than he ever did before, and he masturbates, and grows fat. Then he doesn't masturbate anymore. He just waits. He was so innocent. His innocence was unforgivable. It was a crime. He's a blind man on the bus, an odd expression on his ultimately unreadable face. He sort of smiles. He pats his dog. He can feel the sun he knows it's out. Blind man.

SEVENTY-FIVE

A nobleman had taken Justine away from home, and ravished her, meaning to make her his whore. She struggled, but then acquiesced to fate.

Then, when she could, but with no clear plan in mind, she fled. The dogs of the chateau growled at her. Some barked. She walked off into the night. She had no plan, no goal. She was fairly certain her family would not be happy to see her return. The village priest would not protect her. After all, she was the property of the chateau.

So it was in pure rebellion that she fled. She wept, but all the tears had dried in a short time. She had it in mind to head for Avignon, and then Jerusalem.

If it was her fate to be a whore, then let her be a whore on the way to the Holy City. Yes, she would go to Jerusalem. It was clear to her, after two hours of crisp night air. She would be a penitent, a pilgrim.

But there was someone following her. It was no one human, no one she could name. He caught up with her, and then took her with him, back underground. Catacombs, from forgotten Roman times. After he supped on her, she lay there on the cold stones, far from the light.

She woke up, days later, in ravening torment, and the older vampire was indifferent, he did not care what she did. He did not seem to want her to survive. He had only wanted to see her come alive, to tell her what she had become.

Justine went back to her village. Despicably, in her hunger, she caught a child who had come out to relieve himself against a tree.

Another night, she went back to the chateau. She could quiet all the dogs with a wave of her hand. She began to prey on noble blood, and their minions, taking only a little bit at a time.

It was later that she grew rapacious, and went through a period where she felt the need and the desire to kill, over and above what she required, to walk through habitations like the plague.

Then, in despair, she lived like an animal, allowing herself to become filthy, her face all dirty, leaves clinging to her raggedy clothes. This went on for the very longest time.

Fleur, her sister, had long since had children and died. The village had been burned down. Justine ranged far and wide. Her night senses became so acute and keen. She had as many as ten different places where she could hide during the day.

It seemed like it could go on forever like this, but it did not. Things changed. She met a merchant she liked, and he became her devoted keeper. He helped her get to Paris, and there she flourished for a great many years.

"Were you in Paris during the Revolution?" Keith asks, and her mind is clear enough, it's open, she can reply, "Yes."

The guillotine was never used during the night. She would have liked to have seen it operate, just once.

She nursed a great hatred of the nobility. She was glad to see them pay. At night, she walked the streets of Paris, wearing the red bonnet of a Jacobin wench. But it was a dangerous time for her. There were so many searches of old houses, and openings of tombs, looking for treasure or old bones to desecrate. She got out of Paris just in time, she thinks. Just before the Reign of Terror, under Robespierre.

"I made it to Tours."

And then later, on a ship, she came to the United States. To Baltimore.

SEVENTY-SIX

There is a little scar near Keith's left eye, from an incident in a mosh-pit when he was fifteen. She traces her index finger over the jagged white line of this scar. It is precious to her.

The mere thought that he exists rouses her from inattention: everything becomes more interesting, the world takes on color, it sharpens, it contains the possibility of joy.

She likes it that he has a history, that he for instance loved Renata, who was evil, he experienced sorrow, and suffered—he would not have the same resonance, they could not understand each other in the same way if he was too virginal, it would be impossible for them to connect.

Some part of her even likes it that he murdered the writer, that he was capable of such a thing. It binds him to her, even while it also shows they are similar, they are capable of similar crimes. He has purity, but he is not pure. He is not so pure that his soul recoils from hers.

Their flesh is inside-out. No it's not. It is one landscape, molten, now one thing and then that.

Moments stretch out, time is fractured; a hole is punched through to the blackness beyond.

Then it returns, the drone of lived lives, the smell and sound of the lush, breathing grass just outside the window, in the humid night. She brings her mind back into the room, to listen to Keith's beautiful skin. The beating of his heart. She avoids thinking about the prospect of them staying together, of him growing old, changing, while she stays the same. She could bite him against his will, then see what he felt about it when he reawoke, see whether he hated her.

She doesn't wish to rob him of anything, to steal any portion of him from himself.

To make a plenitude, to overflow. That is love. It comes from and is made of the stuff of God.

SEVENTY-SEVEN

In a garish red room, the SS officer stands over Chase, whom he orders, naked, to fuck the corpse of Michelle. Chase manages, atop the body of the bald girl, to get it in. Somehow he is hard. As there is no lubrication, it hurts his penis, rubs it raw. He moves himself on her, attempts to pull the lifeless thighs up around him in some semblance of a fuck embrace.

Michelle's eyes open. She's incredibly pale. It looks ugly when she bares her new-grown fangs. She is incapable of casting a spell—as Chase tries suddenly to escape, she pursues him, and succeeds in gaining purchase in his neck.

"No!" he cries. "No!"

She sucks him until he loses animation. She continues sucking, gaining color, she's so thirsty, sucks him until he's dead. Sabrina closes her eyes. As Michelle rises, gasping, blood running down her chin, she is helped into a white robe with a big red cross on it, like the Crusades.

David embraces her. Tiff and Jason congratulate her, with awe. She still looks frightened, wild, what has happened to her has not yet sunk in. It is so strange. She burps up some of the salty, rich blood. Gazes longingly at Chase as he is dragged away, offstage. To oblivion.

Michelle manages to say, "I still feel horrible. I'm shaking."

"Sit down," he says. "It will pass."

192

Sabrina weeps for Chase. Silently, without sobbing. David had left it up to her: should Chase be allowed to make the transformation into a vampire? Sabrina said, "No, I don't want that." So his body will be left out, exposed. It will become an ordinary corpse.

The young SS officer walks after Sabrina, following her. He is attracted to her. He thinks they have something in common. The air smells, suffocatingly, of roasted, mysteriously digesting meat. Meat eaten by demons. Invisible, mindless demons. They are everywhere. Sabrina thinks: I am the Queen of Hell.

SEVENTY-EIGHT

In the car, driving, Patrick speaks without looking at Tamara.

"Justine has killed people, hasn't she? She's admitted this to you. You've seen people die at the hospital, in medical school you watched people having open-heart surgery, so this glaring fact, that she kills people—it isn't shocking enough to you. You forgive her for it too easily, because you're fascinated by her. She's a once-in-a-lifetime opportunity. Sure. I grant you all that."

"Then what are you saying?"

"I'm saying that her purposes might not be the same as yours. You get this hit off her, you like her, you find her sympathetic, and I'm not saying you're foolish to respond to her in this way, I just think . . . well, she's probably been manipulating people to her own ends for an awfully long time. How positive can you really be that she won't sacrifice you, or Keith? You tell me she has hypnotic powers. When I hear that, I become suspicious—we don't know how far it goes, do we? How can we know? Maybe you're operating under her spell and you don't know it, you can't tell."

"Patrick, I . . . "

"Okay, okay. I'll shut up."

"No. No, it's good that you're thinking of these things."

She's seems to mean it, sort of. They arrive. In the twilight, shutting the car door, the sound of it, Patrick has an eerie feeling, being here on these grounds. He doesn't know what he wants. Does he need the whole thing to be on CNN before he trusts it, before it's reified for him? Tamara has said that as far as she can tell, to this point, the phenomenon of the vampire is not explainable by ordinary physical means.

This dismays him even as it seems somehow to comfort Tamara, to delight her. Can he not see the metaphysical implications? Is he an absolute materialist, to the point where it becomes nihilism, is that really what he has become?

No, he tells himself. He doesn't want to be like that. It's just that . . . this takes time to get used to, that's all. He's not reconciled, yet, to the new version of reality he's being forced to confront. He doesn't understand it.

They come into the house, let in by Keith, who's wearing a purple shirt. Patrick is still a little bit jealous of him, that is, of Tamara's attitude toward him, and it doesn't really help that Keith is in league with this mysterious creature. In fact, it gives him a sort of glamour, potentially, in Tamara's eyes.

"What has been happening with your hands?" Tamara asks, touching them, and Keith just says, "They've gotten better."

Then they come into the presence of Justine. The object here is to obtain a tube of her blood.

Tamara sticks her several times, but she cannot find a vein. She's embarrassed.

"I'm sorry," she says.

"I don't really feel it," Justine says, trying to ease her mind. Despite himself, Patrick is intrigued.

"Your blood pressure is so low, or nonexistent—the only way to get access to a vein may be to do a cut-down, and I don't want to subject you to that."

"What is it?"

Tamara explains. It's what it sounds like.

"Go ahead," Justine says. "I heal very quickly. Keith has seen," she says, giving him a little smile.

A scalpel is produced from the black bag.

"Are you sure? This will hurt."

"I will survive it, I think."

The cut-down is performed, on Justine's left arm.

The tender, pale flesh. It *must* hurt, Patrick thinks, more than she lets on. He admires her stoicism. He doesn't want to feel drawn to her, to be vulnerable to her, but he is. The blood is like black milk.

SEVENTY-NINE

Jason just wants to get along. He wants things to go smoothly. It's like he is a small child again, trying to be inconspicuous, to avoid drawing unwelcome attention to himself. He is afraid of David, and now of Michelle.

It is he and Minh who keep the household running, who run errands and buy food and make tea. They go during the day to the costume store, and buy costumes. Minh knows what to get.

Jason thinks they should be friends, but they're not. Minh scarcely speaks to him. She is inaccessible. At night, she goes out with David. Jason has gathered that they're keeping an eye on the house where Keith lives with Justine.

Jason feels like a reporter, on a deep deep undercover assignment, in too far, a story he can only hope to survive. Then, if he is still around, he will be a witness, he will know.

Minh says, "I'm going to take Sabrina her tea. Why don't you take a nap?"

EIGHTY

It is *The Two Orphans*. The two sisters come to the big city and are separated. One of them is blind. She has been snatched by the beggar-chieftain, made to be a prostitute. This part is played by Tiff.

Meanwhile the other orphan, Michelle, has become a nun. (There is a nun's costume available, you see.) She asks Ken, the soldier on leave from his regiment, if he will help her find her blind sister, oh please. Ken has changed his name to Rudolph, for Rudolph Hess. Rudolph, from now on.

Jason and some fifteen-year-old kid they picked up off the street, named Plunky, blond dreadlocks, light-blue dirty t-shirt, Jason and Plunky lead the dolled-up blind orphan prostitute to a marble bench, before a fountain, in this cityscape.

David sits with Sabrina, his cold hand in hers. Michelle's boyfriend, Fred, from Saint Agatha, sits nearby, with Minh. Fred is in a bit of a daze.

"Is this your sister?" Rudolph asks.

"Can it be? Oh yes, it's her." Michelle is an inexpressive actor, but David still turns to Sabrina and says, "I love this part."

The two orphans are reunited. They hug and kiss. The wooden figures known as Sam Bell and Lady Maude, exaggerated Norman Rockwell caricatures, impassively look on.

Orchestral music swells, then fades back down where it was before, inconsequent and generic, continuing on.

"I want to thank you for taking care of my sister," Michelle recites, moving toward Jason and Plunky. It is Plunky whom she kisses. The kiss turns into a sustaining bite. Michelle is still not very slick at this. She is learning each time.

EIGHTY-ONE

"You don't understand," Sabrina says, in tears. "I'm half-Jewish, on my mother's side. Rudolph wearing that . . . it just really bothers me. It troubles me. I want to kill him."

David and she lie on their sides. Her dress is up around her hips. He kisses the nape of her neck, around to the side, and she pulls down her lacy underpants to mid-thigh, then to her knees, and then off. His penis glides into her vagina, from behind, as she cries, warm, her eyes closed.

"It's just for effect. I have something planned. Then I'll get rid of him, I promise."

He grasps her breasts. She turns her head toward him, eyes still closed, but seeking a kiss, or something else. She pants, and sobs a different, very different sort of sob.

"Oh God," she cries out, and she bites the pillow, she drools.

She must be sick, she thinks, later on. Doesn't she have a fever? She's still so hot. When Minh enters, Sabrina asks her to touch her forehead, "Does it feel hot?"

Minh does not say. Perhaps she shrugs. She sits down, watches the TV. David is gone, taking Michelle.

"The road to hell waits for no man," the figure named Space-man says, downstairs, to Rudolph and Tiff.

EIGHTY-TWO

They thought of visiting Alonzo and Bridget, but it's such a long drive. Instead, they go on an even longer drive, haphazardly, with no destination, and end up at the ocean. Keith parks the car, and they walk down onto the beach.

They take off their shoes, and walk barefoot in the cool dark sand.

"I've hardly ever seen the ocean," Justine says. "With my own eyes, I've only seen it at night. I've seen it blue on TV."

Keith feels such tenderness toward her—toward what he sees as her fragility, her delicacy. He has a passionate nature; he gives himself unreservedly. He has been able to feel himself in her position, and nothing makes him happier than when, in his presence, she overcomes a certain innate melancholy and otherness, when she is spontaneous, and young, when she experiences things as though for the first time.

She's like someone met in a dream—and yet she's here. Sure, there is an impersonal element to his love, for she symbolizes in her person the existence of all magic, witches and demons, spells. But there are impersonal elements in any romance. One woman represents the wondrous strangeness of all women, of the difference in sex, or simply the miraculous existence of others outside oneself, and that this chasm between oneself and all others can be momentarily bandaged, the wound can be healed.

As they walk into the shallow salty wavelets, the sea foam shining silver and gray and white with phosphorence, they could be anyone, any couple at any time, old or young, ancient or brand new. She laughs, and her laughter mingles with the waves hitting the beach.

Walking back, she murmurs to herself, then sings, "*Well, my Jesus is on the mainline, tell him what you need.*" It's funny how she likes these old blues songs. This one, Mississippi Fred McDowell much of the time just sings part of the line, creating a strange effect. It's like he doesn't see the need to finish, or believes his bottleneck guitar speaks in place of his voice, but Justine likes this, it creates a tension when the resolution is left off.

She sings:

> *Well, he will come in a hur*
> *Tell him what you*

Well, he will come in a hur
Tell him what you

Then:

If you sick
can't get
Tell him what you

Back when Keith used to shoot heroin, "mainline" meant put the needle into a vein. Mississippi Fred McDowell probably meant the telephone, though, Keith tells Justine.

"Jesus is on the *uh*, *uh*," she says, in a hard voice. "Could I be in your band?" she says then, teasing, her voice full of laughter. "You and Alonzo? Really?"

It's so funny. "Sure," he says, and they go to the car, rubbing sand off their feet before putting back on their shoes. She falls over into his arms, in the front seat. Rapturously, they kiss, and look into each other's eyes.

There isn't any real reason why they are so excited, but they are.

"Don't stop," she says, and he drives through the red light. It's a game, to get home especially fast. 2:35.

EIGHTY-THREE

"Something's wrong."

"I feel it too," Keith says, and she touches his arm, just as a light comes on in the house. Somebody is inside, waiting for them, but not choosing to ambush them, exactly. The first notion that flashes into his mind is that it's the other vampire, the one Justine had said she heard. He sees that's what she thinks as well.

But then . . . here is Michelle. Yes, she is with a man. Michelle, her hair grown out to a dark crewcut, with earrings, oh she's very different, Keith sees it, he tenses, the handsome man says something to Justine and they all go inside, "We've been waiting for you," the hairs on Keith's body for a moment, involuntarily, stand quite on end, he shivers. He is the only human being here, and Michelle looks at him with open contempt.

They sit down in the living room, a grotesque parody of two couples meeting socially.

"Do you remember me? Do you know who I am?"

"Of course," Justine says, but beneath her anger she seems unsure.

"What is my name?"

She frowns.

"I understand," the guy says. "There have been so many."

Justine is very beautiful, wearing a slip-like peach-colored dress, one strap down over a pale shoulder, very red lipstick, no eye makeup.

"It's David," she says, with intelligence. "You were an actor."

"Very good."

"You're the one who has been . . . coming around. Spying."

"I was curious about you," he says. "I wondered what kind of company you were keeping. We should be friends. There are not so many of us as all that."

He smiles again, and everyone here, seated, is wound very tight.

"I like to put on shows. I did it in the thirties, and in the sixties, at the very same house. Maybe you will come over sometime, and see. Did you know The Old One?"

"What are you talking about?"

"Oh, there was this Old One . . . he taught me things."

Justine frowns. She waits a few beats, then speaks.

"You'd better go."

"Yes." David stands up, and goes off the wrong way, and Justine rises as well, takes a few steps after him.

Keith remains seated, studying Michelle. It's like she is a wild animal, reacting to unseen currents and signals of the night. She has had a hard time keeping still. It's as if she continually hears things, senses new input that she cannot yet easily sort out.

"Michelle . . ." he says, putting a lot into her name, and she leans slightly toward him and replies, "You're not even worth talking to."

The viciousness is right there, he sees it also in David, David is cool but it's there, regarding ordinary mortals as lesser beings; as he walks back, saying something to Justine, and Michelle rises to join him, to leave, Keith sees something in common, even in his Justine. It's like there may be a limit on their wisdom because of their not aging, never maturing, and the history they so readily develop of taking liberties with people, using them—it's not good. They come to think they are so smart, they know all they need to know, but all they really know is one thing: how to kill. All their cleverness goes into this. How to survive and how to drink blood without getting caught.

Justine returns slowly, as David's car—which must have been concealed nearby—accelerates away, and she looks at Keith as if she understands what he feels, his revulsion at seeing three vampires at once.

"Don't be disgusted by me!" she says, somewhat wildly, she makes a noise that is somewhere between a scream and the cry of an animal, and all the windows and mirrors in the house shatter, it seems a vastly disproportionate effect.

EIGHTY-FOUR

Day passes. Keith would have liked to sleep with Justine, but she won't let him, she never will. She sorrowfully ironically shakes her head and says, "I have to be by myself. I couldn't face you if you saw me like that."

He doesn't know exactly how the windows all broke.

Something about a pressure, a reverse pressure in the air. How it happened is just a detail, it doesn't matter, there are other things to worry about in this world. Bugs come in, though. And having so much broken glass around looks bad.

The lawyer's office calls. There is this lawyer, Philip, who handles all the financial matters. Justine got him when her husband—this thought flares up unpleasantly in Keith's mind, coupled with this David character, the very word "husband" makes him want to go someplace and get drunk—the lawyer is from that time, when Maximilian Durand passed on. All the household bills are paid out of that office. Somebody's going to come by, today, to drop off some papers to be signed.

"How do you know they're not cheating you?" he once asked, and she replied, "I could find out. Do you care?"

Some young woman from the law office comes by about 6:00. She pushes her sunglasses back on her head, looks around, noticing the shattered windows. She's too cool to say anything; she waits for him to explain. He doesn't. He just says, "What are these for? Where does she have to sign?" Let her think whatever she likes.

She says, "Wherever there's a little X marked in red."

The sunlight fades.

After a while he hears a noise, a kind of groan, and he goes in to her quarters, he doesn't know what he expects to find.

"Are you here?"

A movement. She's in the bathroom, the door open, sitting on the toilet, underwear down around her ankles, he can see from here it's soaked with shiny purplish blood.

"I'm sick, a little bit sick." She stands up, staggers a bit, flushes the toilet.

"Are you all right?"

"Yes." She laughs a little, weakly. "I just need nourishment." He sees a fang. "Let me get clean."

It's like she's putting up with him, but there's bad shit she doesn't know if she can trust him to understand. Also, like seeing David has put her into kind of a dark phase, and Keith is jealous, he doesn't want to be but he is.

When she finally comes in, he's sitting in semi-darkness by one of the broken windows, he doesn't look up at first, it's up to her to make the first move to return them to harmony, but she's out of sorts, driven by her vampire nature, she probably wants to kill him and feels like she's doing him a favor as she refrains. She touches his shoulder, lightly, and he understands that she wants to leave, to go out, she needs her sustaining fix.

In the Mercedes, Keith turns on the radio. He'd play a tape or CD but he doesn't want to exercise that much choice.

"What about David?" he says, after a while.

Justine wears sunglasses, at night.

"What about him?"

"I don't like it that he did Michelle, that he was hanging around here, watching. What does he want?"

"I don't know."

"Did he love you? Did you live with him?"

"No, never. He was just . . . I went to his house with him, one time only, and I killed him. I didn't mean to. I was . . . I left him there, I didn't realize he was dead. I lost track of the days, and when I went back, to finish him off, he was already . . . changed. I didn't even want to look at him. Then I never saw him. Until now."

"You never fucked him?"

"No," she says, obviously annoyed. She broods for a minute or two, and then says, "How could you do that with her? Why did you want to? She's fat."

This seems an unfair assessment of Michelle. It pleases him, since they're doing mutual recriminations, that she cares enough to say anything.

"She's not so bad."

It's the worst it's ever been. He doesn't like it, he hates it in fact, his skin crawls, when she gets some guy and takes him in the backseat. The guy moans like he's getting a blow job, and she's taking forever, a long feast, Keith can't stand it and he goes off for a walk, leaving the car.

The victim—a Hispanic, nicely dressed, whom she picked up in a crowded bar—might be dead, or dying; Justine dips the knife into the throat to make a comprehensible wound.

"You hate me, don't you? You loathe me."

"No," he says, but that one syllable's all he can say. They push the body out of the car just around the back of a pizza place, where it's sure to be discovered fairly soon. Who cares? For some reason, Keith worries about the guy.

A woman croons in Arabic over a sensual, hypermodern synth beat. He turns it up, flowing with the traffic, speeding when it's natural, when it fits in. The woman's wailing voice expresses something, just for a moment or two it reaches right into Keith's soul and sets him free.

Then he is back, in a speeding car, feeling surely, drably, like another one of the wanton damned.

EIGHTY-FIVE

It was a nice bar. Mostly Anglo, but sort of in the process of being de-yuppified. Popcorn shrimp, import beer, the music too loud for introspective conversation. A table of Vietnamese students celebrating a dragon-boat victory or loss.

Raul Gutierrez really didn't have any clear conception of having sex with anyone, a pick-up, a one-night stand—no, what he really wanted was a girlfriend, someone to listen to him, someone who would be watching him, who would be aware of him as he led his life. If he had this kind of love, someone who admired him, who saw his finer qualities, then he believed he would be moved to do better, he would be inspired, he'd be a different person, love would transform him in what amounted to a spiritual way.

When he asked this one if he could buy her a drink, if she minded if he sat down, he was already slightly drunk, he was with Cisco and Nick and they always pushed him to drink too much, even in the middle of the week. Alcohol made you outgoing, impulsive, and it was just an impulse, an adventurous impulse, because this girl was not his type at all. It was exciting, but he'd never get anywhere with a girl like that. Her name was Justine.

So when she let him sit down he was glad to, it was a success in front of his friends, they'd be impressed. He'd been on his way back from the can, but at the same time as he reveled in how pretty she was, he was suspicious, frightened even, and this made him more talkative, he felt like there was nothing to do but to get the contradictions out in the open, give them a chance to disagree. Then he would laugh, and ask her for her phone number, he'd be protected when he went back to his friends.

"You grew up here?"

She shook her head, sunglasses in her hand.

"In the Valley," she said.

"Yeah, I have some friends in the Valley."

"I said, do you want to come with me, go for a drive?"

He didn't understand what she meant, but there was only one answer for his honor.

"Sure."

Raul floated on pleasure as he went over with her to say goodbye to his friends. Maybe he was meant for more exotic things than anyone had thought. Guiding her back through the crowd, he touched the nape of her neck, her hair brushed his hand. He was so aware of her ass in that short little black dress. Her legs.

She turned to him outside, he felt like they were already lovers, she turned to him and said, "Look at me, Raul. Do you feel like you know me? What do you see in my eyes?" with this teasing, flirty smile.

EIGHTY-SIX

It's sort of a walk-through of *The Prince of Darkness Tempts Saint Theresa with the Aid of a Waiter from Budapest*. David is the Prince of Darkness, Sabrina Saint Theresa, and Jason is the waiter, carrying a tray of chilled glasses, setting them down, opening a bottle of champagne. The cork flies explosively across the stage.

Saint Theresa throws her bouquet of flowers to the ground.

"Loneliness," David says. "Loneliness in ancient Egypt was very different from loneliness in ancient Greece."

"At this very moment, in a single second," Saint Theresa says, "I've developed a new outlook on life." She tosses off her saintly garb, revealing a glittery, glamorous short gold dress, very low-cut. She drinks a glass of champagne.

The Prince of Darkness joins her. The waiter bows and refills their glasses.

Sabrina throws her glass away, smashing it. Music comes on, romantic music from the twenties. The Prince of Darkness, in tuxedo and tails, begins to dance with her.

She says, "I've been waiting for you all my life. You're a negative particle, highly charged. Your existence means that the universe makes sense."

They dance cheek to cheek.

Minh watches them, just offstage. She closes the curtains at the appropriate time.

Michelle sits in the front row, with Rudolph and Tiff. In a few moments, David comes out between the curtains, sits down in front of them on the edge of the stage.

"What did you think?"

"I want more action," complains Michelle, biting her thumb.

Rudolph and Tiff stay there, as David and Michelle wander

outside. Into the garden.

"Why can't you just keep some, like cattle? Keep them happy and well fed?" asks Michelle.

"The spell loses its charm," David replies. "After a while, you'd have to keep them in chains, and they'd scream every time you came near. It wouldn't be very stylish, or if you decided you liked that sort of thing, you'd still be running a lot more risk of something going wrong while you're asleep."

"You mentioned, the other night, someone you called 'The Old One.' Is he still around?"

"I don't know. I lost touch with him."

"How old was he, anyway?"

"I'm not sure. He had white hair. He talked like he'd been around forever, but he might have been imagining things. I don't know if he knew the truth himself."

Michelle breaks off a rose, letting the thorn pierce her finger. She brings it up to her nose to smell. It looks violet-blue in the night.

"So what do you have against Justine?"

"Nothing. Actually, she did me a great favor."

Michelle is silent, then offers, "Did you know that I fucked Keith?"

"No, I didn't realize. How big is his cock?"

"Why do you want to know that?"

"I'm thinking of cutting it off. I'd like to see the look on her face, see if she cares."

"It would mean, like, total war."

"Then we'd have to kill her, wouldn't we? Killing another one of us is something special, it's a lot more interesting than killing any of them."

"We should do it."

"Of course," David goes on, "Justine might not care. I've never thought of her as being very sentimental. Maybe I was wrong."

"Well then," Michelle says, after a moment, twitching her rose, "we could see."

EIGHTY-SEVEN

When Keith returns, carrying a half-eaten deluxe hamburger in a grease-spotted white paper bag, he comes into this house where all the windows and mirrors are broken, the wind blows into it, and the rain, and Justine looks up at him. In her eyes, her luminous face, there's such an expression, all the pain, and shame, and moral fatigue, and self-consciousness, and hope—she's in his room, with a blanket wrapped around her, the TV on without sound. Halfway through his hamburger, having met Alonzo, talking about music, the escapism of just thinking about tones, tone-colors, and technology, Keith suddenly was lonesome for her, he thought of her, he wanted to see her, and now he's back.

Justine is cold. It's raining out.

They're under the blanket together. It's around their shoulders, as he warms her up.

His love for her is as dense and manifest as a spirit reaching with an arm out of his mouth, a spirit arm reaching to touch her, to find her and help her, caress her, an arm with a hand on it, fingers, fingerprints. And then there is another hand, another arm. One leg, two legs, lips, mouth, eyes, and all the rest.

"We've forgotten what we did," he says, setting the scene, "but it must have been a terrible crime. We wait in the abandoned hotel, wait for them to come and arrest us, lock us away. At the seaside resort, in the off-season."

"We're murderers," Justine says.

"Yes. We're murderers."

A long time passes.

"If you went away, and came back . . ." she says, tentatively, irresolutely.

"I don't know." Keith shrugs.

"Look at those girls," she says, at all these girls in bikinis on the TV.

Then she stands up, letting the blanket fall, and starts outside—into the rain.

Keith finds her, in a few minutes, hair soaking wet, face.

"Was it . . . ?" not saying David's name.

"I think so. He's found me, and he doesn't mean to let me alone."

Keith pulls her to him, both of them dripping, and they go back into the house. They take off their clothes, rubbing each other's body with towels. Justine laughs, her hair is such a mess.

They try to avoid stepping in broken glass.

EIGHTY-EIGHT

It's easy to get Tamara Rothschild. At 3:00 A.M., Friday morning, they ring the front door buzzer at her apartment, and Rudolph says, over the phone, when she sleepily answers, that Keith and Justine are in trouble, and have asked for her. "We'll give you a ride to them, but hurry, it's an emergency. Justine is suffering some very strange symptoms." He hangs up before she can ask him any questions. David and the others wait for her. Either she will come down or she will not. She can try to telephone the house, if she likes, but the wires have been cut. The line will be dead. If Tamara does not come down by 3:30 or so, they will leave, and try something else another time.

Tamara doesn't like it, but she cannot resist. She puts on some clothes. She comes down to see what's going on. The special knowledge revealed about Justine, the mere fact that there is knowledge of Justine's existence—this is the lure.

She comes outside. David says, "You're a loyal friend," and looks into her eyes. Tamara doesn't try to shield herself from or avoid the penetrating gaze. She has a moment of remorse, of exquisite regret, almost relief, and she gets into the van, like a captured deer. She walks and she is not aware of walking. She is bitten, a small amount of blood is taken; she does not feel it. Intensely, she is remembering something from her childhood, a scene in a hallway in Virginia, how the light splashed in, dazzling the shaded area, illuminating the heavy furniture, how at ten she did not want to practice the violin. Her report card is torn, how did this happen, how will she show her parents her grades? She wears a white blouse and navy blue jumper, like everyone else. Her feet are so quick, she has so much nervous energy. She opens these wonderful books that have not been read for many years, heavy big tomes with pictures of strange people living in strange parts of the world, people she's never heard anything about ever since. Tribes who have cameras and automobiles, yet ornamentally tattoo their faces, the women bare their breasts, they're beautiful, the men lengthen their penises with weights and stand there in the brown shade, smoking cigarettes, the smoke swirling lazily in the dusty air currents. The men discuss shipments of densely packed spices and rare dried fruits, fruits no one has ever heard of or tasted over here.

Seeing herself at one remove, as if in a film, she watches as a bee stings her on the neck. It doesn't hurt hardly at all. Honey wells up and oozes out of the hole, as the bee crawls inside. Another one lands there, and her throat buzzes, it suddenly frightens her, there are six or ten bees there in the cavity . . . no, they are her friends. She licks some honey off her index finger. It's wonderful. It numbs her tongue and makes her dream. She goes past fields of brightly colored, swaying flowers, to a little stream, golden reflections shining as the water trickles over the rocks. Somebody whispers something important to her, but she cannot hear. She understands, anyway, as music plays, harpsichords and harmonious flutes. The water runs over her feet. A honeybee with a human face flies past her eyes. It lands on her book, pointing with its stinger. It's like a big dictionary, but she can't read it, it's in a foreign language she has never seen. The words are familiar, but as soon as she sounds them out she forgets what they mean.

It's dark outside on the street. There's a light rain. She must have been up all night. She's with her friends, but she doesn't know who they are. "Why don't you lie down and rest?" someone says, and she agrees. She'll be late for work. No, it doesn't matter. She's too tired. These are her friends. This is where she lives. The bee-sting aches. She is in Germany, with some other students. Some of them, she doesn't like. They leave her alone. She sleeps in her clothes.

EIGHTY-NINE

Since the phone seems to be out of order, Patrick finds no alternative to going over there. He has been very glum over having had to accept that there seem to be vampires in the world, and this glumness has been magnified and inflamed into a kind of incommunicable panic that Justine and Keith might have done something to Tamara, since she did not show up at the hospital today.

Most other conceivable situations of danger, you could talk about it with someone, there would be channels to follow, some kind of a procedure to abandon yourself to, but the only precedent imaginable here comes from trashy old movies. Holding up a cross, or driving a stake through the heart of Bela Lugosi or Christopher Lee. It's both *horrible* and *absurd* to imagine such an outcome, it makes him feel like he's in a nightmare, like he went crazy at some point and didn't know it, and now without Tamara, thinking that Tamara has been taken, and he has to *do* something . . . it's as if he is a child again, playing a made-up childish game, pretending to be an undercover policeman or cartoon superhero. It just does not seem real to him.

Patrick has had an inspiration, based on something Tamara told him. He has put together a custom flashlight featuring an ultraviolet bulb. The idea is that if the vampire cannot stand the light of the sun, it should not be able to stand this flashlight, shone into the face and eyes. It is his secret weapon. The other, more conventional weapon he carries is a handgun, a Glock. He feels nervous in this role, but also very sober, serious, and alert. He has the responsibility to rescue Tamara.

It might not be as bad a situation as all that. There is the possibility that Tamara went over to see Keith and Justine, stayed late, and overslept. Some kind of misadventure. Unlike Tamara, as he has known her, but certainly within the realm of possibility.

The time is 5:45. Patrick did not know Tamara was absent until he tried to phone her, at 3:00. He went to her apartment, used his key to let himself in, discovered nothing in particular—except that her car was still in the garage down below. This is worse than if she drove away on her own, obviously.

Well, if she's not over here, he'll call the police and let them handle it. That some stranger . . . it's not something he wants to think about.

Keith greets him with what seems genuine friendliness, though in a moment this is replaced by puzzlement at Patrick's unconcealable anxiety and fear.

"Where is Tamara?"

NINETY

On the dining room table, there is the invitation, which arrived by messenger this afternoon.

"*The Lost Shepherdess, at 1:00 A.M. Accomplish the deliverance of a friend. No tricks.*" Unsigned, with an address and a simple map.

"What does this mean?" Patrick wants to know.

"I think it means that this guy named David has Tamara. He talked to us about putting on plays, or shows . . . he used to be an actor, in early silent films. Justine bit him, and he's been looking for her ever since. Lately, he's sort of been spying on us, and he must have seen Tamara come and go. How long has she been missing?"

"I talked to her last night, until about 10:00."

"When Justine wakes up, we'll figure out what to do," Keith says. He's thinking, and Patrick is dissatisfied with this seemingly blasé response.

"Fine. I can't just hang out here, waiting. I've got to do something."

"No." Keith grasps him by the arm, hard. "We have to wait." The physical contact seems to communicate more than the words. "David has an entourage. You'll never get anywhere near Tamara unless you go with us."

Patrick stops, but he can't resist saying, "How can you have lived like this?" accusing Keith, by the scorn in his voice, of any number of fucked-up crimes.

It's true. What can he say?

Maybe David . . . no, Keith has looked into David's eyes. He can't deceive himself. David is the worst. Whether he will in this case *do* the worst, or can be persuaded not to, that is the question confronting them now. Will Tamara be sacrificed for their sins?

No, he tells himself firmly. No. We—he and Justine—cannot allow this to go wrong.

NINETY-ONE

Tamara is alone with David. She stands before him, nude. She does not know how she got this way, but she is not ashamed. The spell is on her, but not so heavy as before. She can think, to a degree. If she floats upon it, and does not fight it, she feels all right.

David is sitting in a chair, looking at her. By the slightest of motions, or maybe telepathically, he beckons her to come closer. He touches the skin on the inside of her right thigh, up between her legs, and she shudders a bit, not because she's repulsed, because she's not.

"You're much prettier than I noticed," David says, in a quiet voice. "Some women, until they're naked, you can't see how lovely they are. Your skin is so soft. Isn't there a commercial . . . ? 'Rose-petal soft.' You're beautiful. I like you very much."

"Good. Why don't you let me go free?"

"It's not out of the question," David says, contemplatively, as though half out loud to himself. "Talk to me for a while," meanwhile burrowing a finger half-shyly, taking his time, into her vagina. Tamara finds in herself no power to resist. It's like an interrogation by a bad angel. David seems more inhuman by far than Justine ever did. The hypnotic druglike state she's in waxes and wanes, according perhaps to subtle shifts in the attention David is paying to her.

"What is going on between Justine and . . . what's-his-name? Keith."

"What do you want to know?"

"Well, what do they do? Tell me about them. Give me your diagnosis."

"I suppose they love each other."

"You sound very naive, saying that."

"Maybe I am. That's what Patrick thinks."

"Patrick? Who's that?"

"My fiancé."

"Tell me, Tamara, up until now, would you say you've led an orderly life?"

"I'm sure from your perspective I have."

"My perspective. Yes, there's that. Can you feel this? They used to say, witches that is, they used to say the Devil's cock was cold as ice. There, now I'll make it hot. You like that, don't you?"

"I don't know," she says, shifting her feet delicately, his index and middle finger buried in her sex, playing with her. Making her lubricating juices manifest themselves somehow.

"Can Patrick do this?"

"No. You know he can't."

"Yes. I know he can't. Would he die for you?"

"I don't know," Tamara answers, her brows gathering as she attempts to think about it. "He might. I think he actually would, yes. Yes, he would I think."

"That's very sweet. Have you ever fucked Keith?"

"No, I haven't."

"Have you ever thought about it?"

"Not really."

"Not really. That's fairly ambiguous. Do you wish you had?"

"No. He was a patient of mine. And a heroin addict. So I didn't think of him that way."

"Have you ever heard the expression, 'fate worse than death'?"

215

NINETY-TWO

"There are limits to David's powers," Justine says. "He cannot control more than three or four people at once. I once tried . . . a family of five. It was too difficult, it hurt my head."

She looks so young tonight, vulnerable and young. It's strange.

"What if he . . . puts a spell on me?" Patrick asks.

"Yes. I can protect you from that. If you will let me."

"What?"

She shuts her eyes, and then opens them again, shows Patrick her fangs.

"I won't take more than a spoonful of your blood, but I will give you some of my substance. He cannot hypnotize you when we are linked."

"So . . . you're going to hypnotize me?"

"No. Just . . . keep us in touch. I will be able to feel, if you're out of my sight, in a different room, if you're frightened, or . . ." She looks at Keith.

Visibly, Patrick is dubious, but he holds out his wrist. It is an inoculation.

She bites Keith also, and he thinks of how they came together. She had barely lived, or never lived, or could not remember living. She had instead survived this prolonged inhuman existence, and yet she was not completely jaded, completely dead. She felt the need to show him how she existed, in a sense to try to justify herself, and illustrating herself made her open, enough so that they found a miraculous consonance in each other, a kind of nakedness. Justine opened herself to him, and he recognized her. Both of them shared an asking-for-nothing, an acceptance, and on this some love was allowed to grow.

"Is it true that bullets are no good?" Patrick says, almost a little drunkenly, from the venom, and he shows them his gun, laying it on the table, in the light.

Justine stares at it, for a moment, her face unreadable, more sphinx-like or vamp-like than it's been for a long time. She slowly shakes her head.

"No," she says. "If you blow apart the brain . . . the vampire will die like anyone else."

"I also have this." He shows them a flashlight. No one can decide whether it will work or not. It's not worth the risk to Justine to see. She gives Keith a nervous little smile, looking down at it and back up to his eyes. No, she's not like the other young women out there.

"I'll try to be friends with him," she says. "Maybe he still loves me, and that's all he wants."

"So he loved you," Keith interjects.

"I played a role for him," she says. "A *type* I thought he would like. I don't remember any of it very well."

Patrick, having put his flashlight back in his jacket pocket, says,

"You said, didn't you, that he was in silent films? Anything anyone might have heard of? I took a course on film history once, at USC."

"*Blind Love*, that was one." Justine's face lights up. "And I remember—*Rapture of the Night*! Is that right? Have you heard of that one?"

In the car, of his own accord, Patrick tells them that the blood tests came to naught, if they care. He's nervous, he wants to say everything he knows. The blood turned to soft dark gray dust. A total mystery. It wasn't even sticky. You could shake it up in the tube.

"I hope she's okay," he repeats, forlorn.

NINETY-THREE

At the door, Rudolph and Jason search Keith and Patrick, taking away Patrick's gun. Rudolph says, "What did you expect, to go crawling around in caves, looking for bats?" and gives the flashlight back.

David and Michelle come forward, and David greets Justine, bending over and kissing her hand.

"You're lovely tonight," he says, with a superior smile, as though he sees through all her wiles. She's wearing an emerald green tube top, tightly outlining her round, small breasts, the nipples of which have come erect in the relative cold. She has on a little gold chain, with a gold cross right there on her neck, contradicting all vampire myth. A black skirt, black stockings and shoes. She thought dressing as a femme fatale might possibly disarm David a tad, or make him hesitate, but it doesn't look that way.

Rudolph, in black shirt, gray suspenders, and gray pants tucked into black boots, his brown hair slicked down, points a shotgun at Keith's head. Clicks the hammers back.

"Come," David says to Justine, grabbing her by the bare upper arm, pulling her as she makes a face, as if he is hurting her, "this is just a precaution, so you won't be tempted to interfere. In," he says, and guides her out onto the stage and, so that she has to bend over to get in, into a cage, to which Minh then closes the door.

The shotgun is taken away from Keith's face. Rudolph relaxes, and smirks at him. The cage is about three feet high, with a solid floor, bars all around and over its roof.

Chains connect it up to a pulley, and David now pulls, on his end, a rope, so that the cage rises up into the air. Justine holds onto the bars, staring down, the cage swaying whenever she moves. On her knees, a mournful look catching Keith's eye.

"Stand back, everyone," David orders, and the curtains are opened. There are some people out there, an audience, not many, but enough.

"*The Lost Shepherdess*," he announces, and some music comes on, the lights come up a bit, and Jason is trying to videotape things, walking around.

There is a pastoral backdrop. Green, stylized hills. A yellow sun, outlined in black, with a faint white halo blending into the pale blue of the cloudless sky. Out on the stage are two dark green plastic bushes with many leaves, and a prop oak tree, thick-trunked and tall. A stuffed, or simply fake, blackface merino sheep, with thick, ivory-colored fleece.

Looking zoned-out, or as though she is concentrating on a math problem far away, Tamara slowly emerges from stage right, a bandaid on her neck.

She wears a lavender-blue print dress that doesn't belong to her, and she's barefoot. When she reaches the sheep, she says, "Tolstoy," and pets it, before continuing on her way.

"Go meet her," hisses Michelle, backstage left, and Patrick obeys, coming out, saying, "Tamara! Are you all right?"

Does she know him? She appears interested, at any rate. He embraces her, and she smiles. He leads her offstage. Curtain. They are instructed to go down and join the audience.

"You'll be okay," Michelle says, and Patrick glances at Keith, who still has the shotgun menacingly near him, but he has Tamara, that's what's most important.

She says, "Patrick?" They sit in the front row.

NINETY-FOUR

Minh helps Jason array two of the life-size painted wooden figures. An elderly black man, shirtless, with white hair and beard, smoking a corncob pipe. A Confederate soldier, a common infantryman, with bayonet fixed on the end of his rifle.

And then, a fake little grassy hillock, upon which the naked body of Tiff is laid out, her throat cut ear to ear. She's been dead for several hours. Minh arranges the massy gold ringlets of her hair.

She looks across the stage at Keith, handsome in his white shirt and black pants, and then up at the beautiful Justine, swaying slowly in the cage.

Jason is next to her. They wait for David to re-emerge. At his signal, the curtain will be opened once more.

NINETY-FIVE

"Put this on."

"No," Keith says, and just lets the dark blue Union officer's jacket, with gold braid, fall to the floor. They're not going to kill him over this, and he's not going to cooperate unduly with this spectacle.

"Your funeral," the young man says, and shrugs.

Michelle had said to Keith, "You can leave, you can go with your friends. But leave right now, without Justine."

He wouldn't go.

Michelle was glad. She let him see that she was glad.

Meanwhile Justine, above, is praying, moving her lips, not even knowing what she's saying, her eyes locked on Rudolph, she even knows that is his name. There is no sign that he is connected by blood to David. He is here voluntarily. He likes this. He worships him.

Justine sees, it comes out of him, that earlier this afternoon he was talking to Sabrina, he was suggesting that they could be helpful to one another.

"I'm nothing," he said. "But I can pretend to be something. Obviously, I'm someone. David knows who I am."

"You worthless piece of shit. You scumbag."

"I was standing there, minding my own business, when he came along. All around me," sipped his Coke, "degeneration and decay. I was ready to believe in anything."

Rudolph looks up, now, at Justine. Almost as if he knows, but not quite. He is perspiring, just a little. He smiles at her, as a bed of iron spikes is moved underneath her cage, spikes that would easily pierce the black-painted wood floor if the cage was to suddenly fall.

There are strangers in the audience. People—nobody knows who they are.

NINETY-SIX

The curtain opens.

"Pick it up," David says, resplendent in a Confederate officer's uniform, holding a sword.

Keith decides the bloody knife is better than nothing. You never know. He steps close to the dead blond girl, who is naked but for red high heels matching her painted lips. She stares, all-knowing it seems to Keith, up toward the theoretical sky. Where the sky ought to be, if there is a sky. She doesn't look ridiculous or stupid to him. Rather, she seems composed, you can almost see her leaving her body behind. What is this flesh I was so fond of? How vulnerable it is, how soft.

So Keith has a knife, no match against David's long sword. "You raped my sister," David says, a kind of cruel light in his eyes at this, his joke, seeing it register on Keith. He might not be guilty of this, but he's not innocent, as David well knows. David flicks out the sabre, slashes Keith's left cheek. The laceration feels hot, blood flows inevitably down to stain the white shirt.

"Please don't do this," Justine says, rocking her cage, above.

Keith had forgotten about her, in the moment. He doesn't dare look up now, unreasonably fearing that he might lose one of his eyes.

David, assuming a fencing pose, thrusts forward and stabs him in the ribs.

Justine shrieks; her shriek corresponds exactly to the pain and shock of the stab wound. Keith feels her in him, and is, fighting through the *physicalness* of his fear, conscious of a strength, a vast inner repose. A lack of surprise.

"You raped her, and then you killed her. You . . . fiend—" David waves the sword around. As Keith raises his arms to protect his face he's cut on the right upper arm.

Then David stabs him in the thigh.

"*No!*" Justine screams, and Keith is sorry for her, he wants to comfort her somehow.

He stumbles against the sheep, and feels himself pierced again. This one is in the back, in the shoulder blade, it hurts the worst, and he wonders if this is it, if he's going to die. A sudden swoon of real weakness has him down on one knee, bleeding onto the floor. The pain varies. It suddenly gets worse, say in his side, then he forgets about that one. It is diffuse, a floating negative ball, all of this pain.

When he closes his eyes for a second he catches a vivid glimpse, as fast as that, of an unmoving huge lake, a lake of pellucid beautiful water, green with reflections purple and golden and rose. The water is so deep.

He opens his eyes and turns, feeling suddenly that something is going to change very soon. He looks up to Justine, as Rudolph walks near him, and he notices a big wooden X, with shackles on it, that Rudolph has rolled out. It looks like something you'd find in a torture chamber, and Keith understands.

"If thine eye offend thee, pluck it out," David intones, but there is a disturbance, they all look as, amazingly, Patrick runs up the three steps onto the stage.

NINETY-SEVEN

Several things happen at once.

Rudolph, unaccountably, hands his shotgun to Keith, a solemn, beatific expression on his face. They trade. Keith gives him the knife.

Patrick, with his glasses on, determined, throwing his life away, comes pointing his flashlight, distracting David, drawing also the attention of Michelle.

"I was going to let you go," David says, and Rudolph begins to stab himself in the lower left abdomen, sharply, just as Patrick switches the flashlight on and its light *explodes* in David's face. The face itself is on fire, blackening horribly, as Michelle knocks Patrick aside, her own left arm bursting into flames so that she rolls away, screaming, rolling on it until the flames go out. The flashlight explodes out of his hand.

Minh goes to the rope and begins violently untying it, to cause Justine to fall down on the spikes.

David has backed into the wooden figure's bayonet, the Confederate soldier, the inanimate witness now involved.

Up on his feet, Keith raises the shotgun. He knows how to use one. David, blind but sensing him, throws the sword, but it clatters harmlessly downstage.

Keith shoots David directly in the face, blowing away the best part of his head.

The huge *boom!* startles them all, no one is immune, the sound just makes you jump, it scares you, you can't help but respond. The smell of the powder is, Keith thinks, very sweet, and he smiles at the gory stump of the monster's neck.

Then, with a low wail, Minh succeeds in untying the last of the thick knot, it slips, and the cage falls abruptly, just like that, down onto the spikes.

Lithe as a panther, with such athletically swift responses, Justine jumps as the cage comes apart, one spike catches her leg as she twists free but she manages to land mostly unharmed.

She and Keith embrace, shotgun smoke still hovering, and he loses his strength, dropping the weapon, bleeding all over them both. She is holding him as he begins to ever so slowly collapse from his five wounds.

Rudolph lies on his back, smiling, still breathing, alive. He wants someone to lean over him, to look into his face, but no one will. He has disemboweled himself.

Michelle, one side of her face burned blackish, blistering, one arm worse, has retrieved David's Confederate sword.

"Keith!" Tamara screams, standing at the edge of the stage, but it's too late.

Swiftly, savagely, Michelle stabs Keith in the back, through him and into Justine with inhuman force.

As she pulls the sword back, blood all over, Justine comes up so quickly, Michelle can't help but look into her eyes. Weakened as she is, she's like a child. Justine takes the sword from her. Michelle slips to one knee, whimpering, trembling . . . Justine grasps the sword with both hands, raising it high above her head, and then brings it down, cleanly and heavily, separating head from body. Michelle's head rolls until it's right under the gaze of the big sheep.

Justine tosses the sword, with great force, sideways, so that it sticks into a wall. If Minh, fleeing, doesn't see it, she is aware of it, running out of the house.

Justine holds Keith, kissing him, saying little things to him, as he gazes into her eyes. Tamara comes near, looks at him, but there's nothing any doctor can do.

Cars are driving off, the strangers leaving the scene. Sabrina comes to see David's corpse. Michelle's. The severed head is dignified, at rest. Other survivors, like Jason and Fred, wander about, stunned. They're quite confused.

Justine is kissing Keith when he begins his last breath and then stops.

When he has been dead for several minutes, she looks up to Patrick and Tamara, and asks them if they will help carry him outside. They nod, yes, as the tears slowly run down her cheeks. She looks at them with the history of a species in her eyes, the history of one life.

NINETY-EIGHT

Red hibiscus, white jasmine, yellow penstemon, purple fuchsias. It's a beautiful garden. Justine holds Keith in her arms, there on the grass, wet with morning dew.

She speaks to him. He could be asleep. Dreaming. She asked Tamara and Patrick to leave. The birds are all awake. It's dawn. Nervously, she pushes her hair out of her face, a gesture from when she was a young girl. She prays, but it's hard to remember the right words. She had forgotten how to speak French; now it is all that she knows.

She's so frightened. Every nerve tells her to run. She could flee, and then cherish her love forever, for centuries, build a shrine. Worship him as a murdered god.

But she stays here. She cannot cry anymore. She's dry. She kisses Keith's lacerated cheek. It seems to her that he comes back to life for a few moments, and she murmurs to him, knowing he hears every word.

Oh, she's so cowardly! She can't stand it! To keep herself from running madly, like an animal, she hugs him as hard as she can.

It creeps up on her, the sunlight. Trembly blue swims into silver, her skin sends out warnings, it screams at her, then suddenly it doesn't make any difference if she squeezes her eyes shut tight or not. The world is saturated with white light. She goes blind, burrowing her face into Keith's neck, holding him as though to shield him from the fire that's all around. It is unbearable, atrocious pain. White to black, with an afterimage. Let it end, she cries out to herself, please God. Mercy.

NINETY-NINE

The blood on Keith looks like spilled wine. The tender white flesh of Justine's thigh shows through a large hole in her black stocking, with a long scratch on the skin, as there is above on her bare arm, from contact with the iron spikes. He seems to move his hand, to begin to lift it to her face.

When Justine bursts into flames, Keith's body ignites as well. They burn together there on the lawn. It looks at one point as if Justine is holding flowers, or as if she has wings.

The flames flare up, orange and yellow, the smoke smelling like scorched cake and something else. Gradually the fire settles down to a deep red, until nothing but black ashes remain.

Tamara and Patrick walk out to the burned place. Nothing but ashes, no rib cages or skulls. The birds sing their early morning song. The sun is brighter than it has been for several days.

"Let's go," Patrick says, after a while.

Tamara nods. They walk away.

A hundred black-and-red butterflies dart around, out of nowhere, which they do not see.

Brand New Cherry Flavor

Todd Grimson

'Pierced, tattooed, mirror-shaded and as far off its face as the L.A. it depicts is off the planet'

Charles Shaar Murray, NEW STATESMAN

'Witheringly funny in its satire against cinema, stardom and celebrity'

Andrew Biswell, DAILY TELEGRAPH

'Morally anarchic, image-obsessed and inventively twisted'

ARENA

'Catty, clever and ambitious'

Kodwo Eshun, I-D

'Highly hip, extremely bizarre and darkly humorous — buy it!'

COMPANY

OK, here's the scene: Lisa Nova slept with the film producer to get the job of her dreams and now he's wriggling out of the deal. She's not going to take that lying down — No way! We're talking revenge. So when she hooks up with Boro, Voodoo sorcerer and all round scary freak, it seems like the perfect opportunity for payback day.

  BRAND NEW CHERRY FLAVOR will lead you into scenes of splashy horror and moral distortion that make the most lurid fantasies of today's movies seem inept.

ISBN 0 7043 8057 9   **£6.00**